Never Had

A Spanner

On Her

Never Had
A Spanner
On Her

＊

JAMES LEASOR

HEINEMANN : LONDON

William Heinemann Ltd

LONDON MELBOURNE TORONTO
JOHANNESBURG AUCKLAND

01718290

First published 1970
Copyright © James Leasor 1970

434 41016 0

Printed in Great Britain by
Cox and Wyman Ltd, London, Fakenham and Reading

For Roland Gant,
who thought of the title
and should have written
the book.

1 ❋

That day began just like any other, because, if you think about it, there wasn't any other way it could possibly begin.

The sun heaved itself slowly over the roof-tops and then hung there a bit shakily, like an under-poached egg in the sky, looking down at me. I suppose it was also looking down at eight million other people in London, but I was the one it woke up.

I sat up in bed and blinked around the room which, according to your viewpoint, and whether you are advertising for a tenant, or are the tenant yourself, could be equally truthfully described as 'former groom's residence above Belgravia mews', 'delightful bachelor establishment', 'a pad', or as I call it, a pit. It's all these things, and a bit scruffy as well, with paint chipped around the edges of doors, and stuffing bursting out of the easy chairs. I bought them as a job lot in a second-hand shop in Camden Town. The man wanted six quid for them.

'Tell you what I'll do,' I told him. 'I'll give you four – and I'll take them away.'

He agreed, because he thought I was doing him a favour, until he worked it out in his midget mind that whoever bought them *had* to take them away. But by then it was too late; they were out in the back of my car, and my car was half a mile up the road.

He didn't realize then, though he may have done later, that I also buy and sell.

I live above my shop, and the shop for me is Aristo Autos, which, cut down to its infinitesimal size, is an old stables in the back of the mews in Belgravia, with a tarted-up sign outside, and three or four tarted-up old cars inside, which I buy for as little as possible, and sell for as much as I can.

1

People these days, in this effluent/affluent world (or out of it, for all I know), collect all kinds of things, from match-box labels to steam rollers, and because relatively few old cars have lasted for thirty or forty years – and why the hell should they? – they were only meant to last for a couple of years when they were new – they have also acquired an inflated value as antiques.

Five years ago, to buy a Bentley $4\frac{1}{2}$ litre Black Label would have set me back five hundred iron men; now, I have to pay nearly ten times this sum, and so you can be pretty sure that whoever buys one from me gets the date of his birth and his mother-in-law's age added to it for my profit.

Incidentally, the Black Label badge is another example of the mystique that surrounds old cars – and especially Bentleys. When they were made in Cricklewood up to 1931, the background colours of the big winged 'B' badges on the radiators were there to give a quick indication of the size of engine under the bonnet.

Red meant the Speed Model 3 litre; blue, the ordinary standard model and the $6\frac{1}{2}$ litre; green, the Speed Six; and black, the ordinary $4\frac{1}{2}$ litre. Some Bentleys of those days even had the badge background painted to match the colour of the body, and so it had no significance at all, only I don't put that in my ads.

But now we have these fine cars – the world's fastest lorries as Ettore Bugatti once described them – being advertised as Green Label, or Black Label, as though they were whiskies. Snobbishness, like pre-packed TV meals and frozen foods, are the curse of the age, but it helps to make me a living, so why should I behave like a walking wayside pulpit and denounce it?

I climbed out of bed, looked in the mirror, squeezed a couple of blackheads just for the hell of it, and examined my tongue. I felt three thousand years old and I looked my age. One day nearer the grave, I thought, and wondered where and when and how it would all end. For there's only one thing I can't talk myself out of, if I've a mind to, and that's death. However, this was a gloomy thought, so I didn't think it, but tried to focus my furry mind on better things, like girls with charlies round as brandy glasses, and almost as firm, and wearing trousers so tight that when they bend down you should be able to see the line of their pants, but you can't, so you wonder, are they cheating by wearing tights, or are they wearing nothing at all?

This wasn't all that more cheerful, either, for at my time of life you don't just want to think about such things, you want to be where the action's happening, and it certainly wasn't all happening to me.

I steered my thoughts towards the three old cars in the garage beneath me, standing on the cobbles where the horses used to chew their hay only forty years ago. Business wasn't all that brisk; it never is early in the year – or sometimes, if you're honest – late, either. You have to wait for the Americans to come over for Stratford and the Lakes, and the coach tours of Bonnie Scotland, and when they are stuck for half a day, they may see my ad in their hotel foyer. Right now, even the hotels were half empty, which was one reason why I had been lumbered with these old cars for so long that I practically felt married to them. And marriage, like life insurance, is something that's never greatly attracted me: you have to die to beat them both, which took me back to my gloomy thoughts again.

I washed, shaved, mixed up a couple of eggs, half a cup of milk, and a knob of butter, poured this into a pan, threw in some salt and pepper, stirred them until they went sort of soggy, and ate them with a spoon, standing up, reading the *Daily Express* on the draining board, which is how I eat most meals when I'm on my own. Why mess about laying a table, clearing it up, washing dishes *et al* when there's no need?

3

Police were searching for a masked man in Hampstead, which is as good a place as any to find one, if a masked man is what (or who) you're after; a TV actress had arrived at the Old Bailey for her bankruptcy petition in a Rolls (which, unfortunately, I hadn't sold her); twin brothers, aged thirty-five had changed sex, in Pernambuco, a place I've never been to, and which I thought I'd stay from in case this could be catching.

Altogether, it seemed a pretty normal day outside in the great big world, whatever it was like for me. And, to make things par for the course, no one would turn up to buy any of my stock, a situation which would also be all too normal for my liking. What I wanted was a touch of the old abnormality, with men rushing in carrying sheaves of notes, thick as a horse's neck, all crying out to buy my cars at my prices.

I went downstairs, rolled back the entrance doors, and stood on the cobbles in the mews, wishing something like that would happen, just once in my life.

George, my mechanic, had not yet arrived. He does the real work in my business, and can spruce up an old car as well as those Mayfair beauty clinics tart up some withered old bag to make her look a little less than the hundred years old she must be.

I have had George around for quite a time now. He learned his trade in the Tanks, and we have a sort of love-hate relationship. I hate it when he spends too much of my time and my money on a car, but when he is late, as he was that day, I think how valuable he is, and where the hell would I be if I had to do the hard, hairy work myself, as well as the speaking part?

Another thing about George is that he talks in rhyming slang, which keeps my mind ticking over, for sometimes I can't understand what he means, and if I can't, how can anyone else? Sometimes, of course, I don't think he understands what he means himself, but then that can go for all of us. The

4

great difficulty today is in communicating, as the deaf man told the dumb one.

My three cars, as I say in my old-car ads, were all 'carefully selected, all guaranteed, every worn part replaced'. I suppose that's true, so far as it goes, which isn't all that distance. I'd selected the damn things myself, mainly because I couldn't find anything else to buy at my price, and the worn parts, when they were so obviously worn that they wouldn't work, had been replaced, but only by other parts just a little less worn. Anyhow, my guarantee was carefully drawn up by a Polish lawyer in Bethnal Green, so that when I offered 'guaranteed used cars', all I really guaranteed was that they were used, and after thirty or forty years there was no doubt about that. You could have that in writing if you wanted.

The best of the three to look at was a Marendaz Special, which was quite a nice little car of the 1930s, with a radiator made to look like a little Bentley, and a bonnet with three exhaust pipes sprouting out from one side. Stirling Moss's mother used to win races in a Marendaz, so it could go fast as well as look fast, an ability not shared by all sporting cars at that time.

This car had been made in what we in the car business call The Jam Factory in Maidenhead, because it is now the home of a famous marmalade concern. From the First World War until just before the second, several makes of car, had been made there, from the G.W.K., which took its name from the initials of the three partners who produced it, Mr Grice, Mr Wood and Mr Keiller, to the Auto Electric, which had a battery and *four* engines, one for each wheel, through the rear-engined Burney, designed by Sir Dennis Burney, who pioneered the R100 airship, to one of the more successful, the Marendaz, produced by Captain D. M. K. Marendaz. In addition to the successes of Mrs Moss, Marendaz cars set a twenty-four hour record for both 1100 and 1500 cc cars at Montlhery.

Had they possessed more capital, the end might have been very different, but that's also the story of my life, and maybe yours too, and the fact of the matter is that, having begun in small premises off the Brixton Road, next door to Bugatti's London depot, they travelled West to The Jam Factory, where they unfortunately went out of business in the late summer of 1936 – about the same time as the car that stood next to the Marendaz in my garage, the little open Talbot 10, was coming on to the market.

Mine was the two-seater model, which is very rare, and although it is rather disappointing from an engineering point of view, being mainly a warmed-up Hillman Minx of that time, it *looked* fast, even standing still, and could probably top 60 downhill at full sail.

It was worth a hundred of anyone's money, which would show me a profit, for it had cost me £20. I'd have taken less, too, if I'd been pushed, but no one was around to push me, so I was not doing any business.

The third car was one of those strange sad vehicles that every dealer gets lumbered with from time to time, because they have a certain nostalgic affection for them, largely because of their ugliness. This was a 1935 Chrysler Airflow with a front like a chromium waterfall. When it was new, they said it was a car ten years ahead of its time, but ten years after its time, in 1945, it still looked ugly, because to be honest – and why not, there's no money involved? – it *was* ugly. But like some ugly things – and people – it was also interesting.

It had been built because a senior Chrysler engineer, Carl Breer, motoring home from Detroit one day, saw a flock of geese above him in the distance. As they flew nearer, he realized they weren't geese at all, but a flight of army airplanes, and he thought how close a plane was in design to a bird, how natural it looked in its own element – while car designs still harked back too much and too often to the horse and buggy days.

6

Breer decided to design a car that also took advantage of the air by offering the smallest possible resistance to it; and the Airflow was the result.

Well built, well thought out, it still met the stiffest resistance from a quarter more important than the air – customers. They just didn't like the look of it, and, quite honestly, neither did I. Anyhow, I hoped optimistically that some nutter would fork out £500 for this piece of misconceived modernity of the 1930s. If he wouldn't, then maybe the lead guitarist of a pop group might be persuaded that this was just what he needed for a pre-psychedilic image for himself. Everything has a buyer, if you wait long enough; the only danger is you may die before you meet him.

I was thinking about this and that and the other, but mostly about the other, when a man came round the end of the mews, and walked towards me. He couldn't very well crawl without attracting attention, even in Belgravia, but he could have come running, which might have meant I had a buyer.

When you are in my sort of business, you can tell from a stranger's tread whether he is intent on a deal or whether he just wants to fill in half an hour before his train goes, talking about cars he has never owned.

'You are Aristo Autos?' this man asked, making the thing sound more like an accusation than a question, as though I had been caught flashing it on Hampstead Heath.

'The same,' I told him. 'And you?'

'My name's Kent. Jack Kent.'

'Like the county and the cigarette. Fly your own flag. Be a trend-setter,' I said, because there was nothing else to say, and so far this fellow wasn't adding much to the sum of human knowledge, or even mine.

'Yes,' he said. 'Tell me, do you buy old cars as well as sell them?'

'Depends on the car,' I said. The last thing I wanted to buy was another ancient banger, full of dry rot and rust. I wished that the good Lord had sent me a buyer instead of a seller. Back to the prayer mats, lads.

'What have you got?' I asked him, not meaning in the way of his private parts, but the car.

'A Delahaye.'

As he spoke, he looked at me out of the ends of his eyes, wondering how I would take it.

I took it. A Delahaye has never been my favourite motor-car, but it was a very soundly built beast, although for some reason it wasn't all that easy to sell at a profit.

'What's the model?' I asked, keeping my thoughts out of my voice.

'Two-seater. Type one three five, three and a half litre, overhead valve motor.'

He'd got the facts all pat, almost as though he had learned them off from a book or a catalogue. This could be interesting; not very, but a bit. For years, Delahaye had made lorries, and then someone in the firm decided to put a lorry engine in a car chassis, and dress the whole thing up in Figoni and Falaschi bodies. We always called them 'phoney and flashy' but although they were sometimes the last, they were never the first, and a good two-seater, with enclosed front wheels, could be worth fifteen hundred nicker. Not to buy, of course, but to sell.

'Where is it?' I asked him.

'My place.'

'Where's your place?'

'Belsize Park. I rent a mews garage, Seventeen, Belsize Park West.'

'Why are you selling?'

'I'll be frank with you,' he began, and at once I knew he wasn't going to be quite that. People who talk about honesty and decency and straight-dealing are the ones to watch, preferably with your back against a brick wall, although

8

sometimes things are so rough they'll even stab you in the chest.

'I'll be frank with you. I bought it myself, thought I could make a profit doing it up, as I've read others do, but then found I just hadn't got the time, or the ability. So I want to off-load it.'

'How much?'

'Two-fifty quid,' he said. 'Notes.'

'Naturally.'

I was amazed he thought I'd deal in cheques. I'd read somewhere that it costs you two and six, even to cash a cheque, assuming you have money in the bank. I like notes, because there is no record of any deal, and also you can actually claim the whole transaction as a bad debt, which is useful for putting against those deals when you have had to take a cheque against all your judgement.

'What's the condition like?' I asked him.

'Fair. A runner, anyway. You can drive it.'

This was a step in the right direction, because so many of these old cars are not even towable. Some I have bought have been so rusty that when I tried to move them, the spokes of the wheels collapsed, and they had to be carried away like mechanical cot cases.

'When can I see it?' I asked him, not because I particularly wanted to, but because I had nothing else to say, and for £250 I wasn't being robbed.

'Any time you like,' he said.

'Like now?' I asked.

'Like now.'

'Give me ten minutes for my man to arrive and look after the shop, and I'll be with you. You've got a car?'

'On a meter outside the mews. A grey Cortina.'

'See you there.' He held out his hand, and since he wasn't begging for money, I shook it with mine. He had the firm grip of the insurance salesman, which didn't endear me to him.

9

Professional handshakers want watching; they have a habit of being rather less honest than they seem. Indeed, it's been my experience that their integrity runs in an inverse ratio to the strength and masculinity of their handshake. This man felt as though he were male all over, a phallus in suède brogues and a Dacron suit.

I went back into my garage, and stood for a minute looking at the faded old paintwork of the Marendaz. I always find it hard, when looking at an old car, to imagine how it must have glistened when it was new, in a showroom with potted palms, and those funny nickel ashtrays on long stalks they used to have in the nineteen-thirties. It was like looking at an old face in the mirror – mine, maybe yours – and trying to recall what it looked like when it was young, when life was still an experience to be lived, when time hadn't written its rude name all over it.

I walked into the little hutch at one side of the door, where I do the minimal paperwork my job demands, opened the safe, took out twenty tenners, because you never pay the asking price, folded them double, and buttoned them in my back trouser pocket. I had just locked the safe when George arrived.

'Sorry I'm tiddler's,' he said.

'Tiddler's?' I repeated blankly.

'Yes. Tiddler's bait. Late. Bloody tube got held up.'

'So,' I said. 'Don't lose any sleep. I'm going out to Belsize Park to see some nutter's Delahaye.'

'What about the stock here?' asked George. 'No one's exactly fighting to buy it.'

'Don't tell me,' I told him. 'But we can't keep running on the spot for ever. I've got to go through the motions of doing business.'

I was convincing myself as much as him, and not succeeding. I picked up my set of trade plates, put them in a briefcase, because if there is one person I don't want to look like, that person is a used-car dealer, and walked up the mews.

10

Kent was sitting in a grey Cortina, like he said. He had taken off his hat, and his hair had been cut so short on his skull that it looked like black spray dust. I wondered what his trouble was. Maybe he had lice, or perhaps he just wanted to keep his brain cool.

We sat in silence as we drove north against all the commuters driving south. The car was clean and impersonal; no little gadgets like St Christopher plaques, or chromium vases with plastic flowers, or tiny dogs that nod their head in the back shelf. I used to think that these horrors were a product of the present day, but they've actually been around ever since cars were built to appeal to a wide public.

As long ago as 1928, accessory makers marketed such Freudian monstrosities as a nickel-plated baby's teat for the radiator cap of the Baby Austin (Baby, see?) and cloth figures of a Pierrot, a Sunbonnet Girl, even a Ukulele Girl ('with small spring for suspending') to hang in the rear windows of cars.

You can tell a lot about a person's personality from a glance at their car and the rubbish with which they deck it out. The drivers I hate most have their ashtrays crammed full of sweet papers, and the carpets grey with cigarette ash.

'Had it long?' I asked him.

'Only a few months,' he said noncommittally.

'How did you find it?'

He shrugged.

'Easy to park,' he said.

That was about all we said on the drive, so the great conversationalists of our time weren't in any danger from us. He pulled off Haverstock Hill, down into a welter of streets that had once been gracious, with high gabled houses, all now reduced to hutches for single typists, young provincials up in London for the first time, eager to run in the rat race, and coloured students.

I often wonder how much resentment in coloured countries

stems from leaders who once lived in digs like these, with nothing to do on Sundays except demonstrate; homesick exiles in a grey, rainy land with the gas fire out and never a shilling for the meter.

Kent stopped the car.

'We'll walk the rest,' he said. 'Easier for parking.'

I got out first, and waited for him to lock up. While he was fiddling with the keys, I put my hand in my right jacket pocket and felt for the half-inch pencil I kept there, and scribbled the car number on the back of an envelope. Then I took my hand out of my pocket as though I had just been rummaging for a cigarette.

We went up a couple of alleys to a mews rather like mine, although a bit tattier. A white Rolls, probably belonging to a pop group because it had psychedilic decorations on the doors, was being hosed down outside one garage. Farther down, some characters with cameras and lights were organizing a girl in a mini-skirt to run up an outside staircase. I guessed they were doing a TV commercial. If I'd been on my own I'd have hung about for a while, bending down, lacing my shoe or some damn thing, just to see her going up the stairs, to see what sort she'd got on, but I hadn't the chance. Business before pleasure, as the old pro told the ponce.

'In here,' said Kent. He fumbled in his pocket for a Yale key, and then leaned against the sliding door of a garage. The smell of dry rot and stale air rushed out, but luckily nothing else. Certainly, the Delahaye stayed where it was.

I walked round it, keeping all opinion out of my face. For a car of that age, it wasn't too bad. Agreed, hungry moths had made many meals on the hood, the paint was dull and the chrome pitted and rough as a bear's backside, but it was recognizable as a car, although it hadn't the body I wanted, but a reasonably smart one by Henri Chapron.

When you know people who can chromium-plate quickly, and bring up portable spray plant to work overnight (so long

12

as they are paid in notes) and all those other little short-cuts that can make the difference between success and failure in the old-car business, I figured I wouldn't lose on the deal. But then it is not my business to lose on any deal.

'Can you start it?' I asked Kent.

He lifted the bonnet as though to reassure himself the engine was still there, found it was, and climbed in behind the wheel and pressed the starter. When the engine fired, I put my hand casually on the radiator header tank. It was still warm. Someone must have been running the car only hours before. This is not uncommon when you're trying to sell an old car that's a swine to fire up when it's cold, and it could mean anything or nothing. It didn't mean anything to me. After all, I didn't want the car myself, and no skin fell from my nose if it was difficult to start. Caveat emptor, as my old Polish lawyer liked to say, which means, let the buyer beware; the seller can also be a bastard.

Kent engaged first gear and drove the nose of the car out into the mews.

'I've got the log book,' he said, as though this proved something, and took it out of the door pocket to show me.

The instruments were all there, and original; usually, someone steals the clock, which leaves a sorry hole to fill. I flicked on the lights. They worked. I decided to buy the car.

'It's a difficult model to sell,' I told Kent, because it was true. I'd have told him the same if it hadn't been, of course.

He didn't say anything, but just sat looking at me, with the engine ticking away under its long louvred bonnet.

'Want's a lot of work doing on it, too,' I said. 'It's hard to get people to work on these old cars now. Only a handful of coach-trimmers are left who can do this type of job.'

'Don't make me weep,' said Kent. 'Do you want it, or don't you?'

'Not at two-fifty.'

'How much, then?'

'One-fifty,' I said.

'You're joking?' He sounded hopeful.

'Not with my money. I can't afford fun.'

'This cost me four hundred,' he went on.

'I quite believe it,' I said, although I found it difficult, but why fall out with the nut? It was only his word against mine.

'Two twenty-five,' he said. 'And you're breaking my heart.'

'No good,' I told him.

I shook my head sadly, like a bishop over his favourite curate who had been found after the choirboys again. I knew my cue, now. After all, I should do. I had followed it often enough.

I gave a great sigh, ran one hand in a sort of farewell caress down the old bonnet, and turned away. I generally allow myself three paces on these occasions before I stop and put up my price – if the seller doesn't stop me first. Such is the delicate psychological balance between buying and selling that he invariably does.

Kent let me make two-and-a-half paces before he said hoarsely: 'Two hundred.'

I completed the pace, and turned and stood, head on one side, as though thinking the whole matter over very thoroughly. This was the price I had already agreed in my mind before I'd even left home, but he didn't know that. I kept him waiting, as though this was as serious a matter as General Motors merging with Ford.

'O.K.,' I said at last.

'Good,' said Kent, as though he meant it.

He backed the car into the garage, switched off the engine, climbed out.

I glanced at the log book. His name was the first entry.

'What happened to the old book?' I asked him.

'No more space,' he replied.

This is the answer I'd have given in these circumstances, for in the trade it's not unusual to provide a new book with an

14

old car, in case the buyer tries to contact the former owner and discover the size of the mark-up or, worse, just why the last owner sold it. But, so far, Kent hadn't sounded like a car dealer.

I checked the engine and chassis numbers, and made as sure as I could with my pocket torch that they hadn't been altered from something else. You have to be as careful with old cars as with new, in case they've been stolen. Then I counted out twenty tenners, and bound the trade plates with their elastic bands around the bumpers.

'Feel like a drink?' asked Kent suddenly.

'I feel like anything,' I said. It was a bit early for drinking, but I never refuse a good offer.

'Come upstairs,' he said.

'Do you live here?' I asked him, as I followed him up the wooden, uncarpeted stairs, and a damp, musty smell poured in on me from the walls.

'If I'm in town I sometimes stay here. If like I'm with a bird.'

'I see.'

The room was not unlike mine, but rather shabbier; an old settee in one corner, some filing cabinets, which he had probably bought from a second-hand furniture store, because they didn't match, a table and three dining-room chairs.

He opened the top drawer of his cabinet, took out two glasses and a half bottle of whisky. He measured out two of the smallest tots I'd ever seen, held them up side by side to make quite sure they were of equal size, put down the glasses and carefully screwed the cap back on the whisky bottle in case any should evaporate. Whatever else Kent was, he wasn't fighting to be the last of the big spenders, Mr Host-of-the-Year.

I glanced around the room. There was something anonymous about it, no imprint of any personality or character, not even a trade calendar on the wall to give any clue as to

15

the occupant's business. It could be anyone's room, or no one's. It just happened to be his.

'What line of country are you in?' I asked him.

'Import, export.'

He poured some water from a beater into our glasses. We toasted each other.

'I buy a lot of junk from Hong Kong,' he went on. 'Plastic novelties, rubbish of that kind, dress them up a bit and sell them again, mostly to the Middle East. I've an office in Cairo.'

I nodded, as though I understood this way of making a living, but I didn't, any more than he probably understood mine.

'How did you hear of me?' I asked him. It's valuable to know what advertisements are worth using.

'Someone in a pub,' he said vaguely. 'We were talking about old cars, and he gave me your address.'

'Nice of him,' I said. The man was probably lying. He'd probably read my ad somewhere; in a taxi, an hotel brochure, a newspaper. I like to have saturation coverage, as the man said, when he pee'd all over the strawberries.

'Well, I'll be off.'

I drank my drink and we shook hands. Kent watched me go down the stairs and climb into the Delahaye. Then I heard the door click shut.

I was back in my mews in under an hour. There had been no calls, and we hadn't made any money, but at least we hadn't lost any. George walked round the Delahaye, looking at it, kicking the tyres with the automatic reflex of the old-car dealer, opening and closing the doors to see whether they were sagging on their hinges.

'What are you going to ask for it?' he asked me.

'Four and a half,' I said. 'The paint's not too bad.'

It wasn't all that good, really, but when it had been compounded it would glow like new.

Compound is a mildly abrasive paste that we dealers use to take off the haze from old paint. Years ago, many car polishes contained a good percentage of this stuff, and the advertisements all stressed that although the polishing rag *would* become stained with paint from the car, this was all part of the deep cleansing action, etc. In fact, it was all part of rubbing the paint off, and if you polished the paint too often you'd eventually have no paint left. However, as my old father used to say, you believe what you want to believe, and some of us have been screwed so often that we believe in nothing, not even in ourselves.

George connected up the hose to wash the car. He'd black the tyres, buff up the chromium with some abrasive on a pad at the end of an electric drill to see if we could avoid having it all replated, shampoo the upholstery, and Kent wouldn't recognize the car by evening. I watched him work, and the day passed like any other day.

A few nutters rang up and offered me cars for sale which I didn't want to buy, and an American tourist actually came from the Ritz, where he'd had to stop over for a night on a flight from Los Angeles to Rangoon, and he'd a couple of hours to kill. He told me he owned a dozen old cars in Des Moines, but he was too cautious to make it a baker's dozen and buy another one from me.

Only one thing was different about that day. I telephoned a friend in a hire-purchase company and gave him the number of Kent's Cortina and asked him to let me know anything about it. He was back on the blower within an hour. The car wasn't Kent's at all, but a self-drive rented to him for a fortnight. So why had he lied to me about it? Did he think I'd be more impressed if he said he owned it – and this at a time when three out of four cars on the roads are owned by companies and most of the rest are rented?

I never cease to wonder at the odd ways in which people's minds work, usually activated by greed or sex, or just plain

17

snobbery. Remember what Francis Quarles wrote about them years ago? 'Let the greatest part of the news thou hearest be the least part of what thou believest, lest the greatest part of what thou believest be the least part of what is true.'

He'd have done well in the used carriage trade, would Quarles. I could imagine his ads: 'Every carriage thoroughly restored, new hand-carved shafts, revarnished as necessary, wheels respoked, polished axle caps, leatherwork completely renovated. Never had a hammer on her. Believed former property of Elizabethan courtier.'

About five o'clock, a character turned down the mews in a Mini and stopped just behind my door. He climbed out carefully, locked his door, and came towards me. As I say, you can tell a lot from people by watching how they walk, and also how they drive, how they stop, whether they lock their car doors, or whether they don't bother. This character seemed a very cautious type to me. He was tall, in a dark grey, double-breasted suit, with a wide chalk stripe, carnation in button-hole, white collar with a deep pink shirt and the two-blues of the Old Etonian tie. He might be an accountant; he could be an hermaphrodite so far as I was concerned. His money was the same as anyone else's.

'I'm looking for something open and old,' he began. The way he put it he might be looking for an old lay. One of the lays of ancient Rome.

'How open and how old?' I countered.

'Like this car here,' he said, indicating the Delahaye. 'Haven't seen one of those for years.'

I changed gear gracefully into my spiel.

'Very few left of this model. One of the best ever turned out by the firm. Bound to be a collector's piece in a few years. I've already got three people interested in it.'

This wasn't entirely a lie, either, so don't rush me. This nut had shown some interest, George was interested because

18

it helped to make his living, and so was I because I hoped it would make me a profit. That makes three people, doesn't it?

'How much?' the man asked.

'Four-fifty.'

A shadow of pain crossed his face. He must be an accountant; or maybe he worked for the income tax.

'I can't put it any lower than that.'

I nodded to George across the bonnet. He started the engine.

'Listen to that,' I told the man. 'Everything is balanced dynamically.'

I didn't know what this meant, really, but it sounded good. I'd read it in someone else's advertisement, so it must be true. I believe most things I see in print, unless they're things I put in print myself.

'They don't make them like that any more,' I told him, in case he didn't know. 'It would cost a fortune to get an engine like that built today. Would you like to see it?'

He shook his head. I opened the door, but he didn't even look inside.

'What's your lowest price you would take?' he asked me. 'For cash.'

I signalled to George to switch off the engine. When it grew warm, there was a knock in it like a madman beating on an anvil. That might be serious, or again it might not. I thought it probably was.

'For cash?' I repeated, as though I'd never heard the words before, but believe me, they were music in my ears. 'I'd take four twenty-five.'

'I'll give you three hundred,' he said, reaching into his inside pocket.

'For this?' I asked him in amazement. 'You must be joking.'

'Three hundred,' he said. 'Cash.'

I paused. I could keep the car and ask four-fifty, and I'd

19

probably get it – in time. On the other hand, I'd have my own money tied up in it, and if I could make a quick £100 out of a few hours of George's time, and a trip up to Belsize Park, it seemed foolish not to do so.

But it is always psychologically wrong to give in too easily, as the virgin told the sailor. If you're going to be beaten down on a deal, the man who is doing the beating down likes to feel he's had a struggle. It's a glandular thing. So I wriggled about for five minutes, working out sums in my head, and bringing out a mass of bills which I keep filed under every conceivable make of car. They are all faked, of course, but they look convincing with details of new clutches, reconditioned rear axles, balancing of brakes, and all that crap. Finally, I let him win.

He took out his wallet.

'Cash,' I reminded him.

He counted out thirty ten-pound notes on the bonnet of the car.

'Come into my office,' I said, 'and I'll give you a receipt.'

He came in, and stood over me while I made out the printed form with his name and address, Mr G. A. Snelling, 32 Rosemary Court, Shepherds Bush, W11.

'When will you take it?' I asked him, because when you've done a deal, get rid of the actual physical vehicle as soon as possible, in case the buyer has a change of mind – or something goes wrong with the car. Some of these old motors can break down standing still.

'I'll come back later,' he told me. 'Leave the car outside here with the key in it.'

We shook hands and I watched him climb into his Mini and drive away. He was so careful he even used his flasher at the end of the mews, *and* his right hand, to show he was going to turn, and yet for a careful man he showed surprisingly little interest in the car – he hadn't even wanted to lift the bonnet. I'd have expected him to crawl all over it with a magnifying glass, shining a torch in each corner of the boot. But he hadn't done anything of this. Odd thing, human nature, I thought.

I put the money in my safe and wrote in my cash book: Cash sale, £75. So I had made an income tax loss as well as a cash profit. You couldn't have it better than that, but you could have it more often, as the psychiatrist told the nun.

I went out to the pub for lunch, and when I came back, the Delahaye had gone. Pretty soon after that it began to rain, and I stood looking out at the mews with my mind switched off, waiting for something to happen. It didn't, so I sent out a few reminders to people who owed me money, and was looking through a drawer in my desk for a book of stamps which I thought must be wedged in a crack, when I saw a bunch of keys. They didn't belong to me, and they didn't belong to George. The drawer had been jammed open a couple of inches, and they could easily have dropped in there without anyone noticing.

The only other person who had been in the office that day was Snelling, and so they must be his. I turned them over slowly; a key for a front door, a couple of small silver keys that probably fitted a suitcase, and an obvious ignition key. Snelling had been such a careful man, he must be doing his nut wondering where these were. I looked him up in the telephone book, but there was no Snelling at that address. My good deed for the day, I thought, and the night as well; I'd take them round to him.

A thought crossed my mind, for it had nowhere else to cross.

'Did you find anything in that old Delahaye?' I asked George. I meant, apart from the usual tools, which I always keep – I must have the best selection of car tools in Belgravia – but we also look under the carpets, beneath the seats, and in all the door pockets. It's amazing the things you find – even if it's only razor blades that cut unwary fingers to the bone.

George took up a brown envelope, and shook out the

contents on top of the desk. Two cinema tickets, a half wrapper for Polo mints, a cigarette, squeezed flat and unsmokable, and a small sheet of plain notepaper folded over. This I opened. It was the first page of a letter, but without any address, or date.

It began in a spidery handwriting: 'My dearest daughter. It is many weeks since I heard from you, and I have been thinking of you very much, especially over your birthday. I have only your old address to write to, and I wonder how you have been, and what news you will have to tell me when you come back. I will be here, as always, waiting for you, for . . .'

I turned over the page; it was blank on the other side. The second sheet was missing, so who was it from, and who was it to? An unknown father to an unknown daughter.

I read it through a second time. I should have thrown it away, but I didn't. I thought vaguely I should send it back to Kent; he might have written it, or maybe the daughter was his, or his wife, or maybe nothing. I pushed it into the side pocket of my jacket, and tossed all the other rubbish into the wastepaper basket.

Then I opened the doors and took out my SS100, because I am one of those nutters who believes that you should practice what you preach, and if you're flogging old cars it helps a lot if you drive one yourself, although sometimes, as you pass the Minis and the Minxes with all their windows up, and a good fug flowing through the heater, you wonder if you're doing the right thing.

It was seven o'clock, and the worst of the rush-hour had gone, and so I made fairly easy time down the Bayswater Road towards Shepherds Bush. Rosemary Court was a block of flats that had been modern in the late thirties, when it had been smart to live near Shepherds Bush film studios, but now the tide of fashion had long since ebbed away and the little side streets were blocked with the cars of TV executives at the

B.B.C., ageless young men, with thick black hair, button-down collars and tinted glasses, and I had a hell of a job to slot mine anywhere, for the steering lock on the SS isn't fearfully good.

I managed after a time, and walked back to Rosemary Court. Close to, it looked pretentious, in that rather pathetic way of the nineteen-thirties, with a semi-circular sweep of steps, and four pillars, no doubt hollow, holding up a portico. Two swing doors opened into the building, and to make the entrance more imposing there was a third to the right that didn't swing. This was a telephone booth, and a couple of lovers were pressed together inside so tightly that the glass had steamed over. Whatever they were doing, they weren't phoning.

Thirty-two was on the third floor. I was just about to push through the front door when it burst open and a girl ran out. Her hair was long but tousled, and her eyes were wide with fright. She was carrying a handbag and her coat was open and blowing behind her. She rushed round me and tried the telephone door, but the careful lovers had wedged it closed.

'Oh, God,' she sobbed in desperation, and ran off down the road. I watched her go, past an old woman feeding pigeons from a bag of crusts, past the parked cars. Some other lover, I thought, and went upstairs. She could be the other woman, the sort of girl you see in a restaurant, with a sad-faced, middle-aged man, and she asks: 'Have you told *her* about us yet?' and the man answers carefully, not looking at her: 'Not yet. She's not been very well.'

Only thing was, this girl didn't look that type; she looked too vigorous and positive to accept that situation. But then, you never really knew with people, any more than you are ever really certain with cars.

The stair carpet was dull brown and shabby, with mud trodden into it. The smell of cabbage water and stale cooking hung over the staircase, and on each landing I caught up with snatches of music from an old film on TV. An American male was declaring: 'Honey, this thing is bigger than both of us.' Something, I thought, or maybe he was boasting. I went on up to the third floor.

Thirty-two was half-way down the top corridor, on the right. Three domed bulbs burned dimly in the ceiling, one just outside the door. An illuminated bell push glowed at one side. I pressed it and listened to the chimes. There was nothing else to listen to, no creak of an inner door opening, no feet on the carpet. I rang the bell again. If no one was in, I'd just drop the keys through the letter-box.

Then I thought I'd better scribble a note to say where I'd found them. Then I discovered I hadn't even got someone else's visiting card in my pocket, and no pen, and my stub of pencil, like much of my life, had lost its point.

I rang the bell of the flat opposite to see if I could borrow some writing implement, but no one answered. The only sound of life was a dog that sniffed and snuffled along the bottom edge of the door, and then whined and gave a despairing little bark, as though it had hoped I'd open the door and let it out.

I turned back to thirty-two, and as I did so I saw that the door was about half an inch away from the jamb. I leaned against it, and it opened, as it had every right to do, because someone had fixed the Yale lock so that it could not close.

'Anyone in?' I called. 'Mr Snelling? Shop!'

There was still no answer. I would just go in, see if I could find a pencil on a table, and if not, I'd leave the keys so that Snelling would imagine they'd been there all the time. The hall was very narrow and a door opened off it to the right. I guessed this would be a sort of sitting-room cum dining-room, with a bed in an alcove; I've lived in this size of flat myself.

When I opened the door I saw I'd guessed correctly. I also

24

saw something else. All the drawers in a chest had been pulled open, clothes littered the floor – mostly slips and pants and bras. A cheap writing-desk had been smashed so that the roll-up cover could be opened. Letters, bills, magazines had been rummaged through and left in a jumble.

Sometimes I'm slow as a rheumatic snail, but it didn't take me all that long to realize that Snelling's flat had had a pretty thorough going-over. I looked for the telephone, but the wires had been torn from the wall. I turned back towards the door, and as I turned I breathed a whiff of scent, oily and rich and masculine, in a soft and pampered way. Then I heard a slight intake of breath somewhere behind my left ear; and then the room exploded, and I heard nothing else at all.

*

I must have been swimming or out in the rain, because I was soaking wet.

I moved my head to see where the hell I was, but my head didn't like moving and showed its disapproval by lifting off my body by several feet. When it came back on again, I saw I was sitting in the room with all the drawers and scattered clothes still on the floor. I was wet because someone appeared to have poured a bucket of water over me. At least, I saw an empty bucket on the carpet in a pool of water, and every time I moved, cold water trickled down between my shoulder-blades or under my arm-pits.

The girl I had seen running down the stairs was sitting in a chair, looking at me intently. I tried to look at her intently, too, but this was difficult for my eyes didn't want to focus. Behind her stood two hazy figures. I shook my head again and water sprayed out from my hair.

I saw more clearly now. One man was a policeman in uniform, and the other wore a dark suit with a white open raincoat. For my money he'd be a plain-clothes cop. Why do they choose such plain clothes? They were also looking at

25

me, not with any concern for my condition, but rather as scientists regard a specimen on a slab.

'So, what happened?' I asked, because I wanted to know. 'You tell us,' said the man in the raincoat. 'Who are you, anyway?'

I told him.

'Go on,' they said.

'A man called Snelling bought a car from me this afternoon,' I went on. 'He left some keys behind. He'd given me this address, so I came round with them. I couldn't get an answer at the door, and hadn't a pencil or paper to leave a note. When I saw the door was open, I came inside. Then I got hit on the head.'

'Did you see anyone?' asked the policeman in uniform.

'No one except you.'

I pointed to the girl; it was less painful than nodding to her.

'I saw this man coming into the block,' she agreed. 'I was running out to telephone the police. I'd come home and found everything in a shambles.'

'Where are these keys you mention?' the policeman asked. He seemed to have a lot to say in this show.

I put my hand in my right pocket. Nothing there at all but the lining, not even the letter. I felt in every other pocket, but although I had two five-pound notes folded in my left trouser pocket, and a handkerchief in the right, there were no keys. Like that unsigned letter, they'd gone.

'Gone,' I said.

'Anything to give you any idea who your attacker might be?'

I would have shaken my head again, but it was too sore, so I just said nothing. I didn't add that I'd smelled that strong scent, and I'd recognize it again. There couldn't be two men who smelled like that, even in Shepherd's Bush. After you with that bush, shepherd.

'How did you come here?' asked the plain-clothes man.

'By car. It's parked down the road.'

I stood up slowly and water cascaded everywhere as though I were a collie dog shaking myself. Then I remembered Snelling.

'After all this, does Mr Snelling live here?' I asked all three of them.

The girl said, 'No. I do. I rent the flat furnished.'

'Maybe Mr Snelling's the landlord?' I suggested.

(This man made a certain suggestion, your worship; it all sounded like a court report.)

'Never heard of him,' she said. 'The people I pay rent to are Quendon Leaseholds Limited.'

This didn't sound like Snelling to me, but maybe if I rang them they'd tell me whether he was a tenant of another flat. Perhaps I'd mistaken the address? Perhaps anything, or perhaps nothing.

'I'm sorry about your flat,' I told the girl. 'I hope you find whoever did this.'

'We will,' said the policeman, sounding more confident than I would have been in his position.

I didn't feel like shaking hands with anyone, and they didn't offer to shake hands with me, so I just nodded very carefully so as not to disturb my head unnecessarily, and went out down the narrow corridor under the bulbs, down the stairs. No one stopped me, and I saw no one, either. The same TV programme was playing in each flat as I passed each front door. I might never have been away.

I drove back to the mews very slowly. George had gone, for it was about nine o'clock. I felt tired and had aged at least a thousand years. If Tutankamen had a spare place in his tomb I would gladly have crept in and shared it with him.

I unlocked the garage door, drove inside, shut the door again, went up the stairs, poured five fingers of the old Whyte & Mackay and drank it without adding any water.

Then I sat down on the edge of the bed and tried to make sense out of what had happened. This took a lot of doing.

I checked Snelling's receipt. The address he had given me was 32 Rosemary Court. I knew I hadn't made a mistake there, but clearly I had somewhere. Could the sale of that car have anything to do with the girl's flat being ransacked? It seemed impossible, and even if it were possible I didn't know where to begin to trace the matter through.

Snelling. The name meant nothing to me, but I felt that I'd seen him somewhere in my life, or in another life if you like – for I've always had good luck with girls who are a bit mystical, and who react when you say you feel you've met them in another life, maybe they were slaves at the court of Pharaoh?

His face was as clear to me as the nude calendar on the wall. The Old Etonian tie, the bright red carnation, the dark double-breasted suit, the white collar and the deep pink shirt. A rich man or a rich man's son, or perhaps only someone wanting to appear either of these things? The last could be most likely, for the richest men I've met usually don't look at all as you'd imagine they would look.

In books and films and so on, the main character has all kinds of contacts for just this sort of problem. He'll say; 'It was at that moment that my thirteen years as chief acrobat with the Royal Albanian State Circus proved so useful: I *knew* that this man could only be Count Shagworthy, who had been a three-ball juggler when we played at the Court of King Zog, etc., etc.' And, talking about three-ball jugglers reminds me of George's limerick about that gay young man of Devizes, who owned balls of quite different sizes. The first was so small, it didn't matter at all, but the second won numerous prizes.

In real life, though, I could only think of one man who just might help me if he couldn't think of any reason against it.

I picked up the telephone and dialled old Jacko Jackson,

who keeps an ear so close to the ground he's practically deformed. Jacko lives opposite me in the mews, and he's the biggest gossip since Pepys, though not so well known. I'd have gone over to see him, but I didn't think I could face the journey with the whisky churning round in my head, and my suit still damp and clammy.

Old Jacko has a strange life, but then if we're honest, don't we all? He's an actor in a small way, which means he acts out some of the simpler television commercials, as a retired ambassador, all silver-grey hair and split-arse jacket, sampling some new breakfast food, for he's a good-looking old fellow if you're not close enough to see his eyes, watery as under-poached eggs, or the tremble in his hands that a life-time of cheap gin has given him.

His main acting parts are closely involved with the used-car trade. When a dealer takes a Rolls in part exchange that is just too old to renovate, and yet too young to write off and replace with something superior, he calls in Jacko. And Jacko, after altering the car's registration book so that the last owner appears to have been the Suffragan Bishop of Balls Pond Road, or some such other ecclesiastical dignitary, will put on a chauffeur's gear and, as the late Bishop's chauffeur, will give some innocent buyer a long spiel about the car's sched-uled services, and the gentle driving he has done in it with his Grace, or his Lordship, or whoever, for the last twenty years, only carrying him to confirmation classes, or whatever.

The ringing in my ear stopped, and Jacko's voice, streaked with gin like a verbal rainbow, asked wheezily in my ear: 'Who's this?'

'Me,' I said.

'Oh.'

He sounded disappointed. Maybe he'd hoped I was a client.

'I've got a bottle of gin for you,' I told him, which wasn't strictly true, but I'd buy one wholesale when a friend of mine opened his shop in Soho on the following morning.

'What have I got to do to get it? Bend down?'

He liked a touch of the old sarcasm, did Jacko, for, say what you like about me, and lots of people say plenty, I've never been one to enlarge the circle of my friends this way.

'No,' I told him. 'I want help. Do you know anyone who traders up West use when they want to bid against a genuine buyer to force him to clinch?'

We call this bidding against the wall, and it's not confined to old-car dealers. I know one estate agent in the West End, who's had up to eight dummy bidders at an auction against the two or three genuine buyers. Once, the dummies overdid things and got left with a property they'd pushed up several thousand pounds beyond its real value.

The vendor was beside himself with anger at this and sued the estate agent for malpractice. But the crafty old dealer had already discounted any risk like this. He said that he knew nothing about the dummy bidders; it was all a plot by some disloyal employees – and since he had prudently insured against dishonesty among his staff, he was as fully covered as a bush baptist in total immersion.

But, to return to our mutton, as one lustful shepherd told another.

'I know several dummies,' said Jacko. 'We use 'em for different deals. There's one who looks like a tycoon. Silvery grey hair, hundred guinea suit – he's in the Rolls and Bentley bracket. There's another with string-back gloves, sports cap and all that crap, for the E-types, and a third boyo about forty, Old Etonian tie, carnation, natty suiting, who's useful in the middle range – Daimler, Jag, Jensen – to lean on a dim buyer who can't quite make up his mind.'

This could be my man and I told Jacko so.

'What do you want him for?' he asked.

I began to *ad lib*, because here the truth would be more difficult for him to believe than fiction.

'I've got a fellow who's coming to buy a Bentley

tomorrow,' I said. 'A Mark VI, in quite good nick. I may be able to squeeze him up to four-fifty quid for it, but if this old Etonian character came along and conveniently discovered that this car had belonged to his old uncle, Lord Fornicator, from new, I reckon I could push him up to five or six.'

'The bloke you need's Horatio,' said Jacko firmly. 'The old Etonian tie wallah. No doubt of it at all. Done a bit of fashion modelling in his day. Plays the part of the man about town. Beautiful suit, hand-rubbed shoes, hand-rubbed knob, too, if you ask me.'

'I'm not asking you,' I said firmly. I guessed old Jacko had been drinking, which is what he did most of the day when he wasn't sleeping off the previous day's alcoholic intake, soaking up the stuff like a great soft sponge, and sobbing softly at the sadness of it all. He wasn't my favourite man, but then who is?

'What does he charge, this Horatio?'

'Fiver and cab fare, if it's a local job. If it's out of town, a bit more.'

'This is a local job. Where can I find him?'

'I've lost his number,' said Jacko, 'but I have his address.' Jacko gave it to me.

'What about the gin?' he asked, suddenly suspicious.

'Be at my place tomorrow at nine. I'll give you a couple of quid to buy a bottle at my cut-price bar.'

I knew he wouldn't even be awake at nine. To prise Jacko off his bed at that hour, even for a bottle of gin, was tantamount to murdering him.

'See you,' he promised, but it would be nine at night before he came; if he didn't forget all about it as soon as I rang off.

I poured myself another drink, chewed a couple of aspirins, to ease my aching head, and then went downstairs and opened the garage doors. I took out the SS, and headed towards Chelsea in search of Horatio, who if he didn't hold the bridge, could conceivably hold an answer to my question.

The address Jacko had given me was one of those old Chelsea houses in a side street off the unfashionable end of Fulham Road, with steps going up a pillared porch, and half a dozen push buttons with visiting cards against them by the side of the door. I shone my pencil torch down the names, K. Ahmed, Miss B. Jones, A. Browne (Melbourne) and then a visiting card with a fancy script that spelled out one word: Horatio. I pressed the button and waited. A voice spoke metallically through the speaker grille of the electric lock.

'Who is it?'

'Electricity meters,' I said quickly. 'Sorry it's so late, but you've been overcharged. We're making a special survey.'

'Oh, all right. Come on up. Third floor.'

I thought that if I told him who I was, he might not have asked me in. The door opened, and I was in the hall before the lock could change its mind.

It's my experience of human nature – and believe me, in selling cars you come to learn a lot about the convolutions of the human mind – that most people accept postmen, meter readers, and so on as friendly neuters who will do them no harm.

If Horatio was just a harmless old/young/middle-aged queer, then I'd pretend to have a quick gander at the meter, and tell him that head office would be in touch with him in the morning. The fact that he'd never hear, he'd put down to general British bureaucratic inefficiency, and soon it would be forgotten, as, eventually, all is forgotten. In buying and selling and hearing all the twisted reasons people give you as to why they want to acquire or be rid of cars, you grow a bit devious yourself.

I walked up the steep, old-fashioned stairs to the third landing. The house was a hive of small rooms, all let off, each one the private world of some lonely person, either on the way up or on the way down. You could live here and die here, and the only way anyone outside would know the difference would be from milk bottles outside the front door, or the unclaimed letters in the wire cage behind it.

On the third landing the door was open a few inches, and a wedge of light shone out. I knocked gently at the door, coughed, as I imagined a genuine meter-reader would do, and went inside. A man was twiddling with the controls of a TV set; the picture was very bad. His back was towards me, so I couldn't recognize his face.

'Meter's behind the curtain,' he said, not looking round.

I closed the door behind me, and pulled aside a curtain that hung from a white book shelf. The gas and electricity meters were there all right. The man turned, and I saw he was Snelling. He also recognized me.

'What the hell?' he asked, half in anger, half in surprise.

'My little joke,' I said. 'I thought you mightn't like to see a used-car dealer after hours.'

'What's wrong?' he asked.

'Why should *anything* be wrong? You gave me an address in Rosemary Court, Mr Snelling, or Horatio, or whoever you really are. I went there with some keys you'd left behind in my office. I didn't find you at that address. In fact, you're not even known there, but someone appeared to be waiting for me. They slugged me on the head. Look.'

I bent forward so that he could see the bruise.

'My God,' he said, and his fear and surprise could have been genuine.

'Only God *can* help you now,' I said, 'because I mean to stay here until you tell me why you gave me that wrong address. And did you leave your keys behind in my garage innocently – or on purpose? Did you *expect* I'd take them on to Rosemary Court, and then maybe someone else – or maybe even you, Mr Snelling – would be waiting for me?'

'You've got it all wrong,' he said, backing away.

The picture on the screen trembled suddenly into clarity; it was a commercial for toothpaste. Snelling smiled out at me, with his striped tie and carnation, squeezing a white ribbon of paste on to an enormous brush. No wonder he'd been anxious to adjust the picture. All actors love looking at their favourite people: themselves.

'Just where have I got it wrong?' I asked him. 'Who lives at thirty-two, Rosemary Court, if you don't?'

'I don't know,' he said.

'Come, come, Mr Snelling. You'll have to do better than that. Both of us can't not know.'

It wasn't very grammatical, I agree, but it made sense to him.

I took out from my trouser pocket a foot of coiled copper petrol pipe that I carry when I travel alone; this made even more sense, for there's nothing more innocent for a car dealer to carry – and nothing more useful as an instrument of persuasion, when you put your fist inside the coil, as I did now.

Snelling watched my fingers flex around the polished tube. If he had a brain, he was thinking what damage these hard ridges of copper would make to his face. If they connected, there wouldn't be any more commercials for a few weeks. Even a car dealer wouldn't want to use him if his face was all pushed in; that's how low he'd be placed.

'Who lives there, then?' I asked, taking a step towards him.

'I've told you, I don't know. A stranger rang me and asked if I'd buy the car for him. That often happens. He'd got my name from a fellow in the trade. Warren Street.

'I met him in a pub, The Goat and Compasses. I didn't know him and he didn't tell me his name. I didn't ask him – that's usual too. The less you know the less you can louse things up.

'My fee was a fiver. He pulled out his wallet, for he was paying me in cash, and I saw a letterhead or a card – I didn't know exactly which – with that address. I didn't know who he was. He could be bent, so why get my own address involved? I simply gave you his. Hell, in this business how often do you give your real name, let alone your address?'

'What sort of man was he?'

'Thirty-five. Tall. Wore dark glasses.'

This could describe almost anyone in our business. It didn't describe anyone I know. I made a sudden lunge at Horatio as though I was going to strike him, and he screamed and backed away over the set, and the picture split into a maze of jagged edges and horizontal lines.

'Where did you take the car when you bought it?'

'To a mews,' he replied, so quickly that he didn't have time to make it up.

'Where?'

'Seventeen, Belsize Park West.'

So. That was Kent's address.

'Was the man there who'd given you the money?'

'No. The garage had been left unlocked. My instructions were to drive the car in and close the doors. They had a press padlock.'

'And you've never seen the man again? You've no address for him?'

'No. I usually don't, in these deals. People want to hire me as a front man for all sorts of things. To put up the price, to lower it, to explain why they can't go ahead with some deal. I just take my money, and don't ask questions. It's healthier that way.'

I could believe him. I know of others like him who eke out a precarious twilight existence in the half world of gambling clubs, used-car dealers and shady estate agents, men who spend their working lives pretending to be buyers, sellers, relatives; the only person they can never admit to being is themselves; they are the nothing-people.

'And you swear you know nothing about beating me up?'

'I swear it. I mean, why should I want to do that to you? We've only met once.'

This seemed a novel reason, but I believed him; he wasn't a hard-arm man.

'If I find you've been lying to me, Snelling or Horatio or whatever else you call yourself,' I said, 'I know where you live, and I'll be back. If I find you've got the slightest connexion with this bruise on my head, I'll do my best to make life hard for you.'

'I swear I know nothing.'

He was trembling now, and his face was grey, with the skin stretched tight like parchment over his cheek-bones.

I went down the stairs and out into the street, and drove back to my mews. What had I learned? Simply that Kent had offered me a car, and then, through an intermediary, had apparently bought it back at £100 more. Why?

I thought about going over to see Kent, but if he was straight there was nothing I would learn, and if he was bent he'd be far too clever to tell me. Maybe he regretted selling the car so cheaply, and had unexpectedly received a fantastic offer, so that the best thing would be to buy it back. I'd done that myself once or twice in the past.

I felt like that man in George's story who feels the need for a brain transplant. He goes to the surgeon, and he's told he can have a Jew's brain for £80, or an Irishman's for only £250. All right, he says but why the difference in price?

Because, replies the surgeon, the Irishman's brain has hardly been used.

Nor had mine. I felt as out of my depth as a girl guide in Lisle Street. I know how the boy scouts and the girl guides, but for me, I was very thankful to creep into my narrow slot of a bed and fall asleep.

2 ✳ For the next two or three days, nothing much happened. I agree that there was an earthquake in Peru, a man married his mother-in-law in Bangkok, three peons held up a bank in Mexico City, but in my mews George and I just kept on breathing, and very quietly at that, which shows you how slow business was.

I did a bit of phoning, and answered a few calls from idiots wanting to know what I would give them for their unsaleable vehicles, and so it must have been around Wednesday the following week, when Kent stuck his head round the door, for presumably he'd nowhere better to stick it.

'Got a minute?' he asked.

'I've got more than a minute,' I said, 'and if your money's right, and your sex is right, I've got the inclination, too.'

He looked at me a bit surprised, and I wondered whether this guy might be a lay preacher or President of the League of Anti-Shafters or some such thing. I poured him a Whyte & Mackay whisky to keep him here.

He glanced around my stock; it was the same as when he'd last called.

'So you sold the Delahaye?' he said. 'Make much on it?'

I shrugged. It wasn't his business. Also, if he'd bought it, surely he should know?

'Covered my losses,' I said.

'Well, you can't grumble at that.'

I wasn't grumbling, but I thought this was going to be one of those dreary conversations when we'd start talking about the weather.

It's all right for the ducks when it's raining, and if we have an unexpected sunny day, we're going to pay for it. Mustn't

37

grumble, though. But, why ever not? If people hadn't grumbled, we'd still be living in caves and rubbing sticks together for a flame.

Kent took out a gold cigarette case, withdrew a cigarette very slowly and carefully, lest he should lose a grain of tobacco he'd paid for, and tapped it on the side. He didn't offer me one, which didn't shorten my life span, but it reinforced my original feeling that he wasn't an over-swift man with a coin. He lit his cigarette and looked at the glowing end critically as though to check that it wasn't burning too fast. Then he came to the point of his visit.

'Would you be interested in buying any other old cars?'

'What other old cars?' I parried.

The trouble in my business, or one of the troubles, is that so many people think that an old car must be valuable simply because it is old. This just isn't so, any more than an old wardrobe is necessarily worth more than its weight in firewood, simply because it's old. But if Chippendale or Sheraton or one of those old guys made it, then that's a different deal altogether.

You may own a 1929 Austin-Seven Chummy, and I once refused one at thirty shillings in a part-exchange deal when I was buying and selling newer cars, and today it could fetch five hundred quid. But if you own an Austin Seven a few years newer, say 1934 or thereabouts, I wouldn't give you forty quid for the beast, because I don't know where I could sell it at a profit. All antiques have their fashions and their vogues, and cars are no exception.

'I don't know much about your business,' said Kent, 'but this is the sort of car I have in mind.'

He pulled an envelope from an inner pocket, and shook out four coloured photographs. The first was of a Marmon, one of America's most expensive cars of thirty odd years ago, with the headlights built into the front wings and one of the biggest engines in the business – 16 cylinders, 200 horses – at a

38

time when big engines were far more common than they are today.

Colonel Howard Marmon, who ran a company which always made fine cars, had been facing heavy competition for years, plus sales troubles in the depression. His company was sinking in rough financial seas, and he planned this masterpiece, 'The World's Most Advanced Motor Car', as his ads called it, as a last throw.

He threw and he lost, for Cadillac brought out a V-16 first, and although Marmon's was better in many ways, ten miles an hour faster *and* 150 dollars cheaper, his car was second – and who now remembers the second man to fly the Atlantic or run a four-minute mile ? In this rough old world, you have to be first or not at all.

Like the Chrysler Airflow back in my mews, the Marmon was judged a failure, but it had failed majestically, and if you can't succeed, you can do worse than go down trying.

The second was of a two-seater Fiat Balilla, in bright Italian red, with its tiny vestigial fin behind the cockpit, spidery spoked wheels and minute brake drums. I could sell both easily enough.

The third interested me even more, for it was a 1930 Delage drop-head, with a spare wheel on each side of the bonnet, and big Marchal headlights. The body could be a Chapron, and probably was; this could retail at two and a half thousand iron men with no trouble whatever.

All the cars seemed to have been photographed against the same background; a sandstone wall, rather yellowish, that could look golden in the sun. They were standing on a piece of tarmac, perhaps a road, for sand had blurred its edges. They all wore white number plates with black figures, and each plate had the word 'Privé' on it.

'Where are these cars ?' I asked.

'The Middle East,' said Kent, scooping up the photographs

again. He tapped their edges carefully together, replaced them in the envelope, put the envelope back in an inner pocket, and buttoned down the flap. He was a cautious character, this one. I reckon he probably had two threads on that button, just in case one broke.

'What part of the Middle East?' I asked him.

'Cairo,' he said. 'I have an office there. I told you. Import, export.'

'They *could* be interesting,' I said, and they could at that, if the prices weren't too high.

'Do you know Cairo at all?' he asked.

I shook my head. I had once come down there on a flight from India, where I'd gone to try and buy a half-dozen Phantoms from a Maharajah's stable, hoping unsuccessfully for a discount for quantity. Our plane came down to refuel at Farouk Airport, which shows how long ago that was. I didn't know what they call Cairo airport now, but I'm pretty certain it's not Farouk.

'They have a lot of old cars out there,' Kent went on. 'For one thing, the climate's so dry they never seem to wear out. And if they do wear out, they're practically rebuilt, because Nasser's put a 285 per cent import duty on new cars, simply to stop them coming in. The country's too short of foreign currency to buy them.'

'So what have you in mind?' I asked, guessing the trend of his thoughts, which were about as obvious as the writing on this page.

'This. Why don't we import a few of these cars and flog them here?'

'We?'

'Well, you'd do it. You know the business. I'll help you find them and guide you through all the messing about you'd have with the Egyptian customs people if you tried it on your own. One's got to slip a bit of specie here and there to oil the wheels, and I know the people who take bribes and those who

40

don't. Then, if you make a sale back here, maybe you'll give me a cut.'

'What would you have to pay for that Marmon?' I asked him.

'If we bought it for Egyptian pounds, they're the same as pounds sterling, at the official rate of exchange, so it would cost you a lot of dough, simply because the owner can't buy a replacement.

'But if we could help him, by putting some money for him, say, in a bank in Malta, or paying in dollars, we'd cut his asking price by 50 per cent. On the black market you can get at least a hundred and fifty piastres for a pound sterling instead of the hundred that the Gyppoes will allow you legally.

'The richer ones will do anything to get their money into another country, for then they can travel abroad, or pick up bargains in their own home town, for what everyone needs desperately is foreign currency. I reckon we could pick up that Marmon for two-fifty quid on the nose if we do things my way. What could you sell it for here?'

'Let's have another look at it.'

He brought out the photograph again and I opened the drawer, took out a magnifying glass, and examined the car closely. The paint seemed fairly good, but there were a few bent slats in the horizontal radiator, and a lamp glass was cracked. Still, if it was a runner it must be in fair mechanical order. I could probably shift it for a thousand quid to some old car museum.

So, if I paid two-fifty for it, had the bill of sale made out for, say, seventy-five, and therefore only paid import duty on that seventy-five, and then spent another hundred letting George give it a good go-over, I wouldn't be losing, even though I had to slip Kent something for his trouble.

'I might get five hundred for it,' I said cautiously. Never raise people's hopes where money is concerned; they always remember the highest figure you mention.

41

'It's really impossible to say. You can be lumbered with a car for weeks, and then, on the day after you drop your price and sell, you have a dozen inquiries for it.'

But I was interested, very interested, for the great difficulty in every branch of the antique trade is finding enough antiques. Only so many of anything, from Silver Ghosts to Sheraton tables, were ever made, and the rest are either complete copies or half-copies, by which I mean that they may have the original wheels or contain some bits of wood that Sheraton's chisel could have carved. If I could find a source of old cars that somehow hadn't been tapped, then I could make a killing.

I already had advertisements running every month in *The Times of India*, and in the Calcutta and Delhi editions of *The Statesman*, informing readers that 'an English collector, wishing to augment his stable, urgently seeks pre-war motor-cars in good condition, preferably with open coachwork; highest prices in sterling or dollars.'

But the wily Indians were growing wise to the value of the old cars still within their shores, and they were giving nothing away cheaply.

Spain and Southern Europe had also suffered a pretty good going-over. So had Yugoslavia, where some of my rivals had found several quite extraordinary cars, but, so far as I knew, no one had tried Egypt. I suppose there was some basic resistance to Egypt after the Suez shambles, or maybe because of the Arab-Israeli war, and this could have clouded people's judgement. Yet Egypt might easily be a treasure house of old cars. There had always been rich people in Cairo, the pashas and the beys and all Farouk's hangers-on. And where you have money, you usually find expensive and interesting motor-cars.

Yes, Egypt seemed such an obvious place to look, why hadn't someone done so before? I couldn't think, but there has to be a first time for everything, and the best ideas are often the simplest; look how long it took for someone to think of the safety-pin.

'Are you sure there are no snags about getting a car out of Egypt?' I asked Kent. There might be some absurd ruling he'd never heard of, simply because he'd never tried to export a car.

'Nothing,' he said emphatically. 'I know that. I asked at the British Embassy, and I've checked with the Customs and Excise People in Cairo. It's dead easy – so long as the deal brings in foreign currency. It'd be different altogether if someone in Egypt wanted to do it without money coming in, I give you that.'

Which is about the only thing you'll ever give me, I thought, for words cost nothing and often don't mean much more.

'No strain at all,' he went on. 'Now, what do you say?'

For a moment I didn't say anything, my mind spinning like a Ferrari flywheel. This fellow should know; after all, he worked there. It could just be that I had hit the golden vein.

'It's worth a look,' I agreed cautiously, not wishing to sound too eager. 'What do you want out of the deal, if we can do any business?'

'An agent's cut,' he said. 'Say, 25 per cent.'

'Of what?'

'Your selling price.'

'After all my expenses, renovation costs, duty, and so on,' I said quickly.

'If you want it that way,' he said reluctantly.

We shook hands.

'What's the next step, then?' I asked him.

'Come out to Cairo, spend a few days there, see the cars, make it known you're in the market. I'll introduce you around. Even if you only bought one car, that should cover the cost of your trip. If you bought two, you'd be making a profit.'

'I'll think about it,' I said.

'Well, don't think too long because I'm off myself the day after tomorrow. We might fly out together.'

He poured himself another whisky. I watched him drink it. I don't think he really wanted it, but it happened to be free, and he couldn't resist it for that reason.

He pushed off and I sat down at my desk and wrote £500 for a profit on the Marmon, after all expenses, the same for the Fiat and a whacking big £2,000 profit on the Delage; total, £3,000 net. Kent needn't know I'd made quite that, so I wouldn't have to pay him entirely a quarter. It seemed too easy to be true, but it needn't be. I knew several men who'd bought and sold old beat-up bangers on bomb-sites around London after the war and then suddenly realized what the sites were worth, and so they'd sold them instead and were now millionaires. It's mostly a matter of recognizing a chance, no matter how heavily disguised your chance may be.

I don't know if you are like me, counting chickens before the hens are even pregnant, but the sum looked healthy on paper, and I couldn't see where the arithmetic went wrong. If these cars actually existed in Cairo and could be bought at this price in almost any condition, I must at the very least make this amount.

Now, if I could do it with three, I could do it with thirty, or three hundred – provided the stock was there. If we sold for cash, then we'd have no nibbling at the profits by the Income Tax boyos, and I could finance each new deal with the profits from the previous one.

I imagined how Charles Clore must have felt when the whole wonderful business of sale and leaseback suddenly hit him. This was no harder than printing my own money. Easier, because I didn't even need to buy a press. If I could find enough cars, I could be my own mint. Even so, the fact that it all seemed so easy still struck a wrong note somewhere in my cautious mind.

There are a lot of sharp boys in the car business, so why hadn't some of them tried it before? Or had they tried and run into impossible snags? I decided I would contact one of the sharpest of all, Mossy MacHarris, who'd traded from half a dozen bomb-sites fifteen years ago and now owned a steam yacht a few feet longer than the *Britannia*.

I don't know what Mossy's original name was, or where he came from, but he was so rich I'd go along with him for the journey, whatever his destination. I had known him in the great days when car dealers were making more money in notes than they knew what to do with.

He began by making a speciality of sales of Army surplus equipment, working to a set timetable. Say the Ministry of Supply advertised a sale of three-ton lorries on a Tuesday, and then 1,000 ex-W.D. motor cycles for the following day, Mossy would work out that motor cycle buyers wouldn't bother to turn up for the lorry sale, which was a reasonable enough deduction.

He'd therefore go down on the Monday, the viewing day, chat up some sergeant in charge of the dump, select half a dozen lorries that were in a lot together, and then give the sergeant a tenner to fill up each lorry with motor cycles, when everyone else had gone home, and strap down the canvas covers so that they wouldn't be seen.

Come Tuesday morning, Mossy would cheerfully outbid everyone else for these six lorries – as well he could afford to, because he was also buying fifty or sixty almost brand new motor cycles thrown in, each of which he'd sell for £40 in the trade before that evening sun went down.

You can only do this a few times before someone will split on you, possibly the sergeant, who the second time round wants £20 instead of £10 for his services, and so, having made some capital, Mossy had wisely moved out to the rather more rarified atmosphere of property.

He still controlled a network of about forty garages round

the country, but much of his time now he spent in his house in the South of France, or aboard his yacht, cruising in the Aegean.

I didn't know whether he was happy, but I did know he was rich, which was often the next best thing. Remember, there's only one thing money can't buy: poverty.

I knew Mossy pretty well, and could convince his secretary, his P.A. and so on, that I wasn't on the touch, and thus reached him on the telephone within about fifteen minutes.

'What's the matter?' he asked cautiously. 'You in trouble?'

'Nothing half a million wouldn't see me out of,' I told him. 'Just a proposition that's been put to me. I wondered if I could have a word with you about it. Now?'

'Fine,' he said. 'Come round. But don't mind if I have to dash off in a hurry. I've got a fixed time call to Nicosia that's not come through.'

I didn't mind; I wasn't paying for the call.

It was a sunny afternoon, too nice even to sit in the car, so I walked round to Curzon Street, to one of those old gracious bow-fronted houses, sleeping in the shade of the Hilton, with a metal arch over the front gate and an inverted iron cone where link-men used to snuff out their torches in the days of sedan-chairs.

Inside, it was all terribly, terribly elegant, quite different from the days when Mossy had rented a room in the Earls Court Road and we'd shared a phone box outside in the road as an office.

Here it was striped wallpaper, as thick as fur, white paint as glossy as marble, carpets up to your knees, mirrors and candelabra with real candles. Old Mossy was wearing a suit so tight it looked as though he had been poured into it, and hadn't found the way out, lizard-skin shoes, gold-strapped wristwatch, ingot cuff links. He was going through his millionaire period, and I must say I could have shared it with him. He sat at a desk topped with crimson leather, lined with

46

gold. He looked rather like Napoleon, I thought charitably, but he was probably just that bit richer.

'Haven't seen you for years,' he said, without much regret, pressing a button on his desk, so that a bookcase in the wall revolved to show a cabinet of drinks. He poured two whiskies into gold goblets, in lieu of anything else to pour them into, and added cubes of ice. Then the bookcase turned again and showed us a lot of books. We toasted each other.

'When were you last in Cairo?' I asked him, after all the it's-so-long-since-we-met stuff had died away.

'Me?'

He looked pained.

'Me? With my name? Do you mind?'

'Oh, yes. I'd forgotten that. What I meant, Mossy, was I've been offered a deal out there, and it seems such easy money I felt there must be a snag in it.'

'What sort of deal?' he asked.

He took out a gold toothpick and sawed about between his teeth, now and then looking at the end of the pick as though he expected to find the answer there, while I told him. Then he slipped the toothpick into a waistcoat pocket, and gave his opinion.

'So long as the cars are reasonable, and so long as the Gyppoes let you get them out without any frigging about, you can't lose,' he said.

'That's what I thought. But somehow it just seems too easy. Why hasn't someone thought of it before?'

'When I was a boy,' said Mossy ponderously, as though he was about a hundred and four, '*My* old man used to tell me when I put up a proposition to make money: "If it was as easy as that, Mossy boy, *everyone* would be doing it."'

'In fact, of course, everyone *was* doing it. There's no snag here. Only trouble, the profit's so small. I don't know why you mess about with these diabolical old motors for a few pounds when you can make a thousand times as much with

47

something worth while like land, or shares, or buildings. Now, I've a development just starting in Cyprus. Those bloody Greeks and Turks can't fight for ever, and when all the Swedes and Poles and all those other dreary United Nations characters out there go home, the land values will go up quicker than a young man's fagan.'

Such crude talk sounded out of place in the surroundings, but then Mossy always liked to remind people he'd known years ago that he'd also been poor once; this was one of the ways in which he showed he was still one of us at heart.

'To each his own, Mossy,' I said, and nodded towards the bookcase. He repeated his stuff with the hidden button. I poured myself some more of his whisky, while he sat and watched me rather glumly. He was so rich he could have the stuff piped in, and if I was as rich, I'd have it piped direct from the Mackay distillery. Then I thought of seventeen, Belsize Park West, and mentioned this to him.

He pressed a button on some complicated piece of electronic equipment on his desk, expensively and inexplicably disguised as an eighteenth-century Viennese music box, and gave his orders. Within seconds, or so it seemed, a disembodied voice was giving the answer.

'This mews is owned by one of our companies, Beechwood Freeholds. The tenant of the garage and the flat is a Mr O'Gorman, a street trader. He pays a monthly rent of £84, exclusive of rates. His lease has two years four months to run.'

'Ever heard of a man there called Kent?' I asked the box.

'We have no record of anyone of that name on this file,' the voice assured me gravely. He could have been St Peter doing a Dun and Bradstreet on a stranger at the pearly gates.

'Well, that's it, then,' said Mossy, obviously very pleased at his firm's efficiency. 'Probably this character O'Gorman is subletting.'

48

'Probably,' I said, but so far as I was concerned, he meant nothing in my life.

So we left it like that, for I couldn't leave it anywhere else. I had a few more drinks, but he had none, and it was evening by the time I was back in my mews. The phone was ringing as I unlocked the door. George had gone home long since, so I scooped up the instrument and stood breathing whisky on the window, and then drew a face in the moist breath with a finger. Talk of the devil; Kent was on the line.

'Good bit of news,' he said. 'For you, at least. Fellow who was flying out to Cairo with me has got a slipped disc. Can't move. Flat on his back, pretty well, strapped to his bed. I've got his ticket. Wonder if you'd care to use it? Fly out with me?'

'How about paying?' I asked. He paused and I could almost hear his brain ticking like a cash register.

'Tell you what. Use it now. My firm has paid for it – comes off the tax and doesn't matter a damn. Not as though I was spending the money myself, eh? But if you do a deal, we can talk about it then. O.K.?'

'O.K.,' I said. 'Where shall I see you?'

'London Airport. Nine o'clock. Day after tomorrow. Number three building. At the Air France desk.'

'What's the climate like in Cairo, this time of year?'

'Warmish. So bring a light suit. And some money.'

He rang off. I locked the door behind me and went upstairs. I felt like the cat must feel when he sees a bird on a branch, one he knows just can't get away, and he is savouring that sweet moment before the kill. This could be my lucky day, like the song says, only more so.

The next morning I spent collecting a tourist's visa from the Egyptian Embassy. Then I cabled the Ecclesiastical Bank in Malta, which is an island with certain financial advantages, the most important being that no questions are asked about income tax that you can't answer fairly easily, and where it's not impossible to exchange sterling into any other currency without shortening your life span by filling in forms.

I shifted £1,500 into dollars, and then transferred them to Cairo to await me in traveller's cheques, care of the American Express. Then I went round to my local bank and drew out my meagre £50, which was all Her Majesty's Government allowed me to take abroad legally for a holiday. I then bought three colour film packs for my Polaroid camera, because I might find more cars than Kent had known about, and could possibly buy an option on them, and photograph them and sell them on their pictures before I even had to extract them from Egypt.

On the following morning, early, George drove me out to the airport.

'I'll give you Major Stevens you're going to be done.' George told me cheerfully as we approached the International Building.

'Major Stevens?'

'Yes. Evens.'

'Oh.'

'Yes, oh, indeed. I did years out there, remember. In the Canal Zone. Lot of crafty Jerry Diddlers – fiddlers – there. Running guns, drugs, whirls – girls – anything. Old Farouk set the pace. So, watch it. I'm just giving you an old man's horning – warning.'

'Thank you very much.'

I didn't sound over-enthusiastic, but I had my own doubts, which was why I'd asked George to take me to the airport.

Things seemed to be coming my way, as the politician said when he was pelted with rotten eggs, but, being basically a cynic, I wanted to make sure that Kent was actually at the ticket desk with the ticket in his hand before I was certain.

If he wasn't, then George could drive me back to the mews again. But when we arrived, Kent was walking up and down,

50

puffing at a cheroot, checking his watch with the clock above the gallery.

'Bags of time,' he said. 'I always like to get anywhere early. Saves rushing. Here's your ticket, then. Made out in my friend's name – Cartwright – but that's only a technical point.'

We went through into the departure lounge, where I bought a couple of newspapers. The news was so depressing, nothing but strikes at home, military coups abroad and trade figures falling like rain, that I pushed them into one of those big cylindrical ashtrays rather than read them.

The flight was as uneventful as you expect these things to be, although privately I always marvel at the way one covers prodigious distances in hours, when only a few years back they would have taken days or even weeks.

We reached Cairo airport at about seven o'clock that evening. As we walked through the building, I smelled that forgotten smell of dust, apparently soaked in oil; the scent of a warm day dying, and the arid desert all around, throwing back to the night the heat which that day had forced upon it.

We seemed to be the only people leaving the plane; the rest were going on to Karachi or wherever. An airline official wanted to press a yellow disc into our hands, thinking we must be in transit. When we said we were actually staying in Cairo, he replied in amazement, 'Welcome.'

Welcome to the customs hall like a barn, welcome to some plain-clothes policeman who asked me to fill in a form to say how much money I had brought into the country. I saw Kent look at me in anguish here. He had clearly forgotten to warn me, but I filled in my £50 honestly enough, thinking of my £1,500 at the American Express.

The great snag about being too honest here only becomes apparent when the visitor realizes that two rates of money exchange prevail, the official, at one Egyptian pound to one pound sterling, and the unofficial, which more realistically sets a value of two or even three Egyptian pounds to every English pound.

If you haven't declared all your resources at the airport you can take advantage of this arrangement and literally double your money *and* have a stay for nothing. But if you have been honest, you can only watch others do this, for you must account for every pound you brought in on the way out.

Someone appeared with a trolley to wheel our cases out to the taxi rank. There must have been a hundred cabs, each painted black with white mudguards, all waiting under the sodium lights and the dusty palm trees. A policeman shuffled up and ticked a number in a book. The local war had driven away nearly all tourists from Egypt, but the fewer there were, the fewer possible rivals, I thought, sitting back on the ancient plastic seat of the Mercedes 190D.

The cab was very old and smelled of diesel, grinding along with dim yellow headlights, braying its feeble horn at crossroads. We ran in through Heliopolis, a long, dusty, sandstone suburb, all high walls and square buildings against the mountains of the night. Guttering oil lamps flickered over street-corner stalls. Night watchmen wrapped in blankets waited patiently outside the gates of rich men's houses – for what or who? Enemies or friends?

'Where are we staying?' I asked Kent.

'The Hilton. It's clean and modern, and no dearer than anywhere else – if you take a room at the top. If you don't want the usual American deep-fried golden batter scampi in a seafood basket, farm-fresh, hand-tossed salad, and all that jazz, we can eat out. Also, that might be cheaper.'

The Nile Hilton soared like a cliff against the lingering purple sunset, speckled here and there with lit-up windows. The taxi ran in underneath among pillars and between potted palms.

'You want me tomorrow, gentlemen?' the driver asked

hopefully. 'I give you my price. Three pounds whole day running. With this car I come here? Yes?'

He looked back at us. Trade must be terrible, I thought. Three pounds could hardly cover the cost of fuel.

Kent shook his head.

'No,' he said. 'Not tomorrow, squire, but thanks for the offer.'

We climbed out, and Kent walked ahead, leaving me to pay. He was a slow man, even with a piastre.

We were up on the ninth floor, for the rooms came cheaper the higher you went, and if we'd gone any higher we'd have been out on the roof.

I didn't know what Kent's room was like, and I didn't greatly care. Mine was done out in blue and green hessian, with a decoration on one wall, a sort of plastic frieze, copied from something found in a tomb or pyramid. A big, sliding window opened over Liberation Square. All cities in the Middle East have a Liberation Square, or Liberation Avenue – but what does the name mark except their progress from one tyranny to another? Who has been liberated and who were the liberators?

I hung up my spare light-weight suit in the cupboard, put my shirts into the top drawer of the chest, had a couple of Alka Seltzers for want of anything better to have, and fiddled with the knobs on the bedside table. Taped music of the thirties flooded out in a sugary tide. I slid back the picture window and stepped out on the veranda.

The evening was cool, and the trumpet-calls of car horns, plus the clanging of trams, came up only faintly. Beneath me the lawns of the hotel garden were dark; a fountain played in an ornamental lake across the square. Behind it, red and blue neons for Ethiopian Airlines and Thos. Cooks blazed against the darkening sky.

Somewhere in this city, I thought, lay the cars that were going to make me a fortune. They'd probably been here for thirty years or more; through a war, a revolution, a whole world gone. It was an intriguing thought, and I was just enjoying thinking it, when I heard a knock on the door, and Kent calling, 'Shop!'

I joined him in the corridor.

'What about a meal and then we'll see some belly dancing?' he said.

'Not for me,' I told him. 'My belly's dancing already after that flight. I just want a couple of whiskies and then to bed.'

'You must be getting old,' said Kent.

'Every day, in every way, I grow older and older,' I agreed, which is true, anyway. Every day is a day nearer the grave. You can't beat 'em, and one day we'll all join 'em.

'In that case, I'll have a drink, too, and then I'll go on down to my office and see what's been happening since I've been away.'

'Anyone be there at this hour?'

'Oh, yes,' he said. 'I've a secretary.'

'That's something,' I said. 'I've no one.'

And I hadn't, either. Just a succession of girl friends who left me to marry other men, and sometimes they sent me Christmas cards with such unlikely addresses as Pinner and Penge, and then cards to announce the birth of their various children. I'd no one who cared whether I lived or died, and sometimes I didn't know whether I was sorry or glad. This was one of those times.

We were in the lift now, going up to the roof, to that curious export of North America, the darkened bar. You can't see what you're drinking; you have to feel what's in your glass, and when it hits your stomach, you know.

In the bar, Kent and I sat perched on top of a structure of steel and glass and concrete, mathematically stressed and strained, with Cairo on one side, the ancient Nile on the other, then Gezira Island, and then the long darkness of the desert, punctured here and there by dim and flickering lights. All

54

around us, other people were sitting close together in the gloom. If they were good Muslims they were drinking soft drinks, and if they were more broadminded, they were drinking hard ones. I thought of the indignant retort from a loyal supporter of the old Aga Khan, when someone suggested that, as a Moslem leader, the Aga Khan should not drink champagne: 'When it touches his Highness's lips, the champagne turns to water.'

Kent and I had a couple of whiskies each and they didn't turn to water, but my knees did when I saw the bill, and then I went down in the lift with him to the front hall.

'Just one thing,' he said, as we waited for the doors to open, 'our rooms are probably bugged. Nothing sinister. Simply because we're foreigners. So be careful what you say on the phone. No criticism of Colonel Nasser. It's safer to call him Mr Smith.'

'What would I say about him?' I asked. 'I've never even met the man.'

'These guys might get the idea we're trying to change some money on the side, and maybe even take out their cars at prices less than they think they're worth. If they got that idea, they might put the boot in. They're funny that way.'

'So are most people. Message received and understood. See you tomorrow, down here in the foyer, ten o'clock. O.K.?'

The pneumatic doors opened, and a crowd of package-deal tourists, ancient Americans of various sexes, faces withered and dried by years of air-conditioning, curious Canadians in store suits with wide-bottomed trousers, one actually wearing an overcoat and rubber galoshes, skins wrinkled as a tortoise's neck, thrust themselves unceremoniously on top of us. We fought our way out, through shrill voices complaining to their tour-leader, and Kent was gone.

I walked out of the back door of the hotel, across the road, on to the Nile promenade. Some poor old devil was wrapped in a white sheet like a corpse, asleep on a concrete bench; not a tourist, of course, someone who lived here, if you could call this living. The water lapped and chuckled only feet away. The Nile had seen too many centuries of poverty to show interest now. In the darkness, a number of small wooden boats, all moored at their prows, thumped and creaked against each other. Starving dogs were rooting for food in an overturned dustbin on the bank.

I walked up the street, watching the cars swing past. Apart from one or two modern ones wearing C.D. plates, they all seemed pretty old, an odd mixture of Chryslers and Chevrolets of the nineteen-thirties, with a few small Morrises and Fords of the forties, and then a rash of black and white Mercedes taxis, mostly about ten years old.

Fifty yards up the road, beside the Nile, an old Opel saloon, the one with the horizontal radiator grille, like the pre-war Cord, was pulled into the side under a street light with its bonnet up. I glanced in at the engine as I passed by. It was a bird's nest of wires and string and tubes bound up with tape. By any accepted mechanical standards it should have stopped running long ago, but with a 285 per cent tax on anything new, I knew how the owner felt.

I also felt a bit more confident myself now that I had seen these old cars actually in the streets, dragging themselves along. I had no doubt now that we would be able to pick up as many as we wanted. The only question would be the price, but then this is the biggest question all through life. Is the price of anything – a job, a girl, a deal, a career worth what is offered in return? And who can really say until they've paid it?

I went back to my room, thinking about this in lieu of anything else. The taped music was still playing, apparently the same tune. By the side of the bed lay a sheet of cardboard with a hole in it to hang on the doorknob, listing breakfast guests could order. One was called, safari. This seemed symbolic of good hunting, so I chose that, marked off mango juice, coffee, two boiled eggs, toast and honey, hung it outside the door, pushed a chair up under the doorknob in case too many people had a passkey, and went to bed.

I must have slept like that fellow by the bank of the Nile, because I woke up to hear someone hammering on the door as though the place was on fire. I sprang out, pulled away the chair and opened the door.

'Welcome,' said the waiter. So, it must be morning. He was wearing a fez and a white jacket, balancing a silver tray over his right shoulder. I was wearing nothing, which is how I sleep – I like to think, ready for anything the night may offer, but it hadn't offered much so far in Cairo – so I wrapped a towel round what the old medical ads used to call coyly, the vital organs.

'Welcome to you,' I said.

I ate breakfast on the veranda, bathed, shaved, and by ten o'clock was downstairs. Kent was reading *The Egyptian Gazette,* because it is the only paper printed in English. It seemed full of gloomy news about shelling across the Canal, with statements from Arab leaders demanding this and that, with messages to and from delegates at UNO, the whole thing adding up, in my mind, to a great big nothing.

He threw it on one side, and we walked out through the swing doors, past guides and touts. ('I give you special price in my brother's shop. Not to buy, only to look, just to see. You English? My very good friend, the English'), and all this ageless chat of the sellers.

'Do we take a cab?' I asked him.

'No, we'll walk,' he said. 'No need to throw money away. How have you arranged finance for the deal, by the way?'

'Through the American Express. Do I need the cash now?'

'Maybe an idea. We'll walk that way.'

I thought that if I walked that way some giant Nubian with nuts like oranges would leap on me and beat me to the ground, but I didn't think the thought was worth putting into words.

There was no one in the American Express except the clerks. I showed them my passport, but no one got very excited.

'There should be some traveller's cheques for me here,' I told a man in his shirt-sleeves behind the counter. 'Not in my name, but being cabled from Mr Utos, of Malta. Mr A. A. Utos.'

Just so that you can follow the convoluted turnings of my mind, and to confuse the fellows in Exchange Control, I sometimes send money abroad in different names. So that I won't forget the names, which is easier to do than you may think, I always use an anagram of my firm, Aristo Autos, which, cut down to a name, was, in this case, A. A. Utos.

There was a bit of coming and going and looking through files, all that crap which is inseparable from banks and travel agencies and whatever else, and then the man came up with the cheques for me to sign. I signed them, put them in my pocket, and buttoned down the flap, and we were back in the street.

It felt cold out of the sun, and the wind rattled the pages of magazines hanging by clips in a corner kiosk on the pavement. Here and there, manhole covers had been removed for some unknown purpose, and the holes were blocked with paving slabs. I thought that this would be a hell of a place to go walking around in bare feet at night.

'Are we going straight to your office?' I asked Kent.

He shook his head.

'We're going to one of my contacts first. Fellow who runs a shop. Perfume essences. There's a great trade in that here. Exported all over the world. Sometimes some of the bottles may also contain a bit of heroin or pot, but that's not our concern. He is also an expert on jewels. Sell you a diamond for twenty quid that'd cost you fifty back home.

58

'Just let me fill you in with a little of accepted business etiquette here before we see this character. You probably want to do a deal as quick as Speedy Gonzalez and then over the hill, but, in point of fact, you can't hurry these buggers.'

'You'll have to sit about, drink coffee and chat about the political situation, his mother-in-law's corns and any other damn thing, and then only gradually will the conversation slowly steer round to the object of your visit – flogging these cars. O.K.?'

'O.K.'

We plodded on down to the centre of town. Kent seemed to know where he was going, and I followed him, past shops filled with rubbish like bridal gowns – with, oddly enough, a European dummy as the bride – and then past others selling hurricane lamps and wood carvings.

He suddenly dodged up a side alley and paused astride two swing doors. Men were squatting down on the bones of their backsides in the street, brazing together the ends of great coils of wire, for what purpose I knew not, and didn't greatly care.

We went through these two swing doors like that stock Tombstone City saloon you see in every TV Western, under a sign, Palace of Perfumes, into a narrow corridor, lined with benches covered in shiny black plastic. Rather modestly, they had strips of brocade tacked on to cover up their legs.

The corridor led into a round room with its ceiling concealed by dark red cloth rising to a peak, so that one had the impression of sitting in Saladin's pavilion before going out to do up Richard the Lion Heart, or grab the key of his chastity belt, or whatever else was on offer, in the great crusading days of the Middle East.

The room was ringed by shelves stacked with bottles like an old-fashioned chemist's shop. (After you with that old-fashioned chemist.) There was a photograph of Nasser and a larger, highly coloured one, about three feet square, of a rather blowsy barmaid, blonde with big loose bristols, with a mild smiling man with thinning hair. I was wondering whether he had ever undone that bra and risked disturbing all that soft, loose, crinkled and unlovely flesh, when a curtain parted in the corner of the room and the character appeared.

He was slightly built and beaded, and I recognized him from his photograph on the wall, although he had more hair then. He bowed at us and smiled, showing a lot of gold in his teeth. Then he clapped his hands, and a little boy appeared, and he sent him out to bring back a lacquered tray and the tiny cups of coffee with the glasses of rather cloudy water, over which the Arabs like to talk business.

Kent said: 'This is my English friend.'

He gave the man my name, which cost him nothing. The man bowed.

'It is an honour to meet you,' he said in English.

I thought that was very civil of him, so I said: 'The pleasure is mine,' which shows how unoriginal I can be when someone else isn't writing my lines.

'What is it you want to see?' said this character. 'Jewels? Scents? Essences?'

No one had told me his name so I took up a blue and red visiting card from a side table and read it for myself: Sabry Ahmed. The House of Attar, Perfumes, Scents, Musk, Unguents to make You Young Again, to Light the Fires in Your Blood. Elixirs for all Occasions.

Get away, I thought, this could be interesting, if only it were true.

'You have come here as a tourist, yes?' Sabry asked, pouring the coffee.

I nodded. I didn't want to begin a long explanation for this nut. Let's press on to the real point of our meeting. But there was no hurrying him; he had to follow the rules of a Cairo business talk.

'Then you must take back some perfumes from Egypt. You

60

know that when Tutankamen's tomb was opened, the first thing that the explorers smelled was the perfume? Whatever perfume you buy in America, in England, in France, anywhere, it is almost certain that it has come from Egyptian flowers or herbs. I give you good price. Six bottles for eight pounds. You have any English money? If you have, I give you better price. Six bottles for four English pounds. Yes?'

'No,' I said. 'If I started wearing that stuff it wouldn't be safe to go down the King's Road.'

'Please?' he asked, mouth left open so that we could gaze at all the gold.

'Later,' I said, and looked despairingly at Kent, but he was stirring his coffee.

Sabry picked up a small phial and dabbed some perfume on the cork and then wiped the cork on the back of my hand.

'Just to smell the scent.'

The room filled with the fragrance of crushed flowers, sweet as the bloom of youth, and dying away as soon.

'Just the essence,' he said. 'You need a base to hold it. Alcohol.'

'Very interesting,' I said, and gave Kent a nudge.

Kent cleared his throat rather noisily.

'What my friend wants to discuss,' he said rather unwillingly, 'are old cars.'

'Ah. Have you seen any of the former King Farouk's old cars. Yes?'

'No,' I said. 'What were they, anyhow?'

'Almost every make,' said Sabry, sipping his coffee and straining it noisily through gaps in his teeth.

'He had a hundred and twenty cars, Rolls-Royce, Bentley, Cadillac, Alfa. When he went, the government auctioned them. Some, of course, disappeared. It was a time of disturbance, you understand.'

'I understand,' I said, wondering which sharp car dealer

had got what car, and for how much. Some cars have appreciated fifty times since then.

Sabry poured more coffee.

'You like to buy some musk, yes?'

He opened a small plastic pill box, dug a match stick into the black ointment it contained, and held it at my mouth. I licked the oleaginous mess cautiously; the taste was as vile as it looked, only slightly scented.

Kent and Sabry sat watching me carefully as though I would suddenly rush out like a rutting stag, but as an aphrodisiac it did nothing to me. The oily flavour lingered like the childhood taste of castor oil.

'Make you make love like pom-pom gun,' said Sabry, full of wishful thoughts.

'Charming,' I said, but all it made me think of was George's ancient joke about the young man sent to learn the meaning of it all in Paris. So that he won't alarm his mother, the boy has a code with his dear old dad, who passes the whole thing off as a shooting trip; the boy's affairs will be called bullets. Within days he was receiving his son's urgent requests for more money: 'to bullets, 7,000 francs'; then, 'to bullets, 6,000 francs', and then a pause, followed by a third account, 'to bullets, 6,500 francs. To repairs to gun, 85,000 francs.'

Kent leaned towards Sabry: 'You gave me those photographs of old cars when I was here last,' he began conspiratorially. 'I showed them to my friend here. He wants to see the cars. He may buy them. For English pounds or American dollars.'

'Ah, so you are a man of business. Yes?'

'Yes.'

'Then you must come to my house this evening.'

He spat out some coffee-grounds rather objectionably on the floor.

'Where is your house?' I asked him.

62

'Mr Kent knows. On the road to the Pyramids. I have three cars there.'

'What are they?'

I wanted to get some facts as soon as possible. I didn't go much on all this chatting about, this verbal tennis. Let's get a deal and over the hill, is my motto, or it would be if I had a crest to paint it under.

'A Bugatti, a Marmon, and a Delage.'

A Bugatti was rare indeed. How had such a scarce beast found its way to Egypt? Could it be one of Farouk's cars that someone else had bought and kept? He didn't mention the Fiat I'd seen in the photo, and neither did I in case we confused the discussion. I could buy a Fiat almost any day, but a Bug was a different breed of beast.

'They are all sports cars, then?' I asked him.

'Of course,' he said.

'How much are you asking?'

'Let's not discuss business now. Let's talk like friends now, and like businessmen then. Yes?'

'Yes,' I said, regretfully, and stood up. Kent followed me out of the shop.

'How did you meet that nut?' I asked him. 'Do you work with him here?'

'He's a contact,' he explained. 'His brother is something in the Treasury. He tips me off when quotas are changing, or if there's going to be a sudden tax increase. In my business you need to have contacts.'

'What exactly is your business? What do you export and import?'

'Hong Kong toys. I told you,' he said, aggrieved.

I'd forgotten. But then why should I remember? I know so little of the real world of business that I can't begin to understand how a man in Cairo can make a living exporting plastic rubbish from Hong Kong. Who buys it? And how does he find the fellow in Hong Kong who wants to sell it to him in the first place? The whole mystique of other people's ways of making a living I've always found intriguing.

We had a drink in Groppi's, which I read about in books on the desert war. Waiters wearing tarbushes, yellow belts and robes like white nightshirts served chocolate cakes with silver tongs. There were sweetpeas in silver vases on the tables, and imitation windows filled with frosted glass and lit up from behind to give the impression of sunshine, although we were right inside, at the heart of the building.

Most of the people eating there seemed to be with families, but in one corner a man in a black cloth cap was carefully eating his way through a huge fried flat fish. Maybe, like me, he was the odd man out.

If one could pick up a rarity like a Bugatti that had belonged to Farouk – or which I could say or even hint had been his – and why not? The dead can't sue – I could (and would) name my own price.

A title is always a good selling point. 'Late property of famous peer, immaculately maintained by chauffeur,' would look pretty thin against 'King's car. Unique specimen, preserved with royal disregard of cost.' I could feel the clichés multiplying like amoeba in my mind. The ads. for these cars would also be collectors' pieces.

But if it wasn't Farouk's? Then I should be content with what I already had. Happiness doesn't lie in the extent of a man's possessions, but in the fewness of his wants, as my old father used to tell me.

But what happens when the man's wants aren't few? Samuel Smiles or John Stuart Mill, or whoever else first produced this aphorism never dealt with that, but then most proverbs are very one-sided. 'A rolling stone gathers no moss.' Agreed, but who wants moss on his stone?

'Are you going to your office again?' I asked Kent.

He nodded.

64

'I'll put in an hour or so. Bound to be some letters to answer.'

He sounded more hopeful than convinced.

'Were there any last night?'

'A few,' he said non-committally.

A waiter hovered around us with a folded bill on a plate. Kent looked the other way. I unfolded the bill, put down two Egyptian pounds. The waiter salaamed me, and went off, and didn't come back. We stood up.

'I'll walk with you,' I said.

'There's no need,' he replied. 'Why don't you have a swim at the hotel?'

'I'd rather see Cairo,' I said. 'I can swim anywhere.'

We were standing at the corner of Talaat Harb Street, where the roads went off in a circle like spokes from a wheel. In the centre stood a statue of some pasha in a European frock-coat, trousers and fez, with his back to the sun, ringed in by old houses with shops at the bottom, and balconies higher up, where people had hung seedy grey lumpy mattresses, old corsets, and mercifully unidentifiable washing.

We walked up the street, on the sunny side. A man came towards us very slowly, carrying himself stiffly, as though his joints had locked and he had thrown away the key. He wore an old-fashioned grey tweed suit with wide turn-ups to the trousers, co-respondent brown-and-white shoes, a black beret and a black scarf wound round his neck, like one of a boat race crew. But the only boat he'd ever make now would be Charon's vessel over the Styx.

He held his head to one side as he walked, and I could see the growth under his right ear, huge as a roc's egg, and shining with sweat and distended skin. Every time he came to a sunny patch between the high, gloomy buildings, he stood, turning his face to the sun, warming his cancerous old bones before he shuffled on. I turned and watched him go. The very sight of the man depressed me; I wondered what it did to him.

'Here's my office,' said Kent. He had obviously not even seen the man. His thoughts were entirely on his own affairs.

We turned up some tessellated marble steps, past doors with frosted glass panels pegged apart. Inside, on the left, was a blackboard with names in Arabic script, and, underneath, the names of the firms in the building, in English.

'Which is yours?' I asked Kent; he had never told me.

'Fourth floor.'

He pulled open the lift trellis; we went up. Even on the fourth floor, dust and sand and grit from the desert had blown in under our feet. The soles of our shoes scratched and scraped on the marble.

His office seemed to be one large room with two grey metal desks, topped with plastic. A water cooler filled one corner, with filing cabinets and a telephone on a side table. The air felt stale and old. I wondered what business he could do here. If this was all the equipment one needed, there didn't seem all that much to it. I could see no letters on the desk, no one about.

'Satisfied?' he asked me.

'With what?' I said.

'Well, you wanted to see the office, didn't you?'

'I think I'll go for that swim,' I told him.

'I'd do that thing,' he said. 'You can get a drink at the edge of the pool afterwards. I'll join you when I'm through here.'

The lift had jammed between two floors. I pressed the button, but nothing happened, so I walked down the stairs. On the third floor, I heard the click of heels; someone was coming up slowly.

I turned the corner of the landing. A girl in sunglasses and a cotton dress was coming towards me. She was pretty in a dark way, but it wasn't her good looks that really knocked me out, it was the fact that the last time I had seen her was in that wrecked flat in Rosemary Court.

66

'You,' I said, and, I swear it, my voice trembled.

'I beg your pardon?' she said, as cold as iced lager.

'We've met before. In your flat. Remember?'

She looked at me as though I'd crawled out from under a flat stone, then recognition lit up her face.

'Why, the used-car man,' she said, without notable pleasure.

I felt like an uncle to the Hurdy-Gurdy Man, but all I could say was, 'Yes.'

Then, 'What brings you here?'

'I live here, that's what,' she said, and went on up the stairs.

3 I went on down the stairs and bought a guide book to Cairo from a stall in Liberation Square. On the back was a printed list of the Embassies, with their addresses. I wasn't sure how far it was away, so I hailed a taxi and told the driver, 'The British Embassy.'

I wanted to check whether I needed any special forms before I set about exporting cars, and I thought it easiest to deal with my own countrymen, rather than risk another session with cups of coffee and inconsequential conversation in some Egyptian office. As I drove, I thought about the girl and why the hell she should be in that building and, so it seemed to me, on her way to Kent's office. Maybe she was the secretary he had mentioned? But how could she also be involved with my being beaten up? Or was she involved? In fact, was any of this really happening, or was it all in my mind?

We drove past the Hilton with its flags of many nations, down the underpass and up on the other side. The Nile ran like green oil to my right. We passed the Semiramis Hotel, then Shepheard's. They're evocative names to all who remembered school atlases with red on nearly every map, and then the British Residency on the left, dozing like an old country house that has gone to sleep in the sun, striped shades down over the windows, Queen Victoria's crown still gold on the black iron gates.

Sentry boxes outside the embassies were painted in national colours; no doubt demonstrators found them easier to recognize like that. The British box was in red, white and blue horizontal stripes. I paid off the cab, walked up the path to the crescent-shaped half-moon of a building on the right. It was very cool inside the hall, under the photograph of the Queen and Prince Philip. A man sat at a desk on my left, not English but very nearly so.

'Can I help you?' he said quietly. He might have been a floor walker in some immensely discreet shop.

'I want to export a car from Egypt,' I told him. 'I'd like a bit of advice from someone before I begin.'

'You want the Trade Secretary, then. Please follow me.'

I followed him, like he said, down the corridor into a small room piled with almanacs and trade gazettes. A young man in shirt-sleeves was writing on a foolscap pad at his desk. I introduced myself and told him my problem.

'What sort of car is it?' he asked.

'An old one,' I said. 'I collect old cars. They're my hobby.'

This is always a more promising beginning than to say one actually physically deals in cars, because then you tend to unlatch a floodgate of bitter reminiscence about cars your hearer has been swindled over, with dud clutches, worn big ends and all of the rest.

'What sort of car is it?'

'A Bugatti.' I only mentioned one; if I could export one, I could ship out a hundred.

'Now, that *is* going back a long way. And how do you propose to pay for it?'

'A bank in Malta will provide the money.'

'You are resident there?'

'Look,' I said, not liking the general trend of the conversation, 'I simply want some advice from you about exporting a car – not a discussion about exchange control. This is a perfectly legitimate commercial transaction. It doesn't matter how it's paid so long as I pay for it legally.'

'Quite so, quite so,' agreed the other man. 'Well, what is your problem?'

'Everything,' I said. 'Life is full of problems. When I've bought the car here, I want to know how I can get it out of the country. What port should it go from? Can you recommend a shipping agent?'

'It's difficult to make personal recommendations in my

69

position. You will appreciate that. But your best port is Ismailia. You will need an export permit from the Egyptian Ministry of Trade. Where are you staying – Shepheard's?'

'No, the Hilton.'

'Send a note round by messenger. That'll save you hanging about half the day. You should have no problem. After all, the authorities here are very anxious to have money coming into the country.'

Back in England, if I export a car, I usually hand the whole matter over to a firm that deals with this end of the business. They collect it from my garage, take it to the docks, fill in all the forms, and all that is left for me is to pay their bill, and then wait for the cry of disappointment from the overseas buyer when he finds that all the removable accessories have mysteriously disappeared between my mews and his home. There didn't seem much more to it in Cairo, either, which was comforting to discover.

We shook hands, and I walked back to the hotel. Kent was sitting in the lounge on one of the wide settees set out in a hollow square.

'Where have you been?' he asked me, suspiciously, as though he thought I'd been banging his wife, if he had a wife.

'The Embassy,' I said.

'The Embassy?' he repeated. 'What do you want to get involved there for? Lost your passport?'

'No, just checking about getting the cars out. I don't want to be loused up on the dockside because we haven't some form, and a lot of Gyppoes are screaming their nuts off, and we miss the boat.'

'But I told you,' said Kent, with all the compressed patience of a keeper addressing a lunatic, '*I'll* deal with all that. I *know* these people. It's my business to know them. I work here. Start messing about with the Embassy and all that civil service passed-to-you, up-your-pipe-in-triplicate stuff, in re-yours-of-the-fourth-ult-to-hand, and we'll never get them out.

You leave the details to me. All you have to worry about is whether the cars are any good.'

This was the first time I'd seen him at all animated. I decided to give myself a second time.

'What about a drink?' I said. 'What about that treble whisky you promised me last night?'

He looked as though I had dug a spike into his vitals, and to a man of his meanness it must have hurt him about as much, or even more.

'What?' he asked hoarsely, his eyes bulging like boiled eggs at the horrible suggestion.

'Just joking,' I assured him.

'Don't make jokes like that again,' he pleaded.

I realized then, even if I hadn't before, that Kent was so touched over spending his own money, he'd rather die of thirst than spend a penny – and take that how you like.

'About those cars,' he said. 'That Bugatti Sabry was telling you about really is something. It's a Bugatti Royale.'

'Are *you* joking?' I asked him. I didn't know there was another Royale left in the world, but I did know several people who would pay my price to buy one, for the Royale is unique, a symbol of an unparalleled age that has gone for ever.

Apparently, old Ettore Bugatti had been at a dinner-party in the mid-twenties, when some woman compared his cars unfavourably with Rolls-Royces. He took umbrage at this and decided to produce a Behemoth of a Bugatti, a car built for kings, apparently on the basis that anything Royce could do, he could do bigger and better. He did the first, if not the last. His new car had a 13 litre engine, a wheelbase of 14' 1", and tyres as large as hoops. He charged 30,000 dollars for the chassis alone, back in the 1920s, too, and he was so particular about his potential customers that he invited them – only six or seven cars were built, to my knowledge – to his castle in Molsheim, to stay as his guests, for a few days, just to

71

make sure they were genuinely the right type to own such a car.

Bugatti drove a Royale to Spain for the 1927 San Sebastian Grand Prix, and King Alfonso XIII ordered one immediately, but was dethroned before he could take delivery, which is an occupational hazard of Royalty. Thereafter, though, the Type 41 was called the Car of Kings – La Royale – although in fact, no reigning king ever owned one. King Carol of Rumania and King Boris of Bulgaria both wanted one, but thought that such ostentation was unwise since their countries were so poor.

But while Bugatti's Royale was a commercial failure, its engine was a success. He adapted them to drive locomotives on the French railways, and sold several hundreds for this purpose. Indeed, they were still being made for some years after the war.

With each Royale, Bugatti provided a silver elephant mascot for the radiator, for even although his guarantee ran, not for the life of the car, as with lesser breeds, but for the life of the owner, it was still a mammoth mechanical white elephant.

It has been said, and I'll say it again, that if you owned one of these cars you didn't need to take the dog for a walk, you just walked round the car twice, and that was your lot. I could up the ante to £15,000 for this, and the thought of the profit I would mark up, and the write-down I'd use for tax purposes, and the whole convoluted intricacies and potenialities of the deal excited me.

'You're joking,' I repeated, in case he was.

'About money?' said Kent. 'Never. You speak of the thing I love.'

'Where the hell can you get a Royale from in Egypt? I thought the country was bankrupt?'

'Farouk,' he said. 'When Farouk went, the government took over the Abdin Palace here as a museum. Everything is preserved, just as it was on that Saturday, the 26th of July, when he sailed away in his yacht, pretty well at gun-point. A relic of what they call the bad old days. Every new dictator calls his predecessor's time, the bad old days. They have to, otherwise people get around to thinking that the present days are pretty awful, too.'

'Skip the historical and political stuff,' I told him. 'Where do we come in?'

'Now. Once Sabry was certain you were genuinely interested, he contacted some old retainer that Farouk had around him who spirited away this particular car, just to check exactly what model it was. It's a Type 41, a Royale.'

'You think it's genuine?' I asked him.

He shrugged.

'When you've been as long as I have in the Middle East, you don't talk of these things too much in hotels, in bars, because they're all bugged. Every bloody thing you say in these places is bugged. I told you,' said Kent.

'Then, why are you talking here?'

'Because you can't bug a public place like this so easily, what with people coming and going, piped music, guests being paged, and so on.'

'Thanks for the warning.'

'It didn't cost me anything,' said Kent.

'I know. That's why you gave it to me. What time do we go?'

'I've ordered a taxi for nine o'clock. In your name.'

You would, I thought, in case you had to pay cash.

'It's a bit late, isn't it?'

I don't know whether you are like me, but in some foreign countries I like to be in familiar surroundings after dark. The idea of trailing up some unknown road to the Pyramids to meet unknown people at an unknown house, said to belong to a man who owned a perfume shop, and there to pay over physical cash for three cars, maybe without being able to

73

prove any title to their ownership, didn't entirely fill me with enthusiasm. After all, I'm in business to make money, not give it away.

'You'll be all right,' said Kent, as though he read my thoughts. He stood up.

'Well, I'll get back to the office.'

'How are things there?'

What the hell could he be doing? Banging that girl I'd passed on the stairs? I decided to find out. I said:

'Funny thing happened on my way down the stairs from your office.'

'Like what?'

'Like meeting a girl going up.'

'Dark-haired, in a flowered dress?'

'Yes.'

'Nothing funny about that. She's my secretary, Maria.'

'Nice girl.'

'Good typist, if that's what you mean.'

It wasn't, but I didn't interrupt him.

'She's half French. Was brought up here as a child, so she speaks the lingo and knows her way around. Very useful to me, I can tell you.'

'You are telling me,' I said, but I didn't tell him about the business in Rosemary Court. I don't know why, but I buttoned up my tongue; never give too much away, as one strip-tease girl told the other.

There's a time for speech and a time for silence, and somehow I thought this was a time for waiting and trying to see. After all, if Kent *had* bought the car back again, he must have *had* a reason; I'd find that out first, and then the other questions might also be answered.

'See you outside here just before nine,' Kent said. 'They eat late in Cairo, so it might be an idea to have a snack first.'

Kent didn't offer to dine with me, and I didn't ask him to. I didn't want to be lumbered with his bill; maybe he was

74

having dinner on the free nuts and olives from the bar on the roof.

I watched him walk between the palm trees, under the centre marble staircase and away over the wide tessellated slabs. A Nubian giant in some kind of fancy dress costume opened the door for him, and he was gone, but not forgotten.

I took the lift to my room, picked up the telephone, asked the hotel operator for International, and then gave that operator the number of my garage. I wanted to speak to George. I wanted him to check on the chassis numbers of all known Royales. I didn't want to be lumbered with some fake, although it seemed quite feasible that King Farouk *might* have owned one of these gigantic mechanical extravagances.

'There's just now a delay on the line,' the operator told me. 'I will ring you back.'

I replaced the phone and slid open the windows and went out on the veranda. A long, long way below me, cars, the size of Matchbox models, were happily going round the round-abouts in the gardens in both directions. A boy pushed a handcart, piled with a pyramid of oranges, and behind him an old man was wheeling a blind woman in a handcart. She was dressed completely in black, and even at this distance I could see her blind useless eyes, white and horrible like stones in a statue's face.

I went inside, for the telephone was ringing. I picked it up.

'The line is down,' the operator told me. 'It is impossible to make any foreign calls. Also, it is a holiday tomorrow.'

'Thank you very much,' I said. This was all I needed.

I rang room service for a Whyte & Mackay, then ordered lunch of shish kebab, some fruit and black coffee.

It was one of those days that never seems to end. I had too many hours to kill before I went off with Kent. I took out my travellers' cheques, folded them inside a shirt, put the shirt in my case, and locked it. I left ten English pound notes buttoned in my back pocket, and some loose money in piastres.

I was sorry about that telephone call. There's so much faking in our business, as in all branches of the antique trade, that without knowing the chassis numbers, I felt rather like a gladiator going in naked to fight the lions.

It seemed quite feasible that Farouk or someone close to him *had* bought a Bugatti Royale, I kept assuring myself, but I couldn't be certain. It wouldn't have been impossible for a crafty Egyptian craftsman to have lengthened an earlier, smaller chassis, and made a fake Royale Bug, but would it have been worth while? After all, I had read somewhere that Farouk took 250 million dollars with him when he went into exile, so what was the odd 30,000 or 40,000 for a real Bugatti? It would only be small change to him, almost petty cash.

I lay down on the bed and read *The Egyptian Gazette* that came up with the morning coffee. Like most antique dealers, I am a bit superstitious, so I read what the stars held for me, and they weren't giving much away. I'm Sagittarius, which means I'm never satisfied, and what the astrologer had dug out didn't satisfy me much, either.

'Not everything will go your way today,' I read, 'but an inborn instinct for what the public want should enable you to be successful in the commercial world.' So there you were: you could take it either way, or leave it alone. I left it alone, kicked off my shoes and went to sleep.

When I awoke, the room was cool, and the early evening dusk had painted the sky blue outside. Because of the trouble with Israel, all neon signs had been switched off, and the buildings were black blocks against the hills and sky. A mile above Cairo, an airliner was coming in to land, its red and green wing lights flickering. Oddly enough, street lamps were still burning.

I pulled the curtains, turned on the bedside light, and the piped music. Then I looked at my watch; eight o'clock. Nearly time to meet Kent. I went into the bathroom, washed my face under the cold tap, and rinsed out my mouth to be rid of the taste of sleep.

I had a vague feeling of excitement. If what Kent said was true, this source of old cars had been completely ignored by other dealers. It was like tapping a gold vein, or finding an oil well in your backyard. If things worked out, I might contact a merchant bank on my return and borrow a million quid and buy up every damned old car in Egypt, and ship them to some safe tax haven, like Malta, and sell them from there. I might be rich, yet. It was a good feeling, but nothing like so good as being rich, only a trailer for the main event.

I put on my jacket and shoes, walked down the corridor, waited for the lift, left the key at the desk. The lounge was crowded: another group of package-deal tourists were either arriving or leaving. The impressions of the world a package tourist has must be of too little sleep, too much constipation, too many pre-cooked meals that all taste like warmed-up white rubber, and night-time arrivals and departures in hotels that are the same in every country. They'd be far happier and healthier saving their money by staying at home and watching travelogues on the box.

A black and white taxi was waiting outside the door with the inside light on. Kent sat in the back .

'You're late,' he said accusingly.

'Only minutes,' I told him.

He seemed a bit tense. I eased myself on to the shiny, plastic seat, and the driver took off, dodging between buses with people crowded on the back bumpers and round the doors, out over the traffic lights, and away past the zoo, up the road towards the Pyramids.

It was a wide road, but badly lit. The cars, in any case, all had their headlamps painted blue because of dim-out orders, in case of air-raids, and some had no lights at all. We almost ran down one mule cart piled high with grass, and I heard the driver shouting abuse after us.

77

Big potholes jarred the taxi's old springs. We passed a crowd of men who were clustered round a stall lit by a dim acetylene lamp, eating cakes the shape of quoit rings; then a few night-clubs with dim signs, and then large houses, all stucco, with small lights glowing over the numbers on their gateposts.

The driver slowed near a house behind a high stone wall, with a man standing by the gate. The man waved him in. He held a long stave in his right hand, and I guessed he didn't have that to scratch himself with. For my money – and I wasn't paying any, but I like the sound of the phrase – for my money, he was guarding the place, and if he could stop people coming in, he could also stop them coming out; which was a point to remember if I had to leave hurriedly myself.

The house was like a big concrete box. No lights were showing, perhaps because of the dim-out, perhaps not, and the whole place seemed deserted and uninhabited. Le Corbusier would have done his nut if he'd seen it, for it was so ugly. Three garages were built beneath the ground floor, with roll-up doors. The driver switched off his engine, and we climbed out.

A chill wind was blowing sand, rough as a rasp, against my face. There is no rainfall at all in Cairo, nothing to hold down this pitiless, shifting sea of sand that could bury the whole city if the wind blew strong enough, and long enough, as maybe it will one day.

'Here we are,' said Kent, as though to reassure himself.

'How do you know?'

'I've been often enough before. That's how.'

This was a good start. We went up the stairs, and the door opened before we could ring the bell. The house inside had that oddly impersonal look of a furnished apartment, a shelter from the elements. Some beaten brass pots stood on the marble floor of the hall, with yellow cacti plants, and whoever had beaten them must have been a sadist, for they

78

were covered with dents. The air felt stale and dry; a film of sand covered a table against the wall.

A servant of some kind, looking like a convict in a grey jacket and trousers with brass buttons, closed the door behind us, pulled the black-out curtains, and turned on the main lights. After the gloom, the hall blazed like a film set.

'Welcome, welcome,' said a voice, and Sabry, the man from the House of Attar, a a rogue by any other name would doubtless smell as sweet, came towards us, hands outstretched in greeting. He clapped his hands together, because he had nothing else to do with them, and another man appeared with a tray of drinks. Although they weren't alcoholic, they were liquid, which helped me to get the sand out of my throat. Now, I thought, we'll have all this spiel of bitter coffee and small talk: 'What do you think of Cairo?' and 'Please, how is the Middle East position regarded in England?' and I would make my reply, 'I haven't tried the Middle East position, yet,' and they would look surprised and hurt, and I'd wish I could find a few new gags.

Sabry bowed us into the room he had left. Another man was already there, a cigar as big as a long frankfurter clamped in his face. He wore a pair of grey lightweight trousers, beautifully pressed, black crocodile skin shoes, and a short-sleeved silk shirt. His shoulders bulged under the silk, and he looked just too good to be true. In fact, he was much too good to be true, as I realized when he shook my hand, and went through that bone-squeezing technique.

Close to, his face was much older than it had appeared from the other end of the room. It was pitted by open pores and his eyes were very blue but watery, and the little dab of moustache was flecked with grey. His hair seemed black on his head, but for my money, if I was paying money, it was dyed. Dye now, pay later. As he looked at me, his left eyelid drooped, in a tiny wink. I watched again and he winked again. But he wasn't trying to date me; he just had a nervous tic.

Kent introduced us.

'My good friend Hassan Sayed,' he said. 'He runs a gun-smith's shop in Alexandria.'

'Does he now?' I said. The only Sayed I had heard of had been the one in James Elroy Flecker's poem, and the only line I remembered from that was 'Some to Mecca turn to pray, and I towards thy bed, Yasmin', which didn't carry human knowledge forward very far. After you with thy bed, Yasmin.

'Who buys guns in Alexandria?' I asked to give the con-versational ball a push. It was the only ball I could push decently in that room and that company.

'Not enough people,' admitted Hassan, and his voice was as I expected it to be, just too male, just too deep and throaty like an actor playing an actor playing a he-man.

'In the old days we sold many guns to noblemen. For their protection, you understand.'

'I understand.' We aristos have to hang together, or we'll all hang separately.

'And also there was much shooting. Even today, things are not too bad from the point of view of sport. I go after quail, little small birds, or doves. Very sweet birds to shoot. We wait with our guns in the gardens in the evening, and when they come to settle down to sleep, poom, poom, poom, we go!'

He raised his arms as though holding an imaginary rifle.

'Then there are pigeons. That is a fine bird. They fly in from Europe, all the way, and when they settle down to rest, we are waiting for them, poom, poom, poom!'

'I'm glad I'm not a bird,' I said, and I meant the feathered sort.

'You make the joke?' said Hassan. 'Yes?'

'Yes,' I said. 'If I can't make money or love, I make jokes. They cost nothing and don't tire me out. Show me another pleasure I can enjoy so many times a day without tiring.'

Hassan moved across the room lightly for a man of his weight. I could imagine the trouble he had keeping down his flesh; the chest expanders, the rowing machines, the cycling in some gymnasium and then the massage under steam. Ah, yes, the massage, and not only under steam. I thought of all the small boys who must have been Hassan's close and intimate friends. I thought of the weary pigeons fluttering down the evening sky, a mass of bloodied feathers.

I thought I didn't like Hassan, and when he turned his eyes on me again, small as worm-holes in wood, I thought he didn't like me, either. What the hell was Kent doing with this fellow? Maybe he was Sabry's friend? He certainly wasn't mine.

Kent might have been reading my thoughts through a hole in the side of my head, because he said: 'My good friend Hassan here is related to the Chief of Police for Northern Egypt, and as I told you, my good friend Sabry also has important relations.'

I said: 'Yes?'

After all, even the owner of a perfume palace must have relations of some kind, but if they were important to him, it didn't necessarily mean they were important to me.

'Yes. It is very necessary to have close contacts with the right people. You appreciate that. In the Middle East, things are different from back home.'

Not all that different, unfortunately, I thought, for in how many local council car-parks do you find Rover three-litres, because someone in the surveyor's department has been a useful friend to someone else who wanted to develop a couple of acres over which there had been difficulties for planning permission? But I could see how Kent was anxious to cut his expenditure, and it was obviously helpful to have two locals who would know which officials would have to be paid cash, and those who would only need to be paid compliments.

A servant came in with a silver tray of coffee. He was a

midget with a squeezed-in face, and a head the size of a child's sunk on a small man's body. I was sorry for him, for his hands trembled, and he kept looking at Sabry and licking his lips as though he was afraid of him. As soon as he'd gone, Kent pulled up three chairs.

'We've got the cars,' he said, looking at each of us in turn, with me last of all.

'Where?' I asked.

'Here, in Sabry's garage.'

'What ones have you got?'

'As I said, a Bugatti, a Delage, and a Marmon.'

They sat looking at me, as though expecting me to say something, so I said, 'Let's see them.'

Sabry led us out down a steel staircase into the concrete garage that ran the whole width of the house. Two unshaded bulbs burned in the ceiling. On the right stood a pile of crates and carboys in baskets bearing labels 'Jasmine Essence', 'Oil of Attar' and so on, presumably for use in his scent shop.

I wasn't much concerned with this; what interested me were the three cars, and the first one I checked was the Bugatti. I'd never seen a Royale – not many people have – but the yellow and black beast before me was something much smaller, a Type 57, with a strange open body. Even so, it was valuable; all Bugattis are, but nothing like so valuable as a Royale. The cars had all been driven in, for I felt the bonnets and they were still warm. I examined the tax discs on the windscreen, and they were valid. I wondered who had been driving these exotic vehicles on the Cairo streets. Sabry must have seen my thoughts on my face.

'We asked the owners to leave them for tonight, so you can make any tests you need,' he said.

'Who are the owners?' I asked.

'That is immaterial. They are ordinary people who need some foreign currency.'

'Just how much foreign currency?'

82

'We could probably get a better price if we took the three,' said Kent. 'Each of the owners will come down a little.'

'What do they want?' I asked. 'Last price.'

'Fifteen hundred sterling,' said Sabry immediately, so I guessed he must have a good friend or relation who worked in the American Express, and who had told him the amount of money I had with me. Next time, I'd cable half to Cooks, just to confuse them; if there was a next time, of course.

'It's a lot of money,' I said, as I always do when a seller names a price.

'It is,' agreed Sabry, 'but you know what these will be worth when you get back to England. That Bugatti done up must fetch several thousand English pounds, and what would it cost to renovate – one thousand?'

I didn't say anything, because I was looking under the bonnet. The classic design of the engine, like a solid block of polished metal, looked as good as always, although it was filthy. Oil had leaked out somewhere and the dust and sand blown in and stayed, forming a crust.

'It's not a Royale,' I pointed out. It had a family resemblance, as a little boy can look like his bigger brother, but that was all. There wasn't anything like the profit here I'd hoped for, but there was still a very good profit. The Type 57 was a beautiful machine, but most that I had seen carried Van Vooren or Gangloff bodies; I had never seen one like this. It was probably an Atalante coupé.

The colour-scheme surprised me, black wings and a yellow body, like some kind of wasp on wheels. I bent down and put my nose to the door hinges, where new paint takes longest to dry. I smelled a faint whiff of cellulose. The car had recently been repainted – but why the hideous colour-scheme instead of the traditional bright blue of nearly all the Bugattis I had seen?

'I'll give you twelve hundred for the lot,' I said.

'It's impossible,' said Sabry. 'The owner of the Delage,

for instance, uses it to run tourists out from the Mena House Hotel to the Pyramids. They like to have their photographs taken standing by its side. It's worth keeping, rather than let it go at a low figure.'

'Five hundred is only a hundred more for each owner.'

'Of course,' agreed Sabry. 'But we have already made them cut their prices. Fifteen hundred. Last price.'

I walked round the cars again, wondering where the owner of the Bugatti could find such huge tyres. After the war, one British owner of a Royale fitted 7.50 by 21-inch Goodrich Silvertown tyres – originally intended for an American army mobile gun!

I climbed in behind the wheel of the Marmon, and started the engine. It ran easily, but a bit noisily, but this wasn't surprising for the engine must have been running for very nearly forty years. I switched it off before we poisoned ourselves with exhaust fumes.

'All right,' I said. 'Fifteen hundred. Delivered to the docks.'

I had to make one condition. Never let the seller think he's having things all his own way; that's against any religious principles, and so far as things like this are concerned, I've such strong religious principles I could practically be a bishop.

'That's our job,' said Kent. 'You drive whichever one you want, and I'll take the next, and Hassan or Sabry will have the third.'

'What about the paperwork?' I asked him. 'You said you were going to do that.'

'I've got it all fixed. We've just got to fill in the chassis and engine numbers. Do you want to look over the cars mechanically before we drive them?'

'How far is it to Ismailia, and what's the road like?'

An odd fact about antique machinery is that if you leave it alone, old engines often run for years, but once you begin to disturb them, then things start to go wrong. It's the same with old people who retire from routine jobs; break the routine and you can break them, too.

'We'll never get them out of Ismailia,' said Hassan. 'My cousin tells me that the port is on the verge of closing, because of Israeli shelling. We don't want any trouble with these things stuck on the dockside for weeks, with people stealing pieces off them, or maybe the ship itself getting seized. We'll have to go to Alexandria. That's about a hundred and forty miles, if we take the desert road.'

'We should cover that distance on a tank of petrol each,' I said, 'so long as the tyres and the radiator hoses hold up in the heat.'

All the cars were basically good engineering designs, and without weaknesses. If I'd been buying a Cord, for instance, with its electrically operated gear change that can actually select two gears at the same time, a feat that I have never known any other car achieve, I would have felt far less happy. Even so, it was only common sense to give them a quick going over, but I didn't want to make a production out of it.

I checked the oil in each sump, and although it was the colour and consistency of black treacle, the sumps were full, and there were no bad oil leaks beneath the cars, and surprisingly little play in the steering.

'We'd better have a couple of lengths of rope,' I said. 'Nylon, if possible, in case we need to tow each other. Who do I pay the money to?'

'Me,' said Sabry.

'I've brought nothing with me,' I said. 'I'll have to see you back at the hotel.'

'There's no need,' said Kent. 'We'll see you here tomorrow, at eight. We're ten miles on our way already here.'

'Best make an early start,' Sabry explained. 'It's going to be very hot driving across the desert at midday.'

'I'll be here,' I told him. 'With the money.'

I wasn't too happy about driving the cars all this way ourselves, but then I'm never too happy about anything. Fact is, I tend to look on the gloomy side of things so often that if I'm cheerful it means I've got a temperature.

Heat would be our worst enemy; although these old cars might chug around Cairo quite happily, the long desert journey would loosen the scale and rust of years in their ancient radiators, and could block their withered thermostats and make them boil.

'Eight it is,' said Kent. 'Oh, and there's one other thing. We'll want your signature on the forms. Better do that now.'

We went back upstairs. The servant had cleared away the dirty cups, and clean ones were laid on the tray. I wondered what these people's stomachs were like with all these coffee-grounds swilling about inside them. Their intestines should be the best polished in the business.

Kent opened his brief-case and took out a buff folder of papers.

'We'll need your signature here, and here,' he said pushing forms across the table towards me. I glanced through them. They were the usual import/export declarations in Arabic script with English translations, badly printed, but quite straightforward. The years of registration of the cars seemed right – 1928 for the Bugatti, 1930 for the Delage, 1933 for the Marmon. But the Bugatti was described as a Royale special-bodied roadster, which it manifestly was not. Also, it was probably a 1936 model. They didn't make Type 57's in 1928.

'What's wrong?' asked Kent, watching my face.

'The date and description of the Bug.'

'What's wrong with it?'

'It's about eight years too old here. And it's not a Royale.'

'Does that matter?'

'Only if someone in the Customs notices it.'

'So far as they're concerned, it's a Bugatti, isn't it?'

'If that's all they want, then it's all right.'

'We're very grateful to you indeed,' said Sabry carefully, 'but in my country it is better to make a mistake in a declaration and go through with it, rather than correct that mistake and cross something out. They would immediately become suspicious.'

'You know best,' I said, because maybe he did, and signed the forms. After all, it seemed an unimportant and pedantic point.

Kent took out a rubber stamp, tried it once on the back of an envelope, and banged it down on each page of the forms.

'You think of everything,' I said, and he certainly seemed to have done, for the circular stamp contained my name and the title, Managing Director, Aristo Autos, London, W1, England.

'I meant to ask you if you had a stamp for your firm,' he said apologetically, 'but I forgot. Fellow in the bazaar made this for me this morning. Doesn't mean anything, of course. Just makes it all look a bit more official. These characters in the Customs here go on stamps and seals in a big way.'

I filled in my passport number, signed the last statement, pushed the papers back to him. He read through each one carefully, returned them to his case.

'Well,' I said, standing up, 'thanks for the coffee and the sight of the cars. Are you coming back with me in the cab?'

'No,' said Kent, 'I've some business to do here. I'm not sure how long I will be. You take the taxi back.'

I guessed that this was just a way for him to avoid paying the fare.

Kent followed me out to the cab; the others stayed in the garage. It was quite dark now, and in the dim headlights I saw occasional cyclists, weaving about, then three empty donkey carts running in line, the donkeys trotting happily in the cool of the evening. We swerved for flocks of sheep, and how the driver saw his way I don't know, and didn't like to think.

I was glad when we came back past the zoo, where the eagles were perched high up on the trees in their cages, and ran up the ramp in front of the hotel. I paid off the cab and went up to my room. The telephone began to ring as I opened the door. I picked it up and kicked the door shut. There was a lot of whirring in my ears; voices asked each other questions in French which I didn't understand and then a girl spoke in English: 'You are room 927 ?'

'Yes.'

'Your call to London.'

'My call to London.' I had forgotten all about it. I thought the line was down, or it was a holiday. Not that it mattered now that the Bugatti wasn't what I'd hoped it would be.

George's homely voice spoke in my ear.

'Where's all the action, then ?'

'I've bought three cars,' I said. 'A Marmon, a Bugatti sold as a Royale, but actually a Type 57, and an open Delage.'

'I'm doing the ads for *Motor Sport*,' said George. 'Shall I give 'em gin – put 'em in ?'

'Yes,' I said, 'say they're fully restored, from a foreign collector's stable, regardless of cost, gems of old-world crafts-manship. All that crap. Expected this month.'

'It'll appear about the time you're Pope.'

'I'm Pope ?' What the hell had happened to George ?

'Pope of Rome – home.'

'Oh. Better insure them, too. Get on to the Midland Widows. They're best for these old things. Insure each one specifically for £5,000 agreed price for fire, theft and damage in transit.'

It had to be an agreed price, because otherwise I'd have difficulty when making a claim, for the insurance companies sometimes argue that if the car is old then it is only worth a scrap price.

'Anything else ?' George asked.

'Yes. Couple of other fellows are involved out here,' I told him. 'Locals. One runs a scent and jeweller's shop. Name of Sabry Ahmed. The other seems to have been a playboy in the great days. Must be fifty-ish now. Crinkly hair. One of the lads. Runs a gun shop in Alexandria. Name of Sayed Hassan.'

'Has he a twitch in one kidney?'

'Kidney?' I repeated. George's rhyming slang was often incomprehensible to me, especially over a distance of 2,000 miles.

'Yes. Kidney pie. Eye.'

'Oh. Yes. He has. You know him?'

'Of him, at least.'

'How?'

Even as I asked, I remembered. George had served for twenty-seven years as a regular in the Royal Tank Regiment; his memory for all kinds of things, from chassis numbers to pornographic exhibitions in Bombay, was encyclopaedic.

'I told you,' he said, and indeed he had. 'I was in the Canal Zone during my last posting. They were after him on smuggling charges. Tommy Dodds, mostly. Rods. Guns to you. And some jewels. But apparently there were diplomatic difficulties. He was attached in some way to Farouk's court. No doubt a number of people got their palms crossed with banger. Banger and mash – cash. Remember that case, man in the Hillman Minx with those heavy doors?'

Indeed, I remembered the case of the Hillman with the heavy doors. A provincial bank manager had been driving it through Austria to meet his wife, who had gone on ahead by air. On the way, he picked up an English hitch-hiker, who, hearing that the manager lived in the Midlands, mentioned he had close friends living there, too.

Next day, the manager was unable to start his car, and the hotel owner recommended a garage. Some trivial fault was diagnosed, but the garage man explained he had discovered heavy wear on the steering king pins, and while he hadn't any new spares, he had made some adjustments, which might make it appear hard to steer, so he should contact his local garage as soon as he reached home.

The bank manager never had a chance to act on this advice, for the car was stolen from outside his house on the night he reached home. It was found wrecked and abandoned on its side down a ravine in the west country two weeks later – and both front doors were missing.

That might have been the end of the matter if someone hadn't found a Minx front door of the same colour thrown over a hedge a couple of miles away. Inside, welding marks gave their own explanation. While the car was in its Austrian garage, containers for drugs or jewels had been welded into the doors.

The bank manager – and no doubt other harmless tourists like him – had been a stooge. The smugglers had reckoned on their obvious respectability being good enough assurance that their car would not be searched at any frontier – and if it was, how could they explain the contraband welded into their own front doors? If Hassan had been involved here, then he was one to watch.

'Are you certain?' I asked.

'Absolutely,' said George. 'I'd watch that feather plucker. He's bent as a pin.'

'What's he look like, this Hassan?' I asked George. I had to be certain he wasn't confusing him with someone else.

'Biggish. Tough. Damn great teeth. Likes himself a lot – bags of flexing muscles. And ginger. Ginger beer – queer.'

'That's the boyo,' I agreed, because it was. The ginger man. Then the pips went, so George said goodbye.

I sat down on the edge of the bed, and superimposed that story on what was happening to me. Could *I* be the stooge in this enterprise of exporting three old cars? And if so, how? Or was I simply tired, and imagining the whole thing?

90

I have bought and sold old cars for long enough to know that the reasons people give for buying or selling them are rarely the true ones, although sometimes they genuinely don't realize this themselves. I have also lived long enough to know that the oddest beasts aren't always in the jungle; they walk on two legs – just like you and me.

4
❋
I opened my suitcase on the spare bed, threw in my few shirts, drip-dry socks, and the second suit I hadn't even worn. I can fly around the world in one set of clothes – and often have done, for I wash them out, hang them over the rail to dry overnight, and put them on again fresh in the morning. Why carry more weight than you absolutely need to, as the thin man asked the fat man?

I had another Whyte & Mackay, set my travelling alarm for seven o'clock, wrote out on the hotel card that I wanted breakfast at seven; fruit juice, two fried eggs, honey and toast – it's marvellous what I'll eat when someone else cooks it for me – and hung this on the door.

As I came out of the bathroom with the last of the drip dries, the telephone rang. The desk clerk said a lady was waiting downstairs to see me. I thought of one of George's gags: that was no lady, that was my brother-in-law, he just walks like that – and rejected it.

'How old?' I asked him. No point wasting your time with the sere and yellow when young meat's around.

'I would say about twenty-five, sir,' said the clerk, who had obviously considered the matter.

'You would, would you? Does she look as though she knows what it's all about?'

'Please?'

'Never mind,' I said. 'Send her up.'

Who the hell could this be? Some idiot tourist who knew someone with the same name as me on a package deal, and had confused us? I put the whisky in my case, closed the lid, brushed my hair to add a touch of class. I didn't want to disappoint this girl, whoever she was. I shall not pass this way again, and therefore any good girl I can do, let me do them now, etcetera.

There was a knock at the door. I suddenly felt like Cinderella in the pantomine when she hears knocking outside and everyone in the audience knows it's the big bad fairy or the wolf or whoever is the rascal.

Cinderella calls bravely in her high, shrill voice: 'You can't frighten *me* with that knocking.'

And the other character replies thoughtfully from the other side, in a very deep voice: 'You'd be frightened – if you knew what I was knocking on the door with!'

I opened the door, and if I'd been a jumping man, I would have jumped into the air, for standing there, smiling at me, as though she liked the sight, was the girl I had glimpsed briefly on the way into Snelling's flat when I returned his keys, the girl I had passed on the stairs on her way up to Kent's office. Maria.

'Be my guest,' I said, thinking that she might well have also been the guest of these other two, and where one has been another can also go, which was my thought for the day, and if you've got a better one, drop me a line about it.

She was wearing a light sort of dress, for the day was warm, and she had a couple of worth-while bristols which, being a tit man, interested me, even though they were doubtlessly well shielded from covetous hands. I closed the door behind her. She came into the room and threw her handbag on the bed as though she were going to stay. I decided I wouldn't stop her.

'You don't know me,' she said. 'At least we haven't been introduced formally. I'm Maria.'

'Ave, Maria,' I said. 'Ave atque vale,' which shows I picked up the rudiments of something somewhere, and I don't mean something that I should go to the outpatients' clinic to see about, either. I mean a touch of the old classics. My youth wasn't wasted in bars; not all of it, anyway.

'I'm Mr Kent's secretary.'

'Get away,' I said, not meaning she should actually, but

just to show I can believe all kinds of things, even the truth on occasions.

I gave her my name; I'd nothing else to give at that particular point in time.

'I tried to ring you earlier,' she went on, 'but there was no reply, so I thought I'd better come in person.'

She couldn't very well come in any other way, I thought, but didn't say so. After all, why louse up half a chance if you think you have one?

'There's something I want to ask you. About when you brought those keys back to Mr Snelling in my flat.'

'Yes?'

'Have you told Mr Kent you saw me there?'

'No. Should I have done?'

As I said this, I wondered again why I hadn't, but I hadn't. Maybe there was some subconscious reason, for I couldn't explain it otherwise; and if life has taught me anything, it's never to attempt to explain the inexplicable.

'Then please don't. I can't tell you why now. It's not really important – only to me. And I promise you I will tell you when we're safely aboard that boat, away from here.'

I looked at her a bit sharpish. Either she was having it off with Snelling or with Kent, or probably both, and didn't want Kent to know, or there was some other reason equally important to her. But women are so devious that you rarely learn the real truth about anything from them, only as much of it as they care to let go, and there was no profit in asking questions she didn't want to answer. I would have to wait until we were on that boat, like she said, and then, if she ran true to my experience of women, she'd either tell me nothing or a load of rubbish.

'You're involved in all this?' I asked, to keep the conversation ball rolling.

'All what?'

'Getting these cars out of Egypt.'

94

'It was my idea.'

'So. It's a good idea – if we don't run into any snags.'

'That's why I don't want you to mention about the flat.'

She paused, and so did I. How could what had happened in a cruddy flat in Shepherds Bush affect the export of three old cars from Cairo? I didn't know, but somehow I didn't greatly care for the turn the conversation was taking. Was she trying to warn me of something in a roundabout way? If so, the way was so roundabout that I couldn't follow it at all.

'Does Kent know Snelling?' I asked her.

'I don't know.'

'How well do you know Snelling?'

'I don't know him at all. I'd never heard of him until you mentioned his name.'

'Are you serious?'

If she wasn't, I was. But then she was, too – or so she said.

'Then what can my mentioning him to Kent do to louse up our deal?'

'Please,' she said. 'Don't ask me. I can't tell you yet, but I will. Can you believe me?'

'You don't make it easy.'

She didn't deny this, so I asked her: 'Are you based here or in London?'

'Here. I've worked for Kent for nearly six months. I've been over to London twice. I liked it there.'

I almost gave her my card, but then they cost three guineas a hundred to print, and I could tell her my phone number for nothing. I told her that, just in case it could ever prove useful.

'Are you driving with us to Alexandria?'

'Yes. You've seen the cars?'

I nodded.

'They should make the distance all right.'

'Do you like the Bugatti?'

'It's not my sort of car,' I told her, because it isn't. 'But it's very saleable, though I hate the colours. Kent had told me it was a Royale, and that's how it's described in the export manifests. But it's not. It's a Type 57.'

She opened her mouth as though she was going to say something interesting, but then she changed her mind; maybe Kent had also warned her about the likelihood of my room being bugged, for all she said was: 'I'll see you in the morning. Here. I can charge a taxi to the office.'

'If the office is synonymous with Kent, by all means charge it. That will be the first bill he's picked up on the whole trip. There is a first time for everything, even for that.'

She took her bag from the bed and went out. I watched her walk along the corridor, with the soft carpet and green walls and the piped music, but she didn't look back. If she had, and seen me standing there, I would have taken her up to the roof bar and who knows where it might all have ended. As it was, I couldn't have had a duller night than I had, turning and twisting in bed, wondering whether my alarm had gone off, or how the deal could possibly be crooked, and if it were whether I could lose either my money or the cars or, worst of all, both.

I woke up at about half-past six and switched off the alarm before it could ring, and sat on the edge of the bed, rubbing sleep out of my eyes and scratching my hair, and burping, all those unpleasant things men do on their own, and sometimes not just on their own, when they're only half awake.

Little things, each without any real significance on their own, seemed more important in the early morning. Kent had lied to me when he said he owned the car in which we had driven to Belsize Park, when it was only hired. Was this forgetfulness, or because he wished to impress, or for what other conceivable reason? Was it only wishful thinking that had caused the Bugatti to be described as a Royale, when it wasn't? And what the hell was Maria up to?

I shrugged away these thoughts, ate breakfast, and was down waiting in the front porch when Maria arrived. We drove in silence along the Pyramids road, past the blocks of

96

new flats with their stucco walls all yellow ochre in the early sunshine, past night-clubs shuttered and sad in the same sun, and then green marshes and stalls of such unlikely things as sweetmeats, drainpipes and terracotta chimney pots. Two women sat under a tree, picking nits from each other's hair. Next to them was a huge bamboo cage on a wooden trolley, filled with sorry chickens in several tiers.

The road was wider than I had imagined in the dusk of the previous evening, and lined on either side by eucalyptus trees, their trunks as thick as three men locked together, if you've ever seen three men locked together which, frankly, I haven't.

In the distance, to the left, we saw three grey slag-heaps. I realized with a shock that these must be the Pyramids. As with so much else in life – and maybe in death, too, for all I know – they looked far more impressive in photographs than in fact.

We turned in at the gateway of the house; it was just as deserted as it had been last night. The taxi driver seemed to know his way and blew his horn twice. The man with the stave – or someone who looked just like him – appeared and waved us in. We stopped, Maria paid off the driver and we went up the steps. The front door was open and Kent came out of a room, wiping his mouth with a table napkin.

'Good, good,' he said, as though life was. 'Would you like a coffee?'

I shook my head. I wanted to be on my way. The earlier we started, the sooner we would reach Alexandria, and the less chance of frying ourselves in the desert. I told him so, and he said 'Good', again, and led the way down the steel stairs to the garage.

The doors were already rolled up, and dust had blown in over the cars. The Bugatti appeared even more garish in the daylight in its crude yellow and black paintwork; the other two also looked older in the merciless sunshine, nondescript old shells with tired mechanical hearts that could hardly arouse the interest of even the most inquisitive customs officer. After Sabry's and Hassan's relations had dealt with their colleagues, I hoped they would not be too concerned with questions.

'Sabry will lead with Hassan,' said Kent. 'He does the journey nearly every week from Alex to see his mother here. I'll go next with Maria, then you come behind. If you get into any trouble, break down, that sort of thing, blow the horn and we'll stop.

'Every so often, we'll pass a police post, and the drill is to get out of the car and smile at the policeman, and be pleasant, and if they speak English, say what a wonderful country this is, and how impressed you are. O.K.?'

I nodded.

'When we reach Alex, we'll go right along the front and park outside the docks. We may not clear all three cars through customs tonight, but if we can clear two of them, we'll do the third in the morning. The boat sails tomorrow at noon, by the way.'

It was all rather like being in the army again. I expected someone to shout, 'Any questions?' I had none. All I wanted to see was the colour of someone's money, preferably not my own.

Sabry came down the steps. He was smelling like a polecat with his attar of roses and musk, a rather disagreeable mixture at eight in the morning. He looked at me in a meaningful sort of way, and so I took out my traveller's cheques and signed away £1,500. If I could have beaten him down by even one pound, I would have felt better about it. As I hadn't, I made up my mind that no one in the trade must ever know I had paid three Gyppoes their asking prices for three cars.

He and Hassan had chosen the Bugatti, and it waited on its thick spoked aluminium wheels, the engine ticking over very slowly, like a metronome. Sabry climbed in beside Hassan, folded up my notes, and put them away in a button-down pocket. Kent was starting up the Marmon with Maria by his side as I threw my suitcase into the back of the Delage and then climbed in behind the wheel.

Louis Delage had been physically handicapped in that he had only one good eye, but despite this he had a natural eye for line and for engineering; he'd designed almost as many individualistic cars as Bugatti in his day, and this was one of them. The dashboard was mother-of-pearl, the instruments had pale waxy faces as though they had wilted in the sun of too many summers. The gears felt firm, and there was little side-to-side play in any of the pedals, always a sure sign that a car has been looked after.

The canvas of the hood had split with age, and dust poured in on me like flour as the wind changed. We started off, juddering on our hard springs, a strange enough convoy, but so many old vehicles were either abandoned at the roadside with broken axles, split tyres, or with the driver doing complicated repairs under the engine, for this was old-car country, that we aroused no interest.

We passed a man wheeling a huge block of ice on a sort of railway trolley. The ice was melting as he trundled it along. By the time he reached wherever he was going, he wouldn't have any ice left to deliver, which was his problem. Mine was to hope that our cars, with a combined age of about one hundred and twelve years, would reach Alexandria safely. It seemed enough to have on my mind for the moment.

The road was double-tracked, and on the roofs of some of the flats I saw soldiers and sandbags and machine-guns. Things looked a bit too warlike for my peace of mind. I'd be very glad to be away.

We curved to the right, away from the former Queen Farida's Palace, a passable imitation of a Tyrolean guest-house, and the Mena House Hotel, where Churchill and

Roosevelt held a conference during the war, away from the Pyramids and the camels and the touts with Arab horses who waited for the tourists. The road was a single lane now, with a white line down the middle. Here and there, the wind had blown sand across it, completely covering the macadam, and trees stood dusty and thick on either side. Beyond them, through a haze of sand and dust, the desert shimmered like a burning glass.

We were keeping up a steady pace of about thirty miles an hour, and gradually the buildings fell behind, and then the only links with the city we had left and the one we were going to, were the pylons dragging the electric cables over the hard bright sand.

The desert seemed to run on endlessly, with false peaks, deep ravines, and long valleys of sand. The first police post was a hut on the left of the road. A soldier with a white flag waved us down, and we stopped obediently, climbed up and stood in a row, like naughty children, in front of an old corporal, who sat at a trestle table. His uniform was serge and must have been unbearably hot. His boots looked as though they had been stolen from the British Army dump in the Canal Zone years ago, in the days when George had been a soldier. They probably had been, and never cleaned since.

I glanced at Kent as we stood in line. He was smiling benignly, as though the corporal was a potential client, but neither Hassan nor Sabry were treating the man lightly. Hassan went into a great spiel in Egyptian to him, and then collected up our passports, and handed them over. I couldn't understand what he was saying, and I don't think that the corporal made much of it, either, but he lugubriously compared our photographs in the passports with our faces, and handed them back. The whole exercise seemed futile, about as much use as the bottom half of a mermaid, but no doubt it satisfied him or his superiors.

I didn't have a chance to plug Kent's line about this being a wonderful country, so I decided to save it for next time.

We climbed back into our cars and drove on, the hood of the Delage flapping like a flag. A strong smell of hot oil – holy smoke, we used to call it when I was a boy – drifted up from the direction of the gear box. I had forgotten to check the oil level in the box, and began to wonder whether we would make the distance. The road was completely empty for miles at a time; then the only vehicles we saw were Skoda army lorries, bright and new, driving south, presumably from the docks.

The drive would have been murder in the dark, because the road had no proper edges. Sand had blown over them, sometimes to a depth of several feet. Here and there, on the fringes of the desert, little groups of old army tents, blackened with age and use, whackered in the endless breeze, with a dry, lifeless sound.

Once or twice, we had to make a detour off the road, around a make-shift track, while engineers of some sort were working on the surface. On one of these detours my right-hand rear wheel slipped and spun uselessly in the sand. I managed, by the momentum of the car, to bring it back on the hard surface again, but the experience made me realize that if both rear wheels slid off the road, I would have to be towed out.

On either side now, the sand stretched away to a hazy blue infinity, empty of all life. I had the odd feeling, when the cars in front of me were obscured by their own dust, of being either the first or the last man in the world, with no one else, nothing else, left alive.

We slowed down for the next police post, a more sophisticated affair, with a radio set on the table and a long vertical aerial trembling in the wind. The corporal here actually wrote down our engine numbers, for what reason I didn't discover, but he appeared satisfied, and waved us on.

The wind was now far stronger than it had been near Cairo. It blew empty tins and pieces of newspaper, dropped by goodness knows who, in front of us as though they were leaves. Every few miles, on the right of the road, stood white boards with black lettering in Arabic script, and underneath a stencil of a telephone, and the figure 100, and about 100 yards farther on there was the actual, physical telephone itself, in a yellow box on a pole. I didn't know whether they worked, or whether they were even connected, but they had a reassuring look.

I tended to lose count of time. My eyes kept flickering down to the oil pressure on the dashboard, but the needle stayed firm, although the engine was nearly boiling.

Hassan, as the leader, had turned up the speed to thirty-five, and after two hours by my watch, when I reckoned that if we had nothing worse to meet than we had already passed, we should be all right, he pulled off into a kind of oasis of unexpected trees, ringed round a concrete encampment. There were bushes and advertisements for GMC trucks and Misr petrol, and a rash of big radio masts with a high brick wall round them, and a rest-house with two or three cars parked close together, as though for comfort.

We stopped. I switched off the engine and climbed out. The wind blew my trousers against my legs. It was hot, and yet, because of the wind, cool at the same time; a curious sensation. I felt gritty and in need of a bath. The old Delage engine was happily boiling away now that the fan had stopped turning.

'We'll have a drink here,' Kent explained.

We all walked into the cafe rather stiff-leggedly. It was a relief to be out of the wind. A juke box was playing in one corner, and some other drivers were sitting at formica-topped tables. They looked round at us, wondering who we were, then went on with their meal. A waiter came and wiped the table, produced a menu in script that meant nothing to me.

102

Hassan ordered something which turned out to be five glasses of squeezed lemon juice and water. Kent looked round the room in a conspiratorial way, and pulled his chair half an inch nearer the table.

'We're about forty miles from Alex,' he said. 'Hassan thought it a good idea to have a drink and a wash, for we may have to hang about for hours at the docks. Also, his car is giving a bit of trouble. One of the plugs has oiled up.'

'Do you want me to look at it?' I asked.

'No,' said Hassan, shaking his head. 'My experience of anything old and mechanical is that so long as it runs, leave it alone. That's how it is with old guns, anyhow. I'll nurse the car to Alex, and once we've reached the docks, we'll have no more driving.'

The waiter brought the bill and, as usual, I paid. This was becoming a game, to see how Kent could duck out of paying. I noticed that he managed to be going through his papers, so he pretended he didn't see the waiter. I had a slash and a wash, dried my face on my handkerchief because there wasn't any towel, and then we set off for the last lap.

The heat, the constant faint smell of exhaust, the strong smell of oil, and everywhere the shimmering dancing horizon of the desert, made me feel sleepy. More than once, I dozed off, and jerked myself back to consciousness, just as the front wheel was beginning to dip itself into the sand over the edge of the road.

After about ten miles, great green stretches suddenly appeared on either side of the road, signs proclaiming 'This is a new irrigation project'. We passed a dead camel with a crowd of people standing round it, holding hands. I wondered how they would remove it. There was probably a few hundred piastres in it for some sharp fellow, but I was glad it wasn't my problem.

About twenty miles from Alex, the road forked by a giant model of a Pepsi Cola bottle top, blue and red and white. We took the right turn, and left the desert behind us. Flowers were growing now on either side of the road, yellow flowers like buttercups, cactus plants with wide, fleshy leaves, and trees instead of sand. On the horizon I could see the fingers of factory chimneys, pouring out white smoke, and then a river, then an oil depot with a fence round it, and crates stamped 'Moscow', then a field full of baby camels. They looked just the same as the big ones, only smaller, which wasn't surprising, but the camel is such a strange anachronism of an animal, designed by a committee, so they say, and thus the only beast that never loves its master. When you see his master, you can't really wonder.

On either side of the road, lakes glittered under the sun like mirrors with clumps of reeds and grey brown dry thistles that rattled in the wind. Buffaloes stood up to their stomachs in the water. Here and there men slept at the roadside; their canoes were stuck in the reeds, half ashore, half afloat.

We were almost into Alexandria, white with domes and mosques and minarets, and the tall yellow square buildings of blocks of flats, with the chimneys pouring out their fog of smoke beyond them. The wind carried a strong smell of mud and dung from the drying salt flats. Not at all as I'd imagined Alexandria from reading Lawrence Durrell.

The road was double tracked now, pitted with holes, and grass growing in side streets.

The houses were shabby, and, from windows in blocks of flats, wooden poles pointed out at us, strung with washing. Taxis with yellow bodies and black wings and tops, looking like huge metal wasps, droned past, and men toiled like mules between the shafts of carts of bananas. Everything appeared to be broken down, and yet for centuries Alexandria had been Egypt's second city. Now it looked like a stage-set for a Middle East slum.

We came into the centre of the city, close together, travelling slowly. Boys on cycles with other boys squatting on the handlebars seemed to have a death-wish to disappear under my huge wheels, and I kept my thumb almost incessantly on the horn button.

Hassan led us under the shade of new blocks of flats, up a wide street where litter blew about, whole sheets of newspaper lifting in the wind like sails. In the distance we could see cranes, and the masts of ships, and then a funnel and mast-head flags stretched tight in the wind.

We came through a street clogged with carts and old cars, and the docks were ahead of us. I don't know what I expected – water, I suppose, and ships, but here we seemed to be still in the middle of the city. Hassan stopped, and Kent jumped out of his car and ran back to me.

'There's only room inside the dock gates for two cars at a time,' he explained. 'We're leaving the Bugatti here. Another plug's oiled up and we'll have to clean the lot, otherwise I'm afraid it won't start again. Maria will stay with it, and you come with your papers. O.K. ?'

I had no reason to argue the point. All I wanted was to be out of the heat and fumes. Hassan manœuvred his car behind a two-wheel cart, where a man was selling cucumbers and bottles of lemonade with glass marbles for stoppers, just as they used to sell in South East London, when I was a boy.

I threw my suitcase into the Bugatti. The doors wouldn't lock, but then it didn't matter with Maria there. Anyhow, my luggage was insured. So am I. As I always say, I'm worth more dead than alive, but to whom ?

'You've got the papers ?' Kent asked anxiously.

'Everything,' I assured him.

'Right. The drill here is to say nothing unless you're asked a question direct. Otherwise, let old Hassan and Sabry do the talking. That's what they're here for. What this has cost me in baksheesh is nobody's business.

'All the customs men *should* do is look at the papers, check your passport number, and maybe see that the engine and chassis numbers we've given tally with the plates under the bonnets. On no account say what you can sell these cars for in England, though, in case they want more of a cut.'

I have exported enough cars from other countries, and I couldn't see why Kent was getting so het-up and nervous. Maybe it was the thought that he had actually had to fork out some of his own money, or, if not his own, some he had hoped to make his own for bribes? Or maybe he was edgy because this wasn't really his line of country, and the first time you do anything you feel a bit nervous. Or maybe this business of Maria and Snelling, the man she said she'd never heard of, had some bearing on things, though what, I couldn't imagine.

Hassan and Sabry were waiting for me inside the dockyard gates. To the left was a small building rather like an outsize doll's house. Through a window, two men, incongruously dressed in Army great coats, sat facing each other at a table. They must have been drowning in their own sweat.

One wore a hat, the other was bare-headed. From a shelf behind them a Japanese transistor blared out Arab music. They had empty cups and saucers in front of them, and flies buzzed busily round the rims of the cups.

Sabry went up to the window, pushed aside half a dozen loafers, waved to the men inside as though they were friends from schooldays, and they might well have been, and shook hands ceremoniously with them. Behind us, I noticed a soldier in the customary wretched uniform of fustian khaki and scuffed boots, swinging an ancient Lee Enfield rifle. He was chewing betelnut, and the juice dripped through his lips like blood.

I smiled as brightly as I could, not knowing what I was meant to be doing, or who was in command. I felt rather like an actor pushed out on stage in act two of some drama with no very clear idea of what has already happened in act one. I didn't altogether like the feeling.

The man with the hat stretched out his hand towards me. I

106

took it, thinking he wanted to shake hands, but he waved aside this pleasantry, and instead gripped my document case. I let it go. He unsnapped the case and began to thumb through the papers. Then he said something to Sabry.

Sabry turned to me.

'He wants to know why you want to take the cars out of the country?'

'Because I deal in old cars,' I said, which seemed a sufficiently good reason. After all, it was true.

Sabry translated this. The man said something else. Sabry translated again.

'He wants to know where do you deal in these old cars?'

'I've told him on the form. In London. England. Aristo Autos.'

More translation. More questions, this time between the two characters at the table.

Sabry then said: 'He wants to know why you came here from London to deal in old cars.'

'For Christ's sake,' said Kent behind me, 'What the hell has it got to do with this nut? We're paying for the bloody things, aren't we?'

I nudged him in the ribs. You never know how much English these people understand.

'I came to Egypt because I wanted to see the Pyramids, the Sphinx, and other places I had read about,' I explained, not entirely truthfully. 'Also, there are many old cars in Egypt which we do not have in England.'

As this was being translated, the man nodded and looked at me. For all his shabby appearance, he wasn't a fool. His eyes were hard and small, worm-holes in a middle-aged skull. I held his gaze because I had nothing else to hold, and also I believe childishly that if you let your eyes drop in front of someone they think you are lying, although I had hardly opened my mouth. (If you let your eyes drop right out on the deck, of course, they think you're blind, and quite right, too.)

The first set of papers dealt with the Marmon. He paused over the chassis and engine numbers, and then reached up for a paper book on the shelf behind him, and thumbed his way through with one hand, keeping the other on the papers.

'What's he doing now?' asked Kent nervously.

Before I could nudge him again to silence, Hassan turned and explained.

'He's checking that these numbers actually relate to cars that one can export.'

'What do you mean?' I asked. 'That one can export?'

'Some military vehicles might have been stolen.'

I couldn't imagine confusing that ancient Marmon with a military vehicle, and neither could the man who compiled the book, because the old fool in the hat closed it, and ticked the engine and chassis numbers to show that they had been checked. Then he signed the bottom of each page, banged it with an ancient, battered stamp, and passed the sheaf of papers over to his colleague, who also added something in Arabic script.

The Bugatti's papers gave us a little more trouble. There was more conversation, more searching through the book. Sabry said: 'Did you know that this car was originally registered from the Abdin Palace in Cairo? It was apparently one of King Farouk's cars.'

'Fancy that,' I said, glad that I hadn't been sold a pup, even if it wasn't a Royale. 'There's no snag about exporting it, surely?'

More conversation, arms held up towards the sky as though to catch any manna that Allah might generously cause to descend, then heads laid on shoulders, and much chatter from the layabouts gathered round us at the open window.

Sabry translated this as briefly as he could.

'No reason at all. You've paid for the car. He's just telling you this out of interest.'

'How kind of him,' I said. 'Thank him very much.'

I beamed towards the old man to show my pleasure. He beamed at me. He put out his hand; this time, we shook hands properly. He said something to Sabry, who also grinned.

'He says you've a nice face,' translated Sabry.

'Thank him very much again,' I told him. 'Tell him I'll give him a job any time he asks. I only deal with honest men.'

Everyone laughed when this was translated, and they got through the further nonsensical details about the make of the tyres, the number of miles the car had covered, the tools and type of instruments, very quickly. As the man signed the last page and picked up the papers about the Delage, Kent pushed his way to the window.

'Tell him we've had great trouble with that Bugatti. It's broken down, so we won't actually be able to get it here until tomorrow morning. But we thought we should submit all the papers in a batch, for all the cars and then he can check the numbers against the Bugatti, if he wants to, in the morning.'

All this was translated. The man looked up at us, his eyes cold and stony. Kent's excuse seemed rubbish to me, but I guessed he knew what he was doing. I hoped he did, for I had no idea. There seemed no trouble about the Delage number, though. And after both men had stamped and signed the form, they pushed back their chairs on the concrete floor and came out to look at the cars.

One of the people hanging around the window began to lift the Delage's bonnet. I slipped him a five piastre note, and opened it myself, for I didn't trust his little fingers on the catches. Both men checked the numbers on the brass plate beneath the bonnet and stamped on the chassis frame and cylinder block.

It was all over very quickly and painlessly; I've had more trouble at Tilbury, trying to take out some beat-up pre-war Y-model Ford Eight than I had here.

109

The man in the hat clapped his hands and two other characters appeared in nondescript dungarees and khaki berets. The old fellow tore a strip of paper off the last page of our forms and gave one to each of these men. They climbed into the cars, fiddled with the controls, and, after several attempts, managed to start the engines.

We stood watching them drive off towards the centre of the docks. Then there were more handclasps all round, more translations, and we drifted back towards the gates. When we were outside, I turned to Kent.

'What's the point of saying the Bugatti has broken down?'

'Because it very nearly has, and because I've got an idea for a much better deal,' he said. 'That's why.'

His eyes were glistening now, partly with relief and re-action, and partly at the thought of the size of the deal.

'What is it?' I asked him.

'I'll tell you when we're away from here. I'm taking a taxi. You follow with Maria in the Bugatti. We're going about forty miles out of town. I'll take it easy so you don't drop behind. Those plugs are all fouled up so you can't go very quickly.'

'What the hell is all this about?' I asked him irritably. I'd had enough of driving across the desert. This was like enter-ing for a hundred yards race, and then being told, when you're half way up the track, that the organizers have sud-denly decided to make it a two-twenty.

'I'll tell you when we get there. It's a good deal, I promise you.'

'What about the boat that goes tomorrow?'

'We'll be on it,' he assured me.

Before I could ask anything else, he turned away to hail a cab. I walked back to the Bugatti. Maria was standing against the bonnet.

'Everything all right?' she asked.

'I don't know,' I said. 'The cars went through without any

110

aggravation, but Kent told the man this had broken down. Now we're going forty miles out of town for some reason.'

'He has an idea for a better deal,' Maria said. Her eyes were also shining; if she wasn't excited about this deal, like Kent, then she was excited about something else – or someone else.

'He didn't give me any details,' I said. 'Can you?'

'I'd rather he did.'

I climbed in behind the wheel. She got in the other side. The engine was a bit reluctant to fire; it was so hot that the petrol had evaporated, but it growled into life eventually, missing on one and probably two cylinders. At least Kent hadn't lied about the plugs.

I did a quick, reflex-action check on the controls, ran my fingers along the wires and pipes behind the dash to feel if any were loose. They weren't. One thin pipe showed a faint gleam of copper to the right of my seat. I traced it beneath the floor. It was a petrol pipe. My fingers felt the tap, probably fitted by some previous owner as a precaution against fire when the car was left unattended.

'Let's go,' I said, and let in the clutch.

Kent's taxi, big and brown as a burnished, blown-up bumble bee, began to move. I followed it, at about fifty yards distance. We went out on to the sea front, where waves pounded against rocks behind the stone sea wall, as though angry about something. I found it difficult to realize that this was the Mediterranean which, on the opposite coast of France, has no tide whatever, and whenever I've seen it has seemed to be perpetually placid.

We passed some houses, a café, and here and there, out on streaming rocks and broken chunks of stone and concrete from old anti-invasion defences, men crouched crapping, oblivious of the flying spray. Others, equally oblivious of the crappers, stood fishing. They made a curious and unexpected sight, not the sort of thing that features in the tourist

111

pamphlets about ancient wonders and romantic customs of the Middle East.

On the other side of the promenade, the houses were built close to the road, all shuttered and dusty, with dull, yellow walls where years of heat had burned the life out of the paint. They had English names: The Gordon Hotel, The Cecil, The Carlton, The Ivy, but no English were there now. They had all gone long since; all that they had left behind were their names.

The front doors were closed, although in some downstairs rooms I saw a face, pale and disembodied, perhaps a care-taker, looking through the glass at the angry sea, maybe remembering other years, long ago when the nannies would be out, pushing prams with pale English children under silk sun-shades with scalloped edges.

Behind the harbour wall stood a fortress, white with Moorish domes, and then we were past the town, and the road stretched itself out along the desert by the edge of the sea, so that the sand seemed like one enormous beach. A soldier at a police post waved us through, without even bothering to stop us.

Forty miles, Kent had said. I watched the mileometer turn up the distance on the dashboard, and we had gone forty-three before the right flasher for the taxi began to wink, and he turned away from the sea towards the heart of the desert. We went up a hill, and over the crest lay a gigantic building.

It looked rather like the Palace of Versailles or even the Strand Palace, and wasn't much smaller than either or both, with pillars, archways, gargoyles for water spouts to catch the non-existent rain, and all the other Byzantine archaeological extravagances that come from too much money and too little taste.

At each end of this archaeological abortion ancient cannons pointed useless hexagonal mouths at the hill. Green roller shutters on all the windows were pulled down; the red, white and black tricolour of Egypt fluttered its two green stars from a mast behind the guns. A man in a fez crouched at the base of the pole, picking his nose.

'What the hell is this?' I asked Maria, because it could be anything.

'A former summer palace,' she said. 'It belonged to a member of Farouk's court.'

'And what is it now?'

'Partly a museum and partly an hotel. We've booked rooms here for tonight.'

'So Kent knew all along we weren't going aboard today?'

'Yes.'

'Then why the hell couldn't he have told me?'

'He was very nervous about getting the cars through. He's afraid of his position here in Egypt. Any foreigner lives under the threat of instant expulsion, without even a reason. If he had to go, he'd lose his whole business.'

'That's why he got me to sign the forms, so if anything went wrong I'd be carrying the can?'

'If you put it like that, yes.'

I did put it like that, as the divorcee told the High Court judge, but I still didn't see why Kent had to be so secretive.

'I would have thought it was obvious,' she said, irritated at my dimness. 'If you'd known we were going to switch this old Bugatti for another car, you might have acted nervously, and then the customs people could have suspected something'

'What do you mean, switch it for another car?' I suddenly felt dread, like indigestion, in my guts. What the hell did she mean?

'Kent will tell you,' she said, as though she had already said too much.

I remembered the lie Kent had told me about owning the Cortina when it was only hired; I remembered being beaten senseless in Maria's flat, and her request that I wouldn't say

113

anything about this to him, and I had that unwelcome feeling in my stomach that things were all going wrong for me.

I didn't know where, and how, or why, but as I watched Kent get out of his taxi and hold the door open for Sabry and Hassan, the fact that there were three of them to one of me, with possibly Maria as a neutral, did nothing to cheer me up. My old mother's only son was going to be right up to his neck in it again if he didn't watch out, and the thought brought me no comfort at all.

The taxi turned in a wide arc of dust and was away; someone must have paid the driver, even if Kent hadn't. Sabry and Hassan walked up the steps of the museum, not looking back. Kent came towards me, lighting a cigarette. I cut my engine. It was very quiet out there, and the rim of hill cut off the roar of the waves, so that they seemed like the distant murmur of a crowd.

'What's all this about switching a car?' I asked Kent irritably.

He looked sharply at Maria.

'I said you'd tell him,' she said quickly.

'It's a much better deal,' he said defensively.

'For whom?'

'For all of us. Sorry I had to string you along a bit, but I was scared you might give something away at the Customs if you knew what we were up to. I didn't know how good an actor you were.'

'I'm a method actor,' I said. 'And my method is always to be pleasant to anyone until I know they're heels. Where's this car you want switched?'

'In the garage of this hotel,' he said, nodding towards it. 'It's a long story. Let's book in, get a drink, and I'll see you on the terrace.'

'What's wrong with my room?' I asked. I wanted to get this nut on his own where he couldn't welch on me so easily.

'This is like Cairo. A lot of the rooms let to foreigners are bugged. We don't want to give ourselves away before we start.'

'Can't the terrace be bugged, too?'

'It's less likely. Purely from a technical point of view. Anyway, see you there in twenty minutes.'

I restarted the engine and drove up to the front of the hotel. The man who was picking his nose stopped picking and walked towards us. He was a big flabby fellow in a long brown coat, and a red belt with a huge brass buckle which still bore the Royal Arms of Egypt. He opened the door, took our suitcases out of the back.

'You have a garage?' I asked him.

'Yes, sir.'

I gave him my name.

'Put the car in the garage, then, and leave the key at the reception desk.'

He nodded.

Maria and I walked up the steps together. We might have been lovers, but we weren't. I wanted to keep my strength for whatever the night might hold, like not getting beaten up, like making sure I was aboard that boat on the following morning.

The entrance hall was gigantic. If I'd had a net and a couple of racquets and a tennis ball, we could have had a game. It was furnished in extraordinary style, with a French sideboard about forty feet long, a fireplace with a huge gilt-edge mirror above it, and an Italian ceiling picked out in panels. Red tapestries edged with gold hung from the walls. The floor was marble, and in one corner, looking incongruously insignificant, a reception clerk stood behind a glass-topped desk. Behind him were the key rings and pigeon holes for rooms. If this had been the summer palace for a member of Farouk's court, then what kind of style had Farouk commanded?

I gave the clerk my name, filled in the form, putting my

115

profession as car exporter, which sounds more aristocratic then car coping.

'Room eleven, sir,' said the clerk.

Some webfoot picked up the key and carried my bag. I followed him down the corridor, under pictures of King Farouk as a little boy, and a calendar that stood at Saturday, 26 July, 1952, which was the day he was forced to abdicate, and so presumably a date to remember, either for good or ill, depending on which side of the social or political fence you happened to be.

The landings were thick with tapestries and marble tables, gilt chairs with round cushions embroidered with red roses in the middle of a black centre, and all edged with grey. On one wall was a De Lazlo painting of Farouk as a child, with a red fez and open shirt and jacket, and short trousers, so cunningly executed that his eyes followed me like the eyes in that Lord Kitchener recruiting poster.

The page opened a door on the left, and I was in my room. It was the strangest hotel-room I had ever seen, but then the whole set-up was as odd as a two-pound note, so I didn't fall about. The walls were panelled in pale green wood, picked out with gold. A Persian carpet covered most of the parquet floor. From each wall the Egyptian Royal crest looked down, like crown and anchor symbols. The bed was about twelve feet square. There was a fireplace with a gilt-framed mirror above it, and an ancient gold telephone with a tiny hand crank.

I slipped a handful of small change into the page's grubby fist and locked the door behind him. I had a quick glim around the room in case I could see a microphone, but I wasn't really sure what it would look like, anyhow – certainly not like a microphone.

I didn't see anything odd, apart from a couple of big cockroaches. I turned back the bed quilt quickly so the bugs wouldn't have time to run away, but the sheets were clean. I suppose in a former Royal palace you have different standards from a doss-house in the Earls Court Road.

I opened my suitcase, took out a packet of Alka Seltzer, ran the tap until the water turned from brown to amber, mixed them in a glass, swallowed them and felt a bit better. Then I went out, along the corridor and down the stairs to the terrace. Kent was sitting under a striped golf umbrella at the far end, as far away as he could get, without actually camping on the sand.

'I didn't order until you came,' he said.

I guessed he hadn't.

'I'll take a whisky, then,' I told him.

He frowned.

'It's very expensive here.'

'It'll come off your profits.'

'*Our* profits,' he corrected quickly.

A waiter materialized and then shuffled away and returned with two whiskies already poured out in the glasses. He did his stuff with the syphon, and went back from whence he came, and whence he came was no concern of mine.

Kent looked around in his conspiratorial way, to make sure the man was out of sight, and then jerked his head back to invite me to move a little closer. I shifted the white metal chair nearer to the edge of the table. If I was any closer, I thought, people would say we were in love, and I suddenly wondered who could love this mean man with the soul of an accountant, for so far as making money is concerned, most accountants are like eunuchs: they know how it's done, but they can't do it themselves.

'So what's it about, then?' I asked. 'Why the hell are we here when we could be aboard that boat without any problems at all? What's this better deal you spoke about, and the car you want switched?'

'It's a long story,' he said nervously.

'So you keep saying. But I've got a long time. Maybe we'll

117

both do a long time in some Egyptian jug if your plan comes unstuck. So let's have it all and never mind about my being a good or bad actor. I'm a damn' good audience.'

He cleared his throat, rubbed his chin with his hand nervously.

'I don't know what you remember about Farouk, but it's probably not much, except he was fat and wore dark glasses and had lots of girl friends? Well, that's all true. And as Sabry told you, he had an enormous collection of fast cars. Since he was rich – he left two hundred and fifty million dollars when he died – Farouk could indulge this fancy, and any others, too.

'Well, when he got the heave, General Neguib – who had seized power – auctioned off all these cars. His government wanted rid of them as quickly as possible. They were only an embarrassment to a country trying to work out some more equable scheme of life.

'But back then, prices for old cars weren't very high. Some of them were almost given away. One, in fact, wasn't even sold at all. It wasn't in Cairo at the time, and when it was discovered some time after the sale, no one was interested.'

'Where was it?'

It seemed a good question, and it was all I could think of to say.

'Here. In this summer palace. A courtier was using it.'

He paused, as though all this should make me fall about. I sipped my whisky and sat where I was.

'The point is,' he went on. 'That car's *still* here.'

'So?'

'So I want to switch it for that Bugatti you brought along. It's a Bugatti, too, of course.'

'Of course.'

It could hardly be anything else.

'Why is it here?'

'Because it's become part of the furniture, that's why. If

118

you're a tourist and go round the ex-King's apartments – he had a suite here, just in case he felt like a night by the sea – you'll be shown the ex-King's desk, the ex-Queen's bedroom, his lavatory, her bathroom, even his medicine cabinet with Elastoplast and his old Optrex bottle and a tube of K.Y. jelly. You may also be shown this car. It's an exhibit.'

'What's so special about it?'

'I don't know much about cars,' said Kent. 'But Maria tells me she's seen American tourists go mad when they see it. It's a Royale two-seater, with some kind of special sports body. Bloody great petrol tank which would take you half way round the world, headlamps the size of searchlights, horns as big as bugles. You know much more about all that than I do.

'Once a year, this car is removed from the public gaze, and a crowd of mechanics from Alex set about refurbishing it, putting back the little bits that tourists have stolen, painting over the scratches, and so on. This is what's happening now.'

'Well, how the hell *can* you switch cars? It doesn't seem feasible. The Royale must be too well known. It's bound to be recognized.'

'There's a risk,' he agreed. 'But not very great. Let me ask you a few questions and you'll see how little that risk really is. Tell me, have you ever been to the Tower of London?'

I shook my head.

'Never.'

Why should I go there? After all, I live in London. I can go there any day of my life and so I've never been at all.

'Windsor Castle?'

'No. Only the pub of that name in Notting Hill.'

'The Royal Mews at Buckingham Palace?'

I shook my head.

'Exactly,' said Kent smugly, 'Because you live in London. Only tourists go to places like that. It's the same here.'

'You mean to tell me that those customs men at the docks at Alex wouldn't recognize this car if they saw it?'

'Exactly. Sabry tells me that they're only paid nine pounds a month on which they have to bring up a family. That doesn't leave much over for coming forty odd miles to this Palace just to look over an old car that Farouk owned years ago, does it? How could they get here, anyhow? There are no buses, and they can't afford taxis and they don't run cars and it's too far to walk. Ten to one, they've never even heard of the car, let alone seen it.'

'The customs men aren't the only ones, though,' I pointed out. 'We'd have to drive it there. People on the road would see it.'

'Of course,' agreed Kent. 'That's where you come in.'

That's where I go out, I thought. I didn't like the sound or the smell of this. My name was on those manifests, not Kent's. I would be the one who did time in some underground Egyptian gaol, not Kent.

'You're making heavy weather of it,' he said, as though he'd read my thoughts, and maybe he had. Maybe they were what anyone else would be thinking in my position.

'When I say this is where you come in, that's exactly what I mean. This Royale is painted yellow and black – just like the Bugatti you've driven here. No one stopped me on the way to Alex, or you on the way here, did they? Right. And no one will stop us when we take the Royale to the docks tomorrow.'

I liked the way he used the Royal or editorial plural. How many of us were going to drive the bloody thing, then?

'What about the chassis numbers?'

'We've got the Type 57 here, haven't we?'

I nodded.

'Well, use your loaf. We take off the plate with the chassis and engine numbers from under the bonnet, and screw it on Farouk's car. You can fill in the number that's stamped on

120

the engine block with a bit of putty or some paint. They'll never check that, anyhow – they didn't with the other cars, now, did they? Be fair.'

I was fair; they hadn't.

'Right. We've already established we have three cars, one a Bugatti. We've also established that the Bugatti has broken down, and we've given them the numbers.'

'This will go through very easily. After all, Hassan and Sabry know these people. They've got their contacts, money's changed hands. It'll be days or even weeks before the switch is discovered. By then, we'll be back in England.'

This might be so, but it might equally well not be so.

I sat sipping my drink, thinking, watching the desert still fluid with heat in the distance, shimmering as though the sands were already liquid glass.

I knew now why they had described the car I had driven as being a Royale when it wasn't. Kent had obviously given this scheme a lot of thought and preparation. This, I didn't like. He'd probably had the idea before he contacted me in London. Maybe he'd offered me that old Delahaye so cheaply simply because he wanted to hook me – as he had succeeded in doing.

If this was so, the whole business about Snelling buying the car back for £100 more than I had given for it began to make sense. Kent was so mean he'd skin a turd for a farthing, and he just couldn't bear the thought that he was losing a potential profit, even if he could make a hundred times as much – as he would if we found a Royale.

It's not money that's the root of evil, but, as the Good Book says, the love of money. And the love of money, the prospect of a deal, the hope of an old-car killing so big it was practically a massacre, had lured me here. Kent had held out bait and I'd bitten. I didn't like that, either, for since my name was the only one on all the manifest papers, if anything went wrong, I'd be the only one to fall in the cactus.

Sabry had already taken my money, and they'd simply sail away to take the profit on the two cars aboard ship, while I stayed behind to take whatever punishment an Egyptian court decided. This, I liked least of all. I may bend the truth a little, I may turn back mileometer readings, and I do – and who doesn't, in my business? – but I have never been a ringer, substituting one car for another. This didn't seem a particularly good time to start.

'Why take the risk?' I asked. 'With the Bugatti we've already got, we'll probably make five hundred each, after all expenses, if we split down the middle.'

He looked at me.

'On this one we'll make ten times that amount. Easily. Probably more.'

He could be right, and the way he said it, his eyes narrowed so that their acquisitive gleam didn't show so plainly, I knew he'd hopes of something even higher.

'It's a lot of bread,' I agreed.

'It's a lot of car. Come and see it before you raise more objections.'

We finished our drinks and went into the hotel. Sabry was sitting on a chromium-plated tubular chair, a styling refugee from the nineteen-thirties, turning over the pages of a magazine, obviously waiting for us. He stood up as we arrived. We followed him without a word down a corridor, through a door marked 'Privé'.

It shut soundlessly behind us, and we were in the servants' world, lifted from Edwardian England, with bells hanging on curved springs; the back of the door was even covered in green baize, nailed on with brass headed tacks. A stone staircase led down to some basement. There was a metal rail, and the white-washed walls were cut and gouged where trays had scratched against them as servants had hurried to and fro on their masters' bidding. The good old days, all right; so long as you were on the right side of that door.

We went down these stairs and through another door. Someone had oiled the hinges and locks so liberally that the stuff was actually streaming down the woodwork. I wondered whether this had been Hassan or Sabry.

The garage stretched the whole length of the hotel, and beneath it; three sides were built into the sand. The fourth had the doors. The walls were concrete, and great stains and patches of crystals had formed where dampness had seeped through from the sand. The vast cellar was divided by vertical wooden partitions, each about twenty feet apart, so that a driver or mechanic could work on a car in seclusion, without any risk of being in anyone else's way. Along the far wall was a bench with shelves above it for spares, and spring clips for spanners, all in order of size. Whoever had designed this garage had been an experienced engineer.

Sabry led us past four or five empty booths, their concrete floors stained by oil that had dripped from cars of long ago. I remembered the incident of the Hispano-Suiza that had been driven in 1919 from Paris to Nice in sixteen hours – an immense achievement – and then gone on display in the local showroom, with a clean sheet of white paper under its engine to prove that Hispanos didn't leak oil.

We reached the Type 57 I had driven from Alex, and in the next booth I saw the Royale. It was so large, I would have seen it a couple of miles away.

When the Queen of Sheba visited Solomon, she reported in the Bible that, as regard to his magnificent style of life, 'The half of it had not been told me.' I felt the same when I saw this mechanical leviathan that Le Patron had created, this Brobdingnagian Bugatti.

It looked 400 feet long, but probably was about nineteen; the bonnet, from the elephant mascot to the windscreen, was exactly seven feet. It had a yellow torpedo body with two doors, and two seats so close together the driver would rub thighs with the passenger. With the sort of passenger a young man would have carried in this car when it was new, this would have been no hardship, but rather an earnest of even closer contact to come.

The wings were like black tear-drops, as on the 812 Cord, but with this difference; inside the front wings, two small lockable cupboards had been built, so concealed that you had to look carefully to see their fastenings and their hinges. These were for tools, and maybe even a couple of bottles of Brut.

The body tapered down to a sharp wedge on the tail, and the fins of the wings, sharp as many a knife, trailed slightly behind this. The tail and the wings were ribbed with chromium beadings. I licked my thumb and then rubbed it along the chrome. The plating glittered like new.

The front of the car was imposing, with its high horseshoe-shaped radiator, its giant Marchal headlamps, with mirrored reflectors, the two Zeiss spotlights, a cluster of air horns that could have come from the brass section of an orchestra but hadn't, and on the radiator cap, that mark of luxury, the silver elephant with which the patron had endowed the Royale. Some way behind this, just in front of the windscreen was a green glass Lalique mascot.

You don't see these now, because yobbos in car parks would smash them, or steal them, or tear them off and throw them away, but in the thirties, when these yobbos were still unborn, and their equivalents, confined in tenements and stews and hutches, hadn't the energy or the mind for the senseless destruction of beautiful things, these glass mascots were not only fashionable, but feasible.

This mascot would light up from within at night, and gliding behind that greenly illuminated Indian head, with the hiss of the big carburettor and distant drumming of the exhaust, it must have been wonderful to be alive – and rich. I'm still alive – but rich? Now that's something different altogether.

I walked round the car, examining the body. It was in good

124

nick; rarely can such a long body have held only two people, as the gynaecologist said of the six foot five mother of twins, or, if you prefer to be classical, as Shelley wrote on another occasion altogether: 'Look on my works, ye Mighty, and despair.'

I'd have despaired of ever finding a parking space for this elephantine monster, if it had been mine. One thing puzzled me as I examined it; there should have been a dickey, with a small step behind the driver's door – for mothers-in-law and such other undesirables as the owner had been compelled reluctantly to carry – to mount up into this dickey.

I bent down and examined the curve of the metal at an angle, and could just see where the bolts had been removed and the holes soft-soldered over and rubbed down. The dickey lid had been welded shut, so the car had a completely clean sweep, without any join to mar the line.

On the back of this truly gigantic boot was a small luggage carrier, with its Vuitton travelling trunk still strapped in position, the leather oiled, the nickel buckles polished. How standards have changed, I thought, when today the owner of the most modest car demands a boot large enough to hold luggage for a month's holiday for four, while the owner of this magnificent monster had to be content with cramming his belongings into a small case under the winds and rains of of heaven.

Just in front of the case was a huge petrol filler cap, the size of a saucer. If the tank was commensurate with the size of the filler, the driver could surely make a trip from Cairo to the Cape, without stopping at a petrol station, which might be useful if anyone had such a journey in mind.

Cars nowadays are designed by committees and look that way, but not this car. In the heroic days of the motor-car, when this had been designed and built, one man said how things would look and where they would go; and they went.

I have never been particularly drawn to Bugattis myself, because they are so highly strung they make a racehorse seem as untemperamental as an undertaker's mute. But they certainly have character, inherited from their creator, old Ettore, one of the greatest individualists in the whole history of the horseless carriage.

He was born in Milan, and his father sent him to an art school, where he made as little progress as his brother Rembrandt, who was studying at a technical college.

The two brothers met one holiday, compared failures – and agreed to switch careers. Within a few years, Rembrandt became a distinguished sculptor, and Ettore a manufacturer of classic cars. Father doesn't always know best.

Ettore designed the sort of cars he liked, and lived the kind of life he liked. In hot weather, he wore a beige bowler hat with holes he'd personally punched in it. Sometimes he alternated this headgear with a pith helmet of the kind worn in the French colonies. Around his waist he strapped a leather belt with two holsters, not for pistols, but for carrying his measuring instruments, notebook and pencils.

At the height of his cars' acclaim, he produced fifty cars a month in an extraordinary factory at Molsheim on the fringe of the Vosges mountains.

Originally, this had been a dye works in pawn to a bank. When Bugatti had made his first car, he showed it to the banker, hoping for financial backing, and the banker was so impressed that he offered to rent this factory to Bugatti so he could start production. Here, Bugatti became virtually self-supporting. Not only did he have his own bronze and aluminium foundries, he reared pigs and poultry, prize winning cattle, even ran a private distillery to produce his own liqueurs. He grew his own vegetables, and his table wines came from his own vineyards. For relaxation, he had a stable of thoroughbred hunters, and his own riding school.

After a dispute with the local electricity company, Bugatti built his own generating plant. He cycled round his factory on a bicycle of his own design, and knew all his employees by their first names. During the First War, he buried three of his racing cars in his factory compound in case they should be confiscated. After the war, he dug them up and entered them for the 1920 Le Mans race. Although they were seven years old, one came in twenty minutes before the next arrival. That's how far ahead the Bugatti was, and it stayed out front through the twenties and the thirties.

Then, in 1936, the twentieth century rudely caught up with him; his firm experienced its first labour troubles: Ettore Bugatti was locked out of his own factory. Mortified and humiliated, he withdrew to Paris, and never visited Molsheim again. He ran his factory by remote control – just as Sir Henry Royce ran the Rolls-Royce factory in Derby, for a generation, from Le Canadel in the South of France, after he left England on doctors' orders in 1911, following years of overwork.

When Bugatti's customers dared to complain that some Bugatti cars were hard to start on cold mornings, Ettore retorted that they should be kept in a heated garage. In fact, their engines had generally to be warmed up on one set of plugs, and then another set substituted for running on the road. Only distilled water was advised for their radiators, and an oil of specific purity was ordained for the engines. And if any customers still grumbled at the expense, and inconvenience, then they either couldn't afford to keep a Bugatti as it deserved to be kept, or they weren't the type to appreciate one, and so to hell with them.

I feel the same about some of my own customers, but only seldom do I tell them so.

I walked round the car again. The leather was good and the dashboard was inlaid with mother-of-pearl. The knobs on the switches were the original whalebone. The white faces of the dials had faded to the colour of bleached bone; or maybe they were ivory. They could have been. If they were, some old elephant had certainly not been robbed in vain.

I felt the steering wheel; the linkage had no play, and the four horn buttons were still in place, one under each slender spoke, with an eight-day clock in the centre. The switches I clicked moved with the precision of a hinge on a Fabergé box.

I looked across at Kent. He was looking at me, his face creased like a rumpled suit.

'So, what do you think?' he asked.

'I think it's worth a fortune. Correction. I don't think that. I know.'

'Will you do it?'

'It's a bloody great risk,' I said, but I was wavering. It was a bloody great car. Kent hadn't over-estimated the profit potential. We could get £15,000 in any currency for this. It was one of the real rarities, like the Larz Andersen 1906 Charron with its built-in lavatory, or the old Shah of Persia's gold-plated Pierce Arrow.

I'd like to check the engine numbers, for it could just have been a fake, using one of the later railcar engines, but then I'd easily find out, for the originals had the prefix 'W' on them – just as the numbers of engines in present-day cars often conceal their date of manufacture.

There might be difficulties about advertising this car in case someone in a local Egyptian Embassy recognized it, but this could be arranged. After all, people switch paintings and sell them for fortunes openly in auctions, don't they? There's something snobbish and O.K. about art dealing or even the wine trade, which there certainly isn't about flogging old cars.

I stood looking at the Royale, not really seeing it, wondering about our chances, wondering, odd as this may seem in an old-car dealer, about my own conscience. As I've said, I've never ringed a car before, and although there has to be a first time for everything, even death, I wasn't eager to put a foot on that slippery slope which leads so swiftly down to the dreaded hinterland of stolen cars and forged papers and the whole unpleasant involvement of lies and counter-lies.

'Well?' asked Kent anxiously.

'Let's get out in the open air,' I said. 'This place may have ears, like the hotels in Cairo.'

We went up the stairs and he followed me out on to the veranda, and then down the stone steps to the desert. As we walked, grains of sand filtered through the joints in my shoes and filled my feet. They felt like my conscience, grating on me.

'I don't like it,' I said. 'The risks are enormous for one thing, and it's dishonest for another.'

'Dishonest?' repeated Kent in amazement. '*Now* he says it. What about all those false values we put on the manifest? What about the bribes we're paying. Dishonest? *Of course* it's dishonest. But think of the money at the end, boy. Think of the deal.'

'Think of what happens if it goes wrong,' I said, for I was. 'Think of what the Good Book says. "A good name is rather to be chosen than great riches".'

'It didn't say how great the riches are,' Kent pointed out practically. 'That car must be worth fifteen grand. Think.'

'I am.'

The thought of the profit was already pressing on my mind like a heavy old man on a young girl.

'Well, we haven't got all day,' said Kent. 'If we're going to switch the cars, we'll have to get cracking soon.'

I thought how strange were the different ways in which people react to different stimuli. I've known lethargic men suddenly leap about because a young girl in tight slacks and with big charlies comes on the scene. I've seen the same thing happen when free drink flows like the fountains of Rome, and here was Kent, as mean a man as ever pinched a penny, going ecstatic, adrenalin pouring through his blood, as fast as petrol

129

would stream through the carbs on that car, simply at the prospect of profit.

I left him and went up to my room and sat down in an easy chair, and looked at the wall. I don't want to claim credit for having principles, for maybe the real reason I was holding back was fear that perhaps I'd be left at the docks with my principles and the wrong car, while everyone else went off.

I don't know how long I was sitting there, my thoughts going round and round in my mind like snowflakes in a kaleidoscope, and then jarring up again at the prospect of what would happen if things went wrong. The door opened silently, and Maria came in.

'He's told you?' she asked.

'Yes,' I said. 'I suppose you knew all along?'

She nodded. I wasn't paying her. There was no reason why she should have told me, but I rather wished she had. I always look for one ally when a deal grows complicated; someone I can trust. Here, I had no one I could completely trust, no one I'd like to be alone with if things went wrong. She sat down without being asked. She could have stayed standing for all I cared.

'Let me tell you about that car,' she began.

'Tell me.'

She was going to in any case, so nothing I said would make much difference.

'I had a relation in Cairo who was employed at the Palace. His job was – rather special. He bought this car for King Farouk and he had the body especially made, but he was never paid.'

'That's his problem,' I said. 'Why didn't he put in a bill?'

'He did. Frequently. But it's rather difficult when you're working for a king. You've had this trouble in England with some of your kings in the past. Royalty can be pretty slow when it comes to picking up the bill.'

130

'What you're really trying to tell me is that this car could conceivably be said to be yours – or your relations?'

'Yes,' she said. 'You simplify things a bit, but that's true.'

'So, to ease my aching conscience, you give me this crumb of comfort, that if I stole this car I would actually be helping someone, apart from myself. Is that right?'

She nodded.

'Yes.'

I didn't know whether what she said was true, and I didn't greatly care. I was like the fellow on the psychiatrist's couch, or in the priest's confessional box, who wants to believe that all will be well, and who accepts assurances even when they seem against all reason. After all, you must believe something. I suppose I wanted to believe her.

'Will you do it?' she asked.

'I'll think about it,' I said, and stood up.

Maria got the message, such as it was, and stood up, too.

I watched her walk out of the room, and made up my mind, which had probably been made up more or less since the moment I saw the car, and only confirmed by what she had told me.

To hell with them all. I wouldn't do it.

5
✳

I went to find Kent, to tell him, but he wasn't in his room or in the bar. Finally, I tracked him down on the veranda. He was sitting alone at one of the circular marble tables, drinking a Perrier water, which was the cheapest drink he could find, short of putting his head in the sea.

'I've been thinking it over,' I told him, 'And the answer is No.'

I sat down, facing him.

Kent didn't get up; he just looked across the table at me coldly, as though trying to decide whether I was serious, or whether I could be persuaded, but at no cost to himself, either in cash or kind.

'You're sure?' he said at last.

'Certain. I may be a bit bent, but I'm not circular. I've never switched a car, and I don't want to start now. Even though Maria has told me that legally it could even be hers because some relation was never paid for it.'

'That's true, you know.'

'Maybe. But it seems just a bit too convenient a discovery for my taste.'

Kent stood up, held up his glass in case there was a drop of water left that might escape him when he'd paid for it. There wasn't, so he put it down again.

'Then we'll do it without you,' he announced grandly. 'But, remember this. There's no cut out of this car for you when we get back to London. Right?'

'Absolutely right,' I said, 'So long as you pay me back my five hundred quid. I don't deal in hot cars.'

'The way you go on, like a bloody Sunday School teacher, you're lucky to be dealing in any cars,' said Kent irritably. Then: 'I'll tell the others.'

132

He went up the steps into the hotel. I didn't want to stay where his jack had been warming the seat, so I moved to another table and tapped on the top until a waiter appeared, and I ordered another whisky.

Even if I wasn't any longer personally involved, my name was still on those manifests. I could still be hauled in for questioning if anything went wrong – and I'd still be the only one not sharing any profit, if they succeeded. It was an ironic, heads-they-win, tails-I-lose situation, but there was nothing I could do about it now, so I drank the whisky and watched the sun bedding down for the night behind the hills.

It suddenly grew cold, and I shivered, for I felt that the dying sun was also watching me. I wished I was miles away, aboard that boat, out beyond the twelve-mile limit, heading for home. Most of all, I wished all this aggravation about spiriting away an old car was simply something I'd read about somewhere. I felt uneasy in my bones and my water about the turn events had taken. I had allowed myself to be manœuvred into a position of acute disadvantage, as the nun told the roué, and I didn't like it. If someone has to be pushed, I liked to do the pushing.

There was no one I wanted to talk to, and I'd nothing to read except cheque stubs, which make depressing reading when the money is all going one way – out. Suddenly, it was dark, and dogs were beginning to bark boldly in the empty distance of the desert, and the sound of the sea seemed nearer because there were so few other sounds.

I walked up into the hotel. A few waiters were pattering about in a giant hall that had once no doubt seen embassy receptions and court balls – I mean the ones where there's dancing – and that sort of thing, but it all seemed empty and faded and pointless now. They looked like actors in search of a play.

Under the crystal chandeliers, the tables had white cloths and glittering glasses; red desert flowers floated in silver bowls of water. It looked very romantic, but there was no one to be romantic with, so I sat down, ordered myself a shish kebab and a bottle of iced beer. Both came very quickly, because there were obviously far more waiters and cooks in the kitchen than guests to serve. In fact, only six or seven other people were eating, and about twice this number were standing about, waiting on them.

I hate eating alone, probably because I do so much of it, and it was about eight o'clock when I'd finished. I went up the stairs to Maria's room. A 'Do not disturb' notice was hanging on the handle, and I wondered what she was doing, whether she was having it off with someone. Whoever it might be, it wasn't me, so I didn't disturb her, but went down the stairs again to the garage.

Kent or Hassan or Sabry should be there, which shows how low I'd sunk in my search for conversation. I didn't like any of these characters much, but at least they were people to talk to.

The garage was very cold now that the sun had set. I was reminded of some sort of vault or mausoleum. The air had a chill in it. I tried to find the light switch but I couldn't, so I went down the steps very carefully. A strong smell of quick-drying cellulose hung in the air. I searched around the edge of the stall where the big car was standing until I found a switch, and pressed it. This lit an inspection light that hung in a wire cage on the wall.

The car had torpedo sidelights, the sort that are shaped like pears, with a little red lens at the back, and a huge glass bulls-eye in front.

One of the other Royales, I knew, had not been fitted with any lights, and when this lack was remarked on, it was explained curtly that there was no need, since this particular owner never drove after dark!

These sidelights were ordinary enough, except that some-one had picked out the tiny ruby lens, at the rear of each one,

134

leaving a hole. I began to see why the car needed refurbishing every year. Even in this remote spot, sightseers demanded souvenirs.

I walked around the car, and to my surprise the red lens had been picked out from the other sidelight, too. The big Marchal headlamps were of the type that originally had green tell-tale lights built into their casings, though why these were needed to tell the driver his lamps were on I never have discovered, for they were large as searchlights. But from now on any driver of this Royale would have to manage without them, for these were also missing.

I looked inside the car, over the mother-of-pearl dash and the nickel plated rims of the instruments. Lamb-skin rugs still covered the floor, and the leather felt soft, as though it was waxed every month, as it probably had been. What really interested me was the fact that the little blue and amber and red tell-tale lights in the dashboard, for the ignition, main-beam and oil, had also been prised away, and from their silver sockets the bulbs looked out at me like reproachful eyes.

Usually, when people have a touch of the old kleptos, they will take anything they can remove from the car, and this includes door handles and mats and ashtrays. But here someone had apparently removed all those coloured lenses and yet left the cigar lighter, which is the easiest thing to slip into your pocket from any car.

Why?

I walked over to the other Bugatti and shone the inspection light round it. It still smelled hot from its long journey, and a little oil had dripped out from the crank-case gasket where most Bugattis leak a little, on to the concrete floor. I flashed the torch around the front of the car, and then paused. Someone – perhaps the same person? – had removed the red oval radiator badge, and its screw holes looked at me, empty as tooth sockets.

I don't know why I went back to Farouk's car to examine that radiator badge, but I did. It had greasy finger prints round it. Someone had removed the badge from the car I had driven and fixed it on Farouk's car.

I flashed the torch around the garage to see whether I could see any of the lenses, or the badge that must have been on the big Bugatti, but it was empty except for a moped on its stand and a pile of sacks and rags behind it. Sometimes, in the barns and stables of country houses, one can discover treasure troves of old horns and mascots that have been wrapped in brown paper or rags for years and then forgotten. I once found a set of Stentor air horns, a Grebel searchlight, and a kneeling Silver Lady from a Rolls in a shed in Somerset, so, like the spinster who always looks under her bed every night, I live in hope.

I thought I would just give this bunch a going-over before I left, so I kicked the sacks lightly. Nothing rattled inside them, so I kicked them again, and burrowed through the oily rags, until I found a piece of blue cloth.

The last time I'd seen this, it had been Kent's jacket, and he was wearing it on the terrace outside.

He was still wearing it, but it wasn't doing him any good, and it never would again, either, for he was as dead as the scandal in last Sunday's newspaper.

I bent down and pulled the rags away from Kent's head. He lay, face down, and I could feel no pulse on his wrist or in his neck, which wasn't surprising, because there wasn't one. I turned him over. A little saliva dribbled out of the corner of his mouth. His eyes were open, but they weren't seeing anything now, not even a chance to economize, or the prospect of a profit at the end of the deal.

What had happened to him? Had he fallen, or had he been pushed? From the fact that he was lying buried under rags, I guessed he'd been helped unwillingly over the border to that undiscovered country from whose bourne no traveller returns, and I quote Shakespeare, who died three hundred and fifty four-years ago, so he can't prevent me.

Had Kent collapsed, and then been discovered, and his body concealed by some night watchman or other web-foot who feared he might be accused of killing a foreigner? Or was there something altogether more sinister?

Could he have discovered someone stealing those coloured lenses from the car and become involved in a fight? Of course he could, but this was surely no excuse for murder – if there ever is an adequate excuse for murder.

I felt in his pockets. His wallet was still there, with his passport. I opened the wallet; the notes inside were pressed together close as sardines in a can, but with rather more value. He even had a spring clip on them in case one should slip through his fingers. So he hadn't been killed for his money, and he could carry no currency where he was now.

I covered up the body. If I were asked why in a court of law – and it worried me that I might be – I couldn't give any reason, beyond the basic one that I didn't like looking at a corpse. I hadn't liked Kent much when he was alive, but dead I liked him less.

I didn't greatly like my own situation, either. Here I was in a strange hotel, in a not notably friendly country, with a car that apparently had belonged to that country's former king, and which was now about to be stolen on papers that bore my signature – while the man who had arranged this lay dead at my feet.

I put back the inspection light on its hook and I went up to my bedroom. I washed my hands and face and a very worried me looked back out of the shaving mirror. I filled a tooth glass with whisky, drank it and felt a little more like a human being. I wondered whether the others would still go on with the switch? I thought I'd better tell Maria. Sabry and Hassan struck me as being capable of looking after themselves, but I

137

wasn't so sure about the girl; maybe I could help to look after her? I went along the corridor to her room, wondering what this might involve. The card was still hanging on her door. I banged on the panel.

'Yes?' she said.

'Open up,' I told her.

'I'm in bed.'

'Then get out of bed. It's urgent.'

Something in my voice must have made her realize I wasn't coming in for a quick fumble, for I heard her cross the room and then the bolt slid back inside the door. She opened it a few inches, and I pushed my way in, and locked and bolted the door behind me.

'What's all this about?' she asked.

She wore a dressing-gown. I glanced at the bed; at least she'd been in it alone.

'Have you seen Kent?' I asked her.

'Of course. He's down with the car. Is that all you came to ask me?'

Her voice was edged with suspicion, as mint sauce is edged with vinegar. Surely she didn't think I'd use this just as an excuse to get into her room? Well, I hadn't, had I?

'No,' I said to her spoken question and my unspoken one, and sat down. She remained standing.

'Well?' she went on.

'Well, he's dead.'

'*Dead?*'

She repeated the word as though she had never heard it before, and sat down shakily on the edge of the bed.

'What do you mean, dead?'

'What I say. Mort. Kaput. Finito. The late lamented. Dead. I went down to see how things were getting on, but the garage was deserted. I poked around a bit and found his body under a pile of rags. Dead.'

'Are you sure? Couldn't he have fainted or something?'

138

'Very easily. But if he did, that faint or something proved fatal. If you don't believe me, go and have a look for yourself.'

'Were there any signs of – of a struggle?'

Her voice trembled slightly. For no reason at all, I suddenly thought of her flat back in Shepherds Bush, and being beaten up, and why she hadn't wanted me to mention this to Kent. It would be no use telling him now.

'None that I could see,' I said. 'Should there have been?'

'No. I mean, I don't think so. I just wondered whether maybe someone came in and thought Kent was an intruder or something, and there was a fight. Or it could have happened the other way round. Anyway, what do we do now? Tell the hotel manager?'

'If we do,' I said, 'We'll have to stay here until the police let us go. We'll miss that boat tomorrow. And goodness knows when another one will come that can take the cars.'

'We can't leave Kent here.'

'Why not? We can't take him with us, as he is.'

'Oh, my God.'

She put her head in her hands. I saw that her shoulders were trembling, and I thought with horror that she might be going to cry, but she didn't.

'Have you told Sabry and Hassan?' she asked.

'Not yet. I thought I'd tell you first. After all, you worked with him most.'

'Yes.'

I didn't see any mileage in telling her that the lenses had been stolen from the lamps. Maybe they hadn't even been there in the first place. I couldn't swear to it either way. And they weren't even my lenses. So why should I worry? They'd cost all of five shillings to replace.

'Will you still take that car out?' I asked her.

'Of course,' she said. 'Even if *I* have to drive it myself, we'll take it.'

'All that stuff you told me about some relation of yours having paid for the car – is that true?'

'Yes.'

'Who was the relation?'

'My father.'

I looked at her right in the eyes, as though she was trying to pass me a dud cheque, and she looked right back at me. She had pretty eyes, wide and dark. I didn't know whether she was lying or not. Do you ever, with women?

'Will you help me?' she asked. 'Now?'

'Yes,' I said at once, without really meaning to, and reversing my previous decision without a thought. Hell, I wanted to be involved with that car no more than I wanted a dose of clap. Even less, for clap is curable, and that car could bring infinitely more aggravation. Yet oddly, now I was committed, I felt better, more relaxed. I couldn't think why. I must have needed my head examining, though things in this line of country aren't what they were. Life is so rough, so they say, that the psychiatrists get right down there on the couches with their patients. You don't know who's curing who.

'So what do we do now?' I asked.

'I'll tell the others.'

'What time had Kent planned to move off?'

'Four forty-five tomorrow morning. This place has a night watchman, and he hands over to a day guard then. Kent checked. He was going to settle up the bills tonight, and explain we had an early start to make, so they wouldn't be surprised to hear a car going out. It will still be dark, so even if the new guard is around, he won't be able to see the car too closely.'

This all seemed reasonable enough. Even if some peasant was awake and saw the car go, he'd only have a few seconds to recognize it from its silhouette against the horizon, and if we drove without lights, or on side-lights for the first half mile, this would cut down the risk considerably. I reckoned, too, that I could count the Egyptian *fellaheen* who could distinguish a Type 41 Bugatti Royale from a Type 57 on the fingers of the Venus de Milo. There's a risk in anything, as the eunuch told the pansy; this was the particular one we had to run.

'I'll tell the others, then.'

'Wait,' she said. 'Had Kent been robbed?'

'His wallet seemed to be full.' In death as in life, I thought.

'I'll come down with you. I want to make sure.'

Of what? I wondered, but all I said was: 'You don't want to see the body.'

'He was kind to me,' she said. 'The least I can do is to collect his papers.'

'I'll get them for you.'

She shook her head.

'I want to come down.'

She put on some clothes. I watched her dress and she didn't mind; neither did I.

We went along the corridor, down the stone steps and through the door with the green baize on its back and then down the concrete steps to the garage. I felt I'd been making the journey here so often I'd better start thinking about taking out citizenship papers, or maybe starting a job in the kitchens. The outside garage door was still open, and the stars peered in from several million miles away and saw nothing. We couldn't see all that much either, until I fumbled round and found the inspection lamp switch. I pointed out the pile of sacks.

'Here,' I said.

Maria knelt down beside the sacks as I began to lift them away one by one. Had I been on my own I'd have kicked them to find exactly where the body lay, but this seemed a little indelicate with the girl around. The sacks came away easily enough, like artichoke leaves.

She looked at Kent in the dim light. I reached into his

141

jacket pocket and gave her the wallet. Then I squatted on my haunches in the semi-darkness beyond the circle of light, breathing the cold sandiness of the desert, and the whiff of cellulose and the dust of the concrete.

I didn't know what the hell to do, or what was happening, and I could think of no one who could help me. What an idiot I was to have agreed to help with the car. I could think of no reasons at all for doing this except maybe an absurd wish to appear quixotic, or maybe I wanted to help Maria, or put her in my debt. Or, maybe, I just wanted her.

We stood up and I coiled the flex of the inspection lamp as we walked back to the car. She glanced at it casually, and then bent down suddenly to examine the nearest sidelight; she had seen that the red rear lens was missing. She walked round the other side to examine that light, and then she looked at the diver's helmet tail-lights.

'The red glasses have all gone,' she said slowly.

'Yes. So have the coloured tell-tales on the dash. Some-one's even taken the badge off the car I drove and stuck it on the radiator.'

She shone the light on the front of the radiator, examining the red and white name-plate.

'I don't like this,' she said suddenly, and I knew from the tone of her voice, she wasn't acting; she really was scared. 'Let's get out of here. *Quickly*.'

'Why?'

She didn't answer. We went up the stairs in silence and at some speed. Somewhere in the hotel, piped music was playing a sad, soft, wailing Middle Eastern lament. I suppose it had been in the background ever since we arrived, but you grow so accustomed to piped music that you can forget it's there. We shall have Muzak wherever we go. And, sometimes, too much of it.

'You think your room's bugged?' I asked, remembering Kent's warning.

142

We were in the corridor outside her bedroom.

'I'll tell you here, in case it is,' she said. 'Those glasses in the lights weren't glass at all. They were jewels. Rubies. The others were emeralds and sapphires. They're worth a lot.'

'I can imagine,' I said, and I could.

'Did Kent know that?' I asked her.

She nodded.

'What about Hassan and Sabry?'

'Sabry might have. I just don't know. He was one of Farouk's hangers-on, and knew my father. He was a court jeweller, too. He *could* have known – or he'd have recognized the stones if someone else pointed them out to him.'

'And Hassan?'

She shrugged.

'I wouldn't think so. I don't really know much about him. He's a cousin of the local chief of police. Kent thought he'd be useful.'

'No wonder Kent was anxious to get the car out.'

'Yes,' she said. 'No wonder.'

Her voice sounded flat as a punctured tyre.

'Do you think Kent disturbed someone stealing those jewels – and they killed him?'

'Could be.'

'Can I trust you?' she asked suddenly.

'To do what?' I asked. 'In a crowd, or alone together?'

'I don't mean that. I need your help. I'm desperately serious.'

'So am I. Is this about Kent?'

'Partly.'

'Then don't tell me here,' I said. 'It's too risky. Come outside.'

We were near the lift door. I pressed the button and the gates opened and we went down to the edge of the terrace. The moon was now halfway up the sky and the whole scene looked unreal, as though painted on a stage backcloth. A wind was blowing in from the sea, bringing a fresh smell of salt and seaweed. It felt much colder than I'd expected, and the stars were very bright, which was a lot more than I felt.

We walked a few paces into the desert until the sand, which was trodden down near the terrace, grew soft and feathery, and we began to sink over our shoes in it. We turned round, not speaking, and walked back to the garage. The loneliness of the desert was like a pain; I hated it.

'Now,' I said, 'What's so serious?'

'You don't know who I am, really,' Maria said, 'So I'll go back and explain a few things. My father's French. His name is François. My mother was Egyptian.'

'Was?'

'Yes. She died six years ago. My father had a job in the Abdin Palace in Cairo. He'd worked for various coach-builders in France. Chapron. Figoni and Falaschi. Saoutchik. And others. Farouk liked fast cars and cars with special bodies, and so he was a good customer.

'One of the firms my father worked for in Paris sent him to Cairo to make some modifications to a car Farouk had bought. Farouk became friendly with my father and offered him a job, in charge of his cars. After all, he had a hundred and twenty.

'The two men got on well. My father would organize some special sports car for him with a one-off body, or he'd fix up tickets for Le Mans. Things like that. And as they grew closer, my father organized more intimate things.'

She paused.

'Such as girls?' I asked her.

'Yes. Girls. French. Italian. Roumanian. Even English. Although my father was several years older than Farouk, they liked the same things – excitement, girls, parties. And of course, this worked both ways. Farouk didn't pay my father much, but from time to time, he'd tell him that, say, some foreign firms were going to tender for the contract to electrify

144

the tramways in Cairo, or build new rolling stock for the railways, or some such thing.

'He'd make them slap on an extra ten or twenty or even fifty thousand pounds for what he called special contingencies. This should have covered mistakes in calculations, rises in prices and so on but, in fact, it all went into my father's pocket.'

'Nice for him,' I said.

It was certainly better than horsing around trying to flog cars. I could see the attraction very clearly. What wasn't so clear was where I came into all this, and why I should be trusted. With what – confidence or cash? If I had the option, I'd follow Omar Khayyam's advice and take the cash and let the credit go. But maybe I wouldn't have any choice?

'I was about five when we moved to Cairo,' Maria went on. 'We lived in fantastic style. We had a house with thirty indoor servants and ten gardeners. This was our seaside place.'

'*This?*'

I looked round at the hotel, which was no larger than a barracks, with its spires and balconies and shutters, and the rows of blank windows looking out to sea.

'Yes. My father was very rich.'

'So what went wrong?' I asked her, because obviously something had, otherwise she would still be living in the hotel, not as a paying guest and secretary to a dead man, but as the owner's daughter.

'Farouk was kicked out.'

'Ah, yes.'

In all this, I had forgotten the most important point. Even so, old François must have been worth a bob or two. He'd surely made enough to set himself up in a corner shop somewhere?

'What did he do with the money, apart from living so well?' I asked her. After all, you can only eat three meals a day and most years have only 365 days.

'He sent a lot of it back to France, and the rest to a Swiss numbered account.'

'Did you and your mother know he was taking bribes?'

'Not then. He was always seeing people, entertaining them, having meetings. It was just business, so far as we were concerned. And then Farouk was deposed and it all ended, and we heard what had been going on.'

'Where were you then?'

'Here. In this house. July, nineteen fifty-two. We'd come down for two months, and were actually packing a few things for a picnic. We heard on the radio that Farouk had been forced to abdicate. My mother tried to telephone Cairo, to reach my father, but all the lines were blocked. We just had to wait here and listen to the bulletins which came over each hour.'

'What about your father? He hadn't been forced to abdicate?'

'Unfortunately, no. Farouk was allowed to take a number of his staff with him into exile. My father was actually going up the gangway of the royal yacht when two police officers stopped him. They said he was wanted for questioning.'

'About his bribes?'

'Yes. They knew all about him. After all, everyone in a position of authority was taking backhanders. The new regime wanted to stop this. Their intention was to keep my father in Egypt, virtually a prisoner, as a kind of living reminder that taking bribes has no future. We had a flat in Cairo as well as this house. He was kept under arrest there for several weeks.

'We had a pretty grim time. My mother had some jewels no one knew about, and we sold these to Sabry for about a fifth of what they were worth. He cut them down and got rid of them. He made a big profit, but at least he helped us, when no one else would. Then my father was allowed to come here.

'When Colonel Nasser took over from General Neguib,

146

things eased a bit. I was allowed to go to school in France; my father's sister kept me. After my mother died, I came back here every year to see my father. The authorities didn't interfere with me, but they opened my letters to my father – and they gave me a pretty thorough search each time I came or went through the customs.

'In the meantime, they found my father a job – as a sort of curator in the house he had once owned – a servant where he had formerly controlled so many other servants.'

'If he had so much money in France and Switzerland, couldn't he have used it for a bit of bribery to get out? After all, let's not kid ourselves, it still goes on.'

I was thinking about Kent and his arrangements with the officials in Alexandria.

'My father had told his banks long before this happened that in no circumstances was any more than a thousand pounds to be paid to anyone who asked them for money – even if they presented his cheque or brought a letter from him. Egyptians are the best forgers in the world. He was afraid someone might whip the lot.'

'Didn't he try to get away?'

'Yes. Twice. After my last visit, I smuggled out five separate letters from him to his bank in France and collected a thousand pounds on each. I couldn't bring this money into this country because, as I said, I was searched so thoroughly every time I came through, so I left it in a bank in Marseilles.

'I got to know the manager of a provision shop in Alex whose van comes here every week with food. For two thousand cash, he was willing to drive the van himself and carry my father back to Alex in a laundry basket. For another three thousand, a steward in a cruise liner calling at Alex for a day, was prepared to come ashore, change clothes with my father, give him his pass, and let my father go up the gangway. The steward would jump ship and lose his job, but he reckoned he could get another easily enough.'

'What went wrong?'

Presumably, something had, or she wouldn't be telling me about it.

'My father was discovered at the police post. They searched the van. The driver, of course, said he'd no idea how he came to be there. He couldn't very well say anything else without implicating himself. So my father was brought back here. He wasn't punished. The guards found it all highly entertaining. After all, they were promoted for being so alert.'

'And the second time?'

'I organized that from outside. I still had access to that five thousand, and I found a French pilot who had been with the O.A.S. in Algeria. He'd been running a shuttle service with a small plane, picking up agents.

'His idea was to set out for Tripoli in Libya, flying along the international airline corridor, and then he'd cut his engine and come down here. He was to do this at night. It was a two-seater plane and he'd a dummy in flying gear in the second seat. My father would be out in the desert to meet him; they'd throw away the dummy and then they'd take off.

'Well, he came down on a deserted airfield you British used to have five miles north of here. But the plane had been picked up on radar, and they were waiting for him. They thought he was an Israeli raider, so they didn't take chances. His excuse was that he'd lost his way. They checked his papers, and let him go.'

'Did they find your father then?'

'No. I'd disguised him for the trip as a Muslim widow, in black robes. Luckily, I had an emergency signal arrangement with the pilot in case anything went wrong. He was to switch on his flashing landing lights. I could see these across the desert for a matter of miles, and so we simply turned back.'

'What did that little lot cost you?' I asked.

'Two thousand. I had to pay that before I could get him even to attempt it.'

'Did your father make any other attempts to get out?'

'No. Egypt is a very difficult country to escape from. You can either leave by boat from Alexandria or Ismailia. You can fly out from Cairo, or cross the border in the south into the Sudan, or up north-west into Tripoli.

'That makes only five ways in or out – and each of them is on the watch for my father. There's immediate promotion for anyone who stops him. Instant dismissal, and maybe imprisonment, if he gets through. The rest of the frontier is just sand. No one could cross.'

'There must be foreign tourists down here, people who'd take a risk for a large sum of money?'

'You think so? Well, imagine *you're* a tourist in a museum in a foreign country which is virtually a police state, and suddenly the curator comes up and says: "Actually, old man, I'm *really* a millionaire. If you can get me out of this country I'll give you ten thousand pounds!" You'd think he was a nutter, wouldn't you?'

I had to agree I would. Nothing like that has ever happened to me in any museum; or out of one, either.

'How much freedom does he have now?'

'During the day, he has to keep to this palace or the grounds. There's only one gate he can use, anyway, and that has a watchman on it. At night, he's not allowed out at all. If he were, I might conceivably have organized a boat to pick him up on the beach.'

'Why haven't you tried that?' I asked.

'For God's sake,' she replied. 'Where would I begin?'

I couldn't tell her, so I didn't try.

'If I'd asked about hiring a boat in Alex, they'd be on to me at once.'

'Do the police follow you, then?'

If they did, then they could easily be following me, and with Kent dead in the basement, this thought held no comfort.

'No. Not now. After all, why should they?'

149

It seemed to me that she'd already given me several convincing reasons why they should, but before I could list them, she went on: 'Anyhow, the Egyptians are so afraid that the Israelis will invade, they've a radar station right here in these grounds. Not a very good one, but strong enough to pick up anything at sea.'

'Why choose this place?'

'Because it's here. That's why. And because it has a well for water and a generator for electricity. There's nothing much else along this coast for another fifty miles. Even the police posts up and down the road have to draw water from here or Alex.'

I remembered the anti-aircraft guns at Cairo airport on the roofs of the building, surrounded by sandbags, like something out of a wartime newsreel. I remembered the guns mounted on rooftops along the road into Alexandria, and the troops with binoculars, searching the sky for planes, hopefully or fearfully, according to your political viewpoint and your faith in Egyptian martial qualities.

'Where's your father now?'

'I hope, in bed.'

I wouldn't mind wishing that for myself, I thought, but preferably not alone.

'Is he under guard at night?'

'Yes. The military post in the grounds here has a brick guardroom.'

'I saw it.'

'Well, he's inside. Locked up until seven tomorrow morning.'

'How many troops do they have here?'

'Not many. Probably only about twenty, I'd say, at a guess. In charge of the radar equipment, and an anti-aircraft gun.'

I didn't go much on François or on anyone else who takes bribes, because once you start giving or accepting a touch of

150

the old backhander, corruption becomes infectious. Even so, it seemed to me that he had virtually been a prisoner for the last eighteen years, and this was a long enough sentence. After all, even murderers go free nowadays in half this time. And all François had murdered was honesty.

'What was your plan to get him out?'

'It all depended on Kent.'

'Did you like Kent?' I asked.

She shrugged.

'Not in that way. He was really only a small-time operator on the fringe of other men's deals. But he was useful to me for this one thing. More than useful – essential.'

'What was in it for him if you got your father out?'

'Fifty thousand pounds. Payable in Swiss francs, on a bank in Geneva. He could have had the money anywhere in the world, but that's where he wanted it.'

I wasn't getting it anywhere, but Geneva would suit me, too, I thought. For money, or the other thing.

'Kent was a very careful man,' she went on. 'He covered himself completely. If we couldn't get my father out, if the plan was discovered, *you'd* have taken the blame, for your name was on all the papers. Not his.'

'I know that,' I said.

'Also, if we couldn't get him out, Kent would still have taken half your profits on the two cars already loaded. But if we had succeeded, then he'd have been rich.'

I'm not all that bright in the top storey, but I didn't need to wear a number eight hat to realize that no matter who'd made a profit, I was the only one in this deal who stood to make a loss. And not only a loss of money, but a loss of freedom. The Gyppoes would have had me inside quicker than a chorus boy could slap a guardsman's backside.

'Why tell me all this in the middle of the night?' I asked her, for I could only think of one reason.

'Because I need your help. Like I said.'

'How?'

'I have to get my father out in Farouk's car. It's the only way. We'll never have another chance like this, for there never will *be* another chance. I'll give you ten thousand pounds in any currency you choose once we're all safely out of Egypt.'

'Why so much less than you offered Kent?'

'Because he'd worked for months on the idea. Because his risk was greater. If he'd been discovered, he'd have lost his business in Cairo. It was all or nothing for him. And I *had* to use him. There just was no one else.'

'There's no one else but me now, either. I'll not do it for ten. But I will for twenty.'

'You're serious?'

'Deadly,' I told her, and then thought I might have made a happier choice of word.

'But how can you hope to get him out?' I asked her. 'You tell me the guards at each frontier post are alerted. And we're bound to be stopped at least once on the way to Alex for a police check. And even then we still have to go through Customs. How can you possibly conceal him in this car? There's barely room for two people inside, and no room whatever underneath for him to hang on to.'

'Have you examined the car closely?' she asked.

'Sure. I've been all over it. I've never seen such a large car with so little room. There's not even any spare space under the bonnet, for the engine fills the whole thing. The cockpit's tiny, and the boot is just a joke because of that damn' great petrol tank.'

'Exactly. I'm going to put him in that tank.'

'In the tank? It'll be full of fumes. And how do you propose getting him in? Melt him down and pour him through a funnel?'

'I'm not joking,' she said. 'I told you my father had been a coachbuilder. That car's body was his design. That big

152

petrol tank is a dummy. It was never intended for petrol. There's a tiny tank inside for that. The rest is completely empty. No fumes at all.

'You push forward the seats at the front and the top of the tank opens up. You'd never seen the join, for it's so well made. They used it in the old days for smuggling girls in and out of the Abdin Palace, in Cairo.

'Farouk had some strange ideas, and he hated publicity, which he always seemed to attract whatever he did. It was much easier to bring girls into the Palace hidden in that car, for then no one knew they'd even arrived.'

'Do Hassan and Sabry know about this tank – or the plans for your father?'

'No. They think it's just a straight swop with two cars of the same make. That's why they had the Type 57 sprayed yellow and black, to make it look as much like this as possible.'

'How did you become involved with Kent?'

I felt I wanted to know a bit more before I involved myself too closely. This story seemed like an iceberg; the deeper you went beneath the surface, the more there was of it.

'I came back to Cairo about a year ago, determined to get my father out. I know he had been dishonest, but by the standards of Cairo at that time, he was no worse than a thousand others.'

'I'm sure,' I said quickly, to prevent any further attempt to whitewash the old man. If I didn't, I'd no doubt hear how kind he was to his cat and his budgie and how he looked after an aged spinster sister who had varicose veins, and so on.

I didn't give a fish's tit for all that chat. I wanted to know more about the man as he was now, and by learning this to learn more about my own chances of success. Twenty thousand pounds was a lot of money to pick up, and if I was ever going to pick it up, I had to recognize the risks involved.

As I turned over all this in my mind, slowly, like a man turning a pile of damp leaves with a pitchfork, I heard a tiny noise that might have been a twig creaking. The only odd thing was that an underground concrete garage isn't the place where twigs go to creak.

I jumped for the Bugatti and switched on the huge Bi-flex Marchal headlights. They took a fraction of a second to light – a sure indication of old wiring and corroded contacts – and in that moment, before their blaze turned the far wall amber, I saw the shadow of a man run for the open door. He was out before I could see who he was, but I shouted, 'Stop!'

He didn't act on this suggestion, and since I hadn't anything to throw at him, I threw myself, and sprinted over the concrete floor.

I was blinded by the blaze of lights to one side, and didn't see what tripped me. The floor suddenly whipped up to meet me, and I was down, scrabbling about on my hands and knees, out of breath, and cursing with pain, for I had cracked my shin. Maria was kneeling by my side.

'Are you all right?' she asked anxiously.

This is always a silly question, because being all right can at best be only a relative state of affairs. I sat up, shaking my head, trying to concentrate. I had tripped over a block of wood, the sort that mechanics use for putting under axles when heavy cars are up on jacks.

'Who was that?' I asked her, as though she knew; a right ridiculous question.

'Probably a beggar. They used to come in here from the desert, even in the old days. It gets very cold out there at night. They don't do any harm.'

'There's always a first time,' I told her, and levered myself to my feet. 'Why don't they lock the door?'

'They do sometimes. But there's no need. They've a guard on the gate.'

So they had; I should have remembered what she'd told me

154

only moments before. Or maybe I was just getting jumpy, as one flea told another.

Kent *could* have fallen, or had a heart attack or some such thing, but if he *had* died that way, how had he managed to pull the sacks over himself after he was dead? Perhaps one of the beggars hadn't been so harmless after all.

I glanced at my watch; a quarter to ten, on the same day that we had set out from Cairo, but so much had happened since then that I wouldn't be prepared to swear to it. It seemed to have begun years ago, one of those days I would always remember, one of those days I would far rather forget.

'What if we're stopped on the way, as we were when we drove to Alex?' I asked her. 'You believe that although the police may look over the car, they won't examine the petrol tank? Right?'

'Right.'

'But what if they *do* examine the tank? What if someone has tipped them off? Maybe someone tipped them off about your old man being in that laundry basket. My name's on the manifests. I'll be the one who goes to jail.'

'How often have you been through Customs in a car, all the times you've been abroad?' she asked me.

'Dozens.'

'You've had the boot opened, maybe the carpets lifted up. But how often has anyone looked *inside* the petrol tank?'

'Never,' I had to admit.

'Well, they won't here, either.'

I only had her word for that, but I suppose it was better than no word at all. Not much, but possibly a bit.

'I'd better tell Hassan and Sabry about Kent,' I said. 'After all, Hassan's whole reason for being with us is because he's the police chief's cousin, so maybe he can smooth things over.'

'But don't mention my father. Now Kent's dead, you're the only person who knows of this plan.'

'I've never even seen François. I don't know what he looks like. I never talk about people I don't know.'

We went up the stairs to the hotel. The same music was playing; it could have been the same tune. A long row of dimmed bulbs burned in the empty corridors. There was something unreal about all this faded Edwardian splendour marooned halfway between the sand and the sea. But nothing seemed unreal about the body in the garage, or the risks I would be facing within hours.

I felt the need for a drink, and went into the bar. It was very dimly lit. Half-a-dozen Egyptians sat around a low table in the far corner chewing nuts, with soft drinks on mats. I ordered my usual Whyte & Mackay. As my eyes grew accustomed to the gloom, I recognized Sabry and Hassan among the others. They waved to me. I went over and stood looking down at them. The reception clerk who had booked me in sat next to Sabry. I didn't know who the others were, and didn't greatly care.

'What's happened to you?' asked Sabry.

'Me? Nothing,' I said, surprised. Then I glanced down at my suit, and even in that gloom I looked like a refugee from a flour mill, for it was white with concrete dust, and I'd torn a hole in my left trouser leg at the knee.

'I fell over,' I admitted lamely.

A man at the end of the crowd said something in Egyptian and they all laughed. I didn't like that. When someone is laughing, I like to share in the joke, and not feel I am the joke. I turned to Hassan.

'Could I see you outside for a moment?'

I sounded like a stage policeman, the sort of country cop in a helmet who calls at the back door of The Grange, Act II, Scene III, four weeks later.

'Now?'

156

Even in the dimness, Hassan seemed surprised.

'If you can spare a minute,' I said, trying to keep the irony out of my voice.

'Of course,' said Hassan. He stood up flexing his muscles, just to show he had them. His bad eyelid flickered its semaphore message to no one at all.

We went out into the corridor.

'What's the trouble?' he asked, as though I were a customer who had made a complaint about bad service. Close to, he smelled strong; no wonder he liked scent. Without it, he would smell like a reptile house.

'Kent,' I said. 'He's dead.'

'*Dead?* Where? How?'

His voice stretched tight as a drum.

'He's on the garage floor under a pile of sacks, so it doesn't look as though he died of old age.'

'How did you tear your suit?'

'I went to the garage to see where you all were. Then I saw someone run.'

I didn't add that Maria had been with me.

'I went after them and tripped. That's how.'

'Ah,' he said. 'I should have been with you. With this.'

He slid his hand into the back pocket of his trousers, brought out an F.N. automatic.

'He wouldn't have got away if I'd been there.'

'Maybe,' I said, 'but you weren't. So he did. Now what do we do about Kent?'

'Does the girl know?'

'Yes.'

'Let me deal with this,' said Hassan. 'You may have to make a statement, but it'll only be a formality. After all, my cousin is chief of police. These things help.'

For the first time since I arrived at the hotel, I began to feel more cheerful. For the first time, too, I warmed to Hassan. With a bit of luck, and I could certainly use a bit of luck, or a bit of the other thing, too, we'd get away with it, even with François.

'I'll leave it to you, then,' I said to Hassan.

'You do that.'

His teeth gleamed very white under the lamplight. He looked at me almost pityingly, and I felt I wasn't measuring up to his idea of an organizer, but then what was I meant to organize except to trundle three old cars across the desert to the nearest port?

'I've changed my mind about helping you with the Royale,' I said.

'You have? Good. You drive the little Bugatti, then,' he said. 'There are four of us, and we've all got luggage, so we'll have to take them both. We can dump your car in Alex easily enough. I've a friend there who runs a garage on the sea front.'

'You've got friends everywhere,' I said.

'It comes of having a nice nature,' he assured me. 'People are like mirrors. They reflect how we treat them in the same way. Pleasantly, or, sometimes, not so pleasantly.'

It sounded like something he'd read in a religious calendar or on a Wayside Pulpit board.

'See you, then. Four forty-five in the garage. I've got the hotel manager with me and I've already told him we're leaving early. He's having our bills made out tonight. I'll fix it with the police. If you don't hear from me, take it that you won't hear from them, either. O.K.?'

'O.K.'

I went down the corridor to my own room.

It felt stuffy inside, with the curtains drawn. The heat of the day had stored itself between the heavy drapes and couldn't find a way out. I switched off the light and opened the curtains and looked out over the desert. Under the moon, sand lay white as snow. Dogs were barking somewhere, and the smell of the sea was sharp and strong.

158

I closed the curtains again, and turned on the light, picked a couple of blackheads on my nose, examined my tongue, which looked the same as when I had examined it less than three hours before. I felt uneasy, though why I didn't know, but the feeling of relaxation that Hassan had induced in me by his confidence was evaporating, as the dew on the moonlit desert would burn away under tomorrow's sun.

I sat down on the easy chair to consider what I always consider when I'm worried; a mental profit and loss account. On the profit side, all could go well, in which case I had no problems. On the debit side, François could be discovered, I could be charged with kidnapping him, and with being involved in Kent's death.

But if I went down on any of these charges, then Hassan and Sabry and Maria would go down with me, never mind their influential relations. Hassan and Sabry would wriggle and might probably escape, but I guessed Kent wouldn't have paid them until he was sure all the cars were aboard, so they wouldn't abandon me entirely, for otherwise they would have worked for nothing.

In fact, who would pay them? I suppose this would fall to me, unless Kent had given the cheques to Maria to pay, but remembering how slow a man he was with a dollar, I thought this unlikely.

I wondered about Hassan's reactions to my news of Kent's death; I wondered about my own. I hadn't known him well, and Hassan presumably had known him even less, so there was no question of any private grief. Also, in the Middle East, life doesn't come expensive; a death is a death is a death. We are like wheat that is cut down in the field, and all that, although it's always best to be the cutter and not the cut.

I wondered whether George had been right about Hassan. He has a memory like a photographer's file for odd things like gear ratios and engine numbers, but was this Hassan necessarily the same man he remembered from his service years ago in the Canal Zone?

Hassan wasn't the sort of fellow I'd like to share a room with in Brighton for a week-end in a heatwave, but then no one was asking me to. After this trip, I'd never see him again. That wasn't a threat, either; it was a promise.

Also, it's so easy to be wrong about people or about things. I remember turning down a Daimler Double-Six once because the owner assured me it had only been used to take his maiden aunt to church every Sunday, and again, a Phantom II which had supposedly barely 5,000 miles on the clock because its previous owner, an Indian Prince, had only used it in religious processions.

Trouble was, I'm too suspicious; yet both stories were true. Another dealer believed them and made a couple of thousand quid profit out of a couple of phone calls. Here, George's story could be true, and I rather thought it was.

I prised myself off the bed, opened my suitcase, and began putting in a few more things to save me packing in the early hours. As I threw in my clothes, I couldn't help wondering where I'd be when I took them out again.

I went into the bathroom, collected my electric razor, and then saw the big Dettol bottle in which I carry my emergency supply of whisky when I travel abroad, because sometimes the Customs are funny about people bringing whisky into a country unless you pay duty on it. I poured out half a tooth mug of the stuff, added some water from the tap and drank it slowly, watching my reflection in the mirror.

I finished the whisky and went back into the bedroom. I couldn't be bothered to pack anything else, so I lay down on the bed, my thoughts churning round in my mind like the blades of the Schwitzer-Cummins supercharger on the old SJ Duesenberg. What with the whisky, the reaction from a hot drive across the desert, and the worry over finding Kent's body, they must have churned to a halt, because the next

160

thing I remember was lying with my eyes open, looking at the light burning down on me from the ceiling.

Where am I? I thought. What's happened? Where's the action, then?

Wherever it was, it had passed me by. I had a headache, because I don't like lying on my back, and the light had been burning for four hours by my watch. Hell, I must have been tired to drop off like that. And why had I wakened so suddenly? I felt stiff and cold, and my feet were tight in my shoes. I wished I hadn't made that drink so strong.

I glanced towards the windows. The curtains were billowing out so that they looked like the brocade sails of some land-locked galleon.

There was nothing at all strange about this – except that I clearly remembered shutting the windows.

I had that sudden premonition of danger, which must have been what awakened me, and not my bursting bladder. Someone else was in the room with me, someone who wasn't a friend.

I swung up from the bed and the quick motion made me dizzy for a second, and then I shook sleep from my head. The room was empty; I was imagining things. Possibly the wind had blown the window open. I stood up, and went towards it, telling myself I was becoming altogether too melodramatic, and my nerves were bad as a result of the life I led.

I had taken exactly two paces across the carpet when the lights went out.

My head still felt fuzzy, and after the blaze of the bulbs, I saw a raw red mist instead of darkness. Then I heard the slam of the bathroom door, and I knew whoever had been in the room had been hiding there, and I jumped to the right and so missed the first blow aimed at me.

A fist punched into the plywood front of the wardrobe, and I heard a man's cry of rage and anger, and also the same scent

161

I had smelled just before I had been attacked in Maria's flat. It was underlaid with sweat, which I had noticed when talking to Hassan earlier on, although the scent had been different then.

So now I knew who had hit me then, and who was in the room with me now. Hassan.

'Help!' I shouted, which was ridiculous, for the only fists that could help me were right at the ends of my own two arms.

No one answered. I hadn't really expected them to. I heard breathing and I slugged out with my boot in the direction of the breather. It connected with a shin bone. Suddenly, the breathing was much nearer to me, and I knew where he would probably be, and I brought up both my fists locked together against his face. If the blow had connected that would have been his lot, but it didn't, and the next thing I remembered was someone on my back, and my arms being bent to my sides, and my head forced back with the crook of an elbow under my chin.

I reached down and back to where this attacker kept his cobs, and I squeezed like I was wringing water out of a Shetland wool sweater after a day in the rain.

He screamed – as I would have screamed, too, for I was reducing them to the size of wrinkled raisins – and he let me go smartly. I jabbed my elbow back in his gut to remember me by, and jumped for the bedside table. I flicked on the light, tossed it on the bed in case it fell and went out, and then threw the table, legs first, like four spears, at Hassan.

'Are you bloody mad?' I shouted at him. 'What's got into you?'

Hassan dodged the table, and half crouched, facing me, lips drawn back over his china teeth. His right hand moved as quickly as a snake dodging the charmer in Old Bombay (or New Delhi, for that matter) and when I saw it again, he was holding the F.N.

162

He came towards me, and for the first time I realized how he hated me; hatred was written as large on his face as the news on that neon sign in Piccadilly. But why, for God's sake?

I picked up the lamp and threw it at him, and leapt on to the bed as he fired. I kicked out with both my feet and heard his grunt of pain, and the gun clatter to the one small square of floor not covered by carpet. Then we fought in the darkness.

Hassan's sweat, overlaid by the scent I had last smelled in Maria's bedroom in Rosemary Court, filled the room as we slugged away at each other, like two blind men in a coal cellar, fighting by ear, each aiming at the other's breathing.

I hit and hit and went on hitting, and then I paused. I couldn't even hear Hassan breathe. Either he was dead, which I doubted, or he was deliberately holding his breath – and this could mean nothing good for me.

It didn't.

I suddenly sensed someone behind me and then, as I turned, hands hard as a King Dick wrench went around my throat. I kicked and gouged and hit nothing, only using up air in my lungs that I could have saved for a better purpose.

Against my reddened eyelids, I saw a quick run-through of nothing, and heard a loud humming in my ears. My lungs were bursting, but I had no air and I could make no noise, utter no cry, for help or mercy. I couldn't even breathe.

Then, quite suddenly, there was an end to it all; no pain, nothing at all, but a deeper darkness, soft as a Moseley Float-On-Air cushion in a 1930's car.

6 ❋ Equally suddenly, there was also a lot of pain, and my sweat was gluing my shirt to my body in a rather uncomfortable way, and my nose and lips were cracking with dried blood, also mine, unfortunately.

I stretched my legs and my arms – remembering that gag about the old man who recalled how, when he was young, he had four supple members and one stiff, but now he was old, he had four stiff members and one supple.

In stretching, my fingers felt the roughness of concrete. They were scratched and raw and sore, which was also how I felt all over.

I lay where I was, because for the moment I could do nothing else, and I wasn't quite sure where the hell I was, but gradually, as consciousness returned from wherever it had been, I realized I was lying on a concrete floor. It felt very cold; wind was blowing sand in under a door that didn't fit very well, and I could see a horizontal slit of pale blue light beneath the woodwork, so the dawn couldn't be too far away, and no doubt was coming closer.

I shivered and sat up slowly, for if I moved quickly I thought my head might leave my body altogether. It stayed where it was, so I pushed my luck even further and stood up. I could make out the dim shape of a pile of sacks, then the dim glittering roundness of a car radiator. I was back in square one, in the garage beneath the hotel.

I took a few hesitant steps towards the switch, turned on the inspection light, unhung it from the wall and looked at myself in the driving mirror of the small Bugatti. My face was a mass of blood, my eyes puffed up like an adder's, and vomit had stained the front of my jacket. I shone the light around the garage.

The Royale had gone, which didn't surprise me. I'd take a

164

lot of surprising now. I carried the light over to the pile of sacks. Kent's body hadn't gone. This didn't surprise me, either. It lay there, face down, taking no interest in anything. I glanced at my watch. The glass had smashed, but the mechanism was still working: three-thirty-five. It must be in the morning, but which morning? The morning after I found Hassan in my room, presumably.

I sat down on the running board, my head in my hands, trying to recap what had happened.

Presumably Hassan and Sabry had stolen the Royale. If so, how could they get it through the Customs? I had all the papers upstairs in my suitcase. But had I? Or had Hassan and Sabry come into the room to steal those papers? This seemed so possible that it was almost a certainty. I stood up shakily, switched off the light, and closed my eyes to accustom them to the darkness, which had turned an unhealthy red against my aching lids.

I turned the handle of the door that led to the back stairs. The handle moved easily enough, but the door didn't; it had been locked on the other side. I crossed the garage to try the roll-up doors, but they were padlocked down.

So here was a right turn-up; locked in a garage with a dead man, both of us showing signs of having been in a fight. Whoever discovered us would understandably assume we had been in the same fight, and that I had killed Kent. And I'd be hard pushed to prove otherwise, for it was such an easy and obvious solution that I couldn't see the Egyptian police not jumping at it.

Hassan and Sabry could get the Royale through the Customs on the papers they'd no doubt taken from my room, and make a killing on the jewels in the lights, as well as the three old cars.

Of course, if I ever caught up with them, I could sue – but no one but an idiot would bother to pour good money after bad in such a cause. If Hassan was related to the chief of

165

police, no doubt he also had a good friend or relation among the judges.

Meanwhile, I was imprisoned here until someone let me out, but before that happened, I'd no doubt that Hassan would tell the hotel manager how a mad Englishman, who'd made all sorts of threats against Kent, was locked in his garage. I had to get out before that happened. But – how?

Wild ideas of driving the little Bugatti at full bore against the wooden doors and smashing my way through, of hacking a hole in the side door with the crank handle, or soaking rags in petrol behind the door and burning away the wood around the lock poured through my mind, and poured out again. They just wouldn't work.

Perhaps a spare key would be left hanging on a nail somewhere? After all, this was an hotel garage, and some other customer might innocently lock themselves in it.

I switched on the inspection light again and shielded it with my hand to direct its faint rays all round the walls. A hose hung coiled from a hook, some tins of grease and polish were piled neatly on a cobwebby wooden shelf, and two ignition keys were suspended from a piece of string on a nail; otherwise, nothing.

I pressed my hands to my head, forcing myself to think of a way out. This was a problem for George's motto, which he says he heard from a juggler: keep your balls in the air. It means, of course, that you have to keep the action going, like the three-ball juggler. Lose command of the situation for a moment and you've lost the battle.

In the great days, when this had been a private house, how would François order his chauffeur to bring the car to the door? He could send a servant, or there might be a speaking tube, as I had seen in Edwardian motor-houses in England, but more likely there would be a telephone. This gave me new heart. A telephone. If there were, I could ring Maria in her room.

I searched the walls; no telephone. I couldn't even see any wires entering the garage. Then I looked behind the Bugatti, and set into the wall I saw a small cupboard with a grey-painted door. I opened it. On a ledge stood a telephone, and behind the door was pasted a list of numbers in Arabic script, which meant nothing to me. What meant more was the fact that, to put the telephone out of action, the three wires of the flex had been neatly cut.

However, this was not an insuperable problem. I opened the Bugatti tool-box, took out a pair of wire-strippers, ripped off the red and green and yellow plastic insulation from the wires, and twisted the bare copper ends together.

Then I picked up the telephone, jaggled the rest up and down. A sleepy operator answered: 'Hello?' I gave him Maria's room number, and heard the bell buzz, and then her voice, equally sleepily, saying *'Oui?'*

'Never mind the French chat,' I said. 'It's me.'

'You?' she said. 'What's the time?'

'Time for you to be out of bed and down in the garage,' I told her.

'Why? There's nearly an hour yet.'

'Not for me, there isn't. I'm locked in here.'

'Locked in? Who by?'

Disbelief touched her voice, like a frame around an old-fashioned photograph.

'Never mind the Socratic dialogue. Come down *now*. I'll be waiting behind the door.'

I put back the telephone, turned off the inspection light, and waited. The gap beneath the main door showed lighter now. I wondered where Hassan was, whether Sabry was with him. I could picture them in that big old car, humming down the empty road, the desert merging with the dying darkness on either side. It could be an exciting drive. I just wished I was making it.

167

I heard footsteps on the stairs, and then the click and turn of the lock. The door swung open. I let myself through.

'My God,' said Maria, when she saw me. 'What happened?'

'Hassan came into my room. We had a fight. I got knocked out, and came to here.'

We went up to my room. All the clothes had been tossed out of my suitcase. My passport and the car manifests had been under them in a brown envelope. I didn't need to have Sherlock as my middle name to see that they weren't there.

'Are you sure it was Hassan?'

'Certain. No two men could smell like him, or even look like him.'

'But why?'

'The Royale. That's why. He's stolen it. Maybe he and Sabry knew about those jewels, after all. Perhaps one of them was that fellow I chased in the garage.'

'But what about my father? How can we get him away?'

'We can't,' I said. 'Without that car, it's impossible.' Anyhow, I thought, never mind about dear old dad; what about us?

'I can't leave him here,' said Maria.

'What else can you do? If we all three pack into the little car we'll be stopped at the first police post up the road. You told me yourself how they all know about him.'

'We could try to move him on Kent's passport,' she said.

'Absurd. He looks nothing like Kent. Even a passport photograph can't be that bad.'

Also, for all I knew, and I knew damn-all, Hassan and Sabry might have warned the nearest police post up the road, that if two men and a woman *did* come past in another old car, one of the men was François. It would be an obvious thing to do, and Hassan wasn't the sort of man who'd miss such a chance.

'Well, what are we going to do?'

168

'I don't know what *you're* going to do, but here's my plan for today.

'We'll get right into the Type 57 and drive to Alex ourselves – now. I've no papers for this damn' thing because Hassan's stolen them. But I'll trust my luck to get through the customs myself on Kent's passport. I'll put on a pair of dark glasses, and to these fellows one Englishman looks much the same as another. Just like Chinese all look the same to us.'

I'd had enough of this horsing about. I wanted to be out of this hotel and aboard that boat in the shortest possible time. If we delayed much longer, the boat would already have sailed. Without money, I couldn't buy a plane ticket, and who would lend a penniless, passportless Briton the cost of a flight to London?

'But, my father. I'll never have another chance like this. It's all geared for us to leave.'

'It was,' I agreed, 'but how the hell can we possibly smuggle him out?'

'If we can only move him from the guardroom, we're halfway home. We might hide out in the desert somewhere. Maybe you could lay on a boat?'

'And what would I use for money?' I asked.

'I'll pay you what I was paying Kent if we're successful.'

'*If* we're successful, I'll earn what you were going to pay Kent. But now there's no conceivable chance of succeeding. Your whole plan hinged on moving him in the dummy petrol tank. How can I, without money or influence, possibly hire a boat big enough to sail down the Red Sea? Be your age.'

'Maybe we could hide while you had a special tank made for your car?'

'That's just not on. There's much more to it than simply having a big petrol tank made. The body on the Royale was designed specifically for the purpose. It would take weeks to have such a body made again – even *if* I knew a coachbuilder who would attempt it, and *if* I had the money. Cash. Not promises.'

'Twenty thousand,' she said. 'It's a lot of money.'

'It's a lot of talk,' I said, but I was thinking all the same, it *was* a lot of money. To keep as much in what is laughingly called legitimate business, I would have to make more than twice that amount. The ethics weren't bothering me, only the risks, for every man has his price, and no one had priced me so expensively before.

But the chance of succeeding here seemed less than minimal. I tried to cheer myself up by thinking that *if* we could spirit François out of the camp, and *if* Maria could hide up somewhere in a shack in the desert for a few days, *if* I could hire or steal a boat from Alex, it might *just* be possible to pick up dear old dad on the beach and go south after dark under sail, in case the engine were picked up by a listening post.

Allowing all these hopeful possibilities, it was then just conceivable that we could make Dar-es-Salaam with a following wind, *if* the currents were right. But as Churchill said feelingly about the catastrophic landing in Gallipoli in the First World War, 'The terrible "ifs" accumulated', and right here I could see nothing but ifs crowding in as close as sardines in a can.

I didn't know the country, and I didn't know the people, but, even so, I guessed we'd have no help at all from the locals. After all, what would be in it for them, apart from promises and the far more likely opportunity of a long stay in some Egyptian dungeon? We'd be on our own, so how could Maria and her father keep alive for several days in a shack in the desert – if they could even find a shack?

Equally, Maria and her father might be prepared to ditch me if things went wrong – and I wouldn't be in that shack to know whether things were going well or badly.

170

Someone once said that if all the beards in the B.B.C. were stretched from end to end, they'd reach from Sodom to Gomorrah, and I wouldn't necessarily disagree with that viewpoint. Twenty-thousand pound notes, on the other hand, stretched end to end, would make a wonderful green path to a life of young girls and old wines; of sunshine, amusing conversation and, possibly, even larger ads in *Motor Sport* and *Exchange and Mart*.

Maybe it could also open the way to a chain of Aristo Autos in the more pleasant parts of the world, places where income tax was low, and where money, once made, could be kept more easily than in Belgravia.

I was weakening. Maria could see that, and so could I, but there was still the basic problem we hadn't discussed; how to get her old man out of the guardroom, past the guard, over the barbed wire and into my car – and then where to take him without being seen.

'How was Kent going to spring him?' I asked her.

'He was going to create a diversion and then spirit him out.'

'How?'

'He brought a Verey pistol out from London with a couple of cartridges. He'd opened up the ends, and packed them with tiny, torn-up pieces of silver paper from cigarette packets and chocolate bars.'

'What the hell for?'

I found it hard to imagine Kent doing this in that shabby flat in the mews in Belsize Park, but then he might have been doing things even more useless; like tarting up old cars he couldn't even sell, for instance.

'He'd been a bomber pilot during the war,' she said. 'Apparently, to confuse enemy radar they'd throw out masses of these silver paper fragments. These would drift down to earth and show on radar screens as points of light – like parachutists falling, if you like. They called it window.'

This didn't sound a convincing scheme to me, transposed nearly thirty years on and substituting, for Dortmund, a desert by the Red Sea.

'Kent had worked things out on a strict time schedule,' Maria continued. 'At four-fifty, he was to drive the Royale south along the road for a couple of miles, then fire off these shots towards the hotel.

'We had a trial run with a silver paper cartridge over a field in England, and counted how long the pieces took to fall.'

'And then?'

'Then he'd hare back here. He'd switch off his engine for the last couple of hundred yards before he reached the hotel and coast along in the dark, so he wouldn't be heard.

'By then, the falling silver paper should be showing on the radar screen. The troops would be ordered to stand to.

'Kent would cut the telephone line so they wouldn't be able to alert anyone else, and the fact that they couldn't get through to Alex on the phone would heighten their fears that this was an Israeli invasion, the real thing.

'Meanwhile, I'd have taken a tin of petrol from the garage a couple of hundred yards into the desert, with a mass of old rags and a timing device Kent has also brought from London. At exactly five minutes past five, this would explode and the rags would keep burning.

'Kent worked out that the troops, already jittery, would now be absolutely certain the invasion had begun. They'd bang away with their ack-ack gun into the sky, or shoot at the flames in the desert. Under cover of all this, Kent and I would go through the back of the camp, cut the wire, kick in the door – and get my father out.'

'Wouldn't you be stopped driving away?' I asked.

'Who by? The soldiers would all be watching the south, facing the fire. We'd be going north.'

It sounded ingenious, and just feasible. I could imagine the

172

horror in this tiny garrison of reluctant soldiers, all anticipating annihilation by parachutists. They'd keep firing away madly at anything or nothing, making as much noise as possible to conceal their own fear.

'Twenty thousand,' Maria said, seeing my thoughts in my face, as those soldiers would see the terrifying, falling flecks of light on their radar screen.

I was being an idiot, a mad, stupid nutter who should be certified and join all the other Napoleons and poached eggs and handstanders who fill our asylums, but it was a big sum, and it could just possibly be mine.

'Well, what do you think?'

'I think it's a bloody silly idea. But with some luck, it *might* work.'

'You mean, you'll try it?'

'I mean, I'll try it,' I said. 'But get this straight right from now. I'm no hero. I'm in this strictly for cash, and I want it in writing that I'm paid as soon as we reach some other country.'

Actually, it's useless having an agreement in writing, as any lawyer will tell you (for a fee), for if someone means to screw you, it doesn't matter a fish's tit whether the contract is written on vellum with crown-and-anchor seals and red ribbon and signed over five bob stamps and all that crap, they'll still screw you. But something from my lost youth or my south London background still clung pathetically to the mythical strength of the written word.

Maria pulled an old envelope out of her pocket and wrote on the back: 'I promise to pay the bearer £20,000 cash if we all reach a foreign port safely.' She signed it and gave it to me. It wasn't worth the envelope she had written it on – and even that was worthless because it had been used – but it was at least some kind of promise, though I'd have an easier job skinning an amoeba than making this arrangement stick if she changed her mind.

My promised twenty grand seemed a long way off, but,

173

even so, the promise was better than nothing, as the mother superior told the abbot – which reminded me of a terrible joke George told me just before I left, about a nun in a convent in the French vineyard country, who went to her mother superior in some dismay.

'I've discovered another case of Lesbianism in the convent,' she told her.

'Never mind,' replied the Mother Superior cheerfully. 'Let's open a bottle. It *can't* be worse than this Beaujolais we've been having.'

Things might be worse for me, but not a lot.

Anyway, I put the envelope in my back trouser pocket and buttoned down the flap.

'When do we start?' I asked her.

'Now,' she said. 'I'll get you the gun from Kent's room.'

She left me alone in the garage. I poured one can of petrol into the Bugatti's tank, dumped another behind the seats, with some sacks, then climbed in behind the wheel, drawing comfort from the now-familiar controls, trying to keep my mind off the innumerable things that could go wrong – and the horrible consequences to me if they did. She was back before I'd succeeded.

She handed me the Verey pistol. It felt rather like a small blunderbuss. The two cartridges had brass bottoms and red plastic sides; their ends were crimped in and bound over crudely with strips of Sellotape.

'If the watchman's at the gate, just wave to him,' she told me.

'Thank you very much,' I said. 'Any curfew here?'

'No. Anyhow, you're a tourist and a foreigner, and all the police and officials have orders to be pleasant to tourists.'

'I hope they carry them out,' I said. Maria glanced at her watch.

'I'll open the door,' she said. 'I took the key off its hook behind the reception desk. You start the engine.'

She crossed the garage floor and rolled up the bureau door. A cold breeze blew in from the sea, stirring the concrete dust and flapping the rags around Kent's body. I turned on the ignition and pressed the starter. The Stromberg UUR-2 carburettor hissed like a captive snake and then the engine fired. I kept down the revs to make as little noise as possible, so that the exhaust sounded like very small strips of calico being torn by a timid maiden lady instead of its usual throaty bark. I drove through the door and Maria rolled it down behind me.

She climbed in and we went down the short drive and through the gates. An old man with a stave in his hand raised up his arm in salute.

'Salaamo,' I called to him, and waved as Maria had told me. He waved back and hawked in his throat and then spat on the sand, as though the effort had been altogether too much for him.

'Get it off your chest, lad,' I said to myself and immediately felt better. The waiting was the worst; now that things were happening, even small unimportant things like driving along a coast road with a girl by my side, there was less time for doubts and dreads.

We had no lights burning, but enough reflection from the moon on the sea for me to see my way. The desert lay like lava, grey and uninviting, faintly tinged with pink in the distance as the sun struggled over the edge of the world to put in another day's warmth. I glanced behind at the hotel. Dim lights were burning at one or two of the upper windows that didn't face the sea; the early-turn staff must be going on duty soon.

I drove for about two hundred yards, and then Maria nudged me to stop. She climbed out, and I humped the petrol can and the sacks across the sand for her.

'It'll do here,' she said, after we had walked down to where the sand felt firm and damp, near the breaking waves.

I threw down the can and sacks thankfully.

'Let's set our watches,' she said.

Mine was three minutes fast. I turned back the hands.

'Everything's been timed to within thirty seconds,' she said. 'I'll see you two hundred yards south of the hotel. In the car. Don't forget to coast past the hotel, so they won't hear the engine.'

'Don't you forget that twenty thousand quid,' I told her, in case she did.

On the way back to the car I looked back once, and Maria was standing in the sand, dark against the phosphorescence of the sea. I waved to her, but she didn't wave back, so I climbed into the car and set off down the road.

I watched the mileometer clock up one and nine-tenths, and then slowed and turned carefully in case my back wheels went over the edge of the road into the sand. I stopped, loaded the pistol, and aimed it out of the window up in the air and towards the hotel. I squeezed the trigger. Luckily, there was very little noise from the cartridge. I broke the pistol, reloaded it with the second cartridge and fired again. Then I threw the pistol away into the sand and hared back along the road.

I saw the glow-worm glitter of lights in the hotel windows when I was still half-a-mile away, and gave one last burst of throttle, then switched off the engine and coasted past the gate. As the car's momentum slowed, I pulled over to the right of the road and stopped. I opened the tool box, took out a pair of pliers and a hammer, shoved them into my pocket, closed the box and began to walk back to the hotel.

I climbed the first telegraph pole I saw. The first six inches were murder, as the actress told the bishop, because I had to climb with my legs wound round the rough and splintery post, but after that the Egyptian authorities had thoughtfully fitted metal steps, so I went up easily enough, to where two wires swung from their porcelain insulators. Close to, the

176

wires sang like enormous violin strings. I snipped one of them and its song ceased. One broken wire would be an accident; two would almost certainly spell sabotage.

Down on the ground, I kept as close to the wall as I could, for there was no other cover. The only sound was the thunder of the surf and the rattle of the wind in the reeds; or maybe it was the sound of my teeth chattering.

I glanced at my watch. Two minutes to go.

By now, that falling silver paper should be showing on the radar screen. But what if no one was watching it? What if the operator was asleep? I hadn't too much faith in the soldierly qualities of the troops I'd seen. We might be going through all these complicated motions of deception without even an audience of one.

I imagined Maria also waiting out there in the darkness. I wondered what her dear old dad was thinking about in the guard house, and what was happening to Hassan and Sabry. If they knew the value of the jewels on that Royale, they'd probably be thinking about their good life ahead, or – more likely – how to double-cross each other. And me? I was thinking that if I extracted myself safely without losing either my skin or my money, I'd settle in future for a quieter life.

One minute to go.

Suddenly, I heard voices from the tents: then shouting; then shadowy figures began to mill about, climbing up into the gun emplacement. The snout of the anti-aircraft gun moved slowly round until it was pointing over the sea. I'd wronged these Gyppoes. Someone had been watching the screen, after all.

Forty seconds to go. Out towards the sea, the darkness suddenly erupted in an orange ball of fire, so bright, so unexpected that I could see the long line of empty sand dunes, the white froth of the waves, and even the black oily smoke that ringed the flames.

The sound of the explosion followed a second later, rattling the hotel windows, and the shock wave blew my shirt hard against my body. The blaze died down slightly, but against its glare I could see soldiers rushing frantically about in the compound. Some were holding machine guns, which they began to fire wildly towards the flames, swinging their weapons as though they were hoses. This could be dangerous, for none of them was taking aim. However, so long as they kept their weapons pointed away from me, I'd be safe enough, as the young housewife told the amorous milkman.

I ran through the gate; the night watchman had prudently absented himself in the commotion, which was fortunate for me. The fence presented three strands of wire, each about a foot apart. I snipped these through easily with the pliers, and ran on, half-doubled, towards the guard house.

François should have been waiting for me, framed in the doorway, but he wasn't: the doorway was just filled with the door.

I kept back in the shadows for a moment, hoping he'd come out. Maybe he had overslept, though how he could sleep through the cacophony of noise seemed incredible to me. Soldiers had formed a line near their anti-aircraft gun, handing up shells from ammunition boxes. The gunner was aiming at nothing at all, but looking very determined about it, and firing away recklessly. I suppose each shell must have cost a fiver, but it wasn't his money, so why should he worry?

No one was looking my way, so I ran up the two steps to the door, and threw my weight against it. The door threw its weight right back at me and almost put my shoulder out. This door was meant to keep prisoners in, not to let unwanted visitors through. I took the hammer from my pocket and smashed the lock.

The door swung open. I closed it quickly with me inside. The noise of shouting and firing and the banging of the gun was fainter now. I groped for the light switch and flicked it on.

The windows were blacked out, the bed was empty, the sheets pulled back as though whoever had been in it had left hurriedly and hadn't rung for room service – presumably dear old dad.

So where the hell was he? I couldn't guess, but he certainly wasn't there. I looked under the bed just in case, but two cockroaches looked back at me reproachfully, so I left them.

I switched out the light, and ran back across the compound. This time, a soldier saw me and swung his rifle towards me and fired. He was a bum shot, for he missed, and, as he tried to reload, the second bullet jammed halfway into the breech. I suppose it was blocked with the sands of the Nile, like the Sphinx's backside.*

I threw my pliers at him, and he screamed with alarm, dropped his rifle and fled.

The ack-ack gun was firing now like a pom-pom and I heard the shrapnel hissing down. I sprinted through the gate, along the road, and jumped into the car. Maria was waiting in the front seat, with the ignition already on. I pressed the starter; the engine whirred and caught, and we were off.

'Where's dad?' she asked.

'God knows,' I said. 'I don't. He wasn't there.'

'He must have been. I saw him go in this evening.'

'Well, take my word for it. Someone else took him out, or he's made a balls of the arrangements and gone off on his own.'

*Another of George's rhymes:

> The sexual desires of the camel
> Are greater than anyone thinks,
> And at the height of the mating season
> He'll even fancy the Sphinx.
> Now the Sphinx's posterior passage
> Is blocked by the sands of the Nile,
> Which accounts for the hump on the camel
> And the Sphinx's inscrutable smile.

Maria didn't say anything. I think she was simply beyond speech. This was the moment for which she'd been working and waiting for so long, and something had gone wrong, what and how she couldn't comprehend. She sat like a zombie, staring out of the windscreen, seeing nothing but her own failure.

I didn't know where François was, but my bet was that Hassan had loused things up for us somehow. Maybe he'd told the guard commander that I was a dangerous character, and the commander had switched François elsewhere – just in case?

The more I thought about this, the more I wished I was somewhere else. If Hassan didn't catch me on one hook, he was obviously determined to do so on another.

As we drove, not speaking, only thinking, which was worse, the sound of the firing sank to a distant crackle, like November fireworks in someone else's back garden.

I glanced at my watch; twenty-five minutes to five. At this rate we would be in Alex by seven. I decided to drive straight to the docks. But then I remembered I had no papers for the car, and no passport for myself. We'd stop in the café I'd seen on the sea-front on the way down and have breakfast, and ask the owner where the consulate was, and I'd tell the consul I'd lost my passport and the papers, which was true, up to a point. He'd curse me, no doubt, but he'd still help me. He'd have to, wouldn't he? That's what consuls are for, surely? I tried to convince myself, but not very successfully.

The road stretched on, grey across the desert, and without lights I couldn't make out any landmarks I remembered from the run out. I glanced at the dials on the dash for assurance; oil pressure at 30; petrol at 10 gallons; speed, 55 m.p.h., which was fast enough. Maria was sitting hunched up in her seat, staring straight ahead through the fly-spotted windscreen. I didn't know what she was thinking about, but I hoped her thoughts were more cheerful than mine.

180

Then I had another idea. To hell with the consul and all that horsing about – ('And what was the number of your passport? Where and when was it issued? You don't *know*?'). Instead, I'd bluff my way through Immigration on Kent's passport, but I'd have to leave this car behind. What a way to make a living, and me a car dealer! Buy three cars and only collect two.

The road began to turn and twist like a tarmac corkscrew through sand-dunes, speared on either side with green reeds and rushes, now dropping between them, so that they soared twenty or thirty feet on either side of the car, then rising above, so that the full force of the wind buffeted us and made the hood flap like a punctured drum-skin.

I'm so accustomed to driving on the crowded roads of southern England, that to have no other car to pass or follow seemed somehow sinister. I wondered vaguely and irrationally whether a terrible tragedy had overtaken mankind, whether Armageddon had begun (and was over, somehow missing me) – or maybe the Chinese had exploded too large a hydrogen bomb?

There was an emptiness about everything, the quietness of death, only broken by the creak of the Bugatti's springs over occasional potholes, the flap of the canvas roof, and the muted crackle of the exhaust.

The road dipped suddenly between two dunes, and turned sharp left, away from the sea. I braked and dropped down a gear, into the hairpin bend. Then I stopped. A rock, about the size of a dustbin, had come loose from somewhere and blocked the road. I heaved the steering wheel to the right to miss it, but it still caught the hub of the front wheel and the force of the blow spun the steering wheel out of my hands.

I stopped to climb out and see what damage I'd done. At that moment I sensed rather than saw a movement from the reeds on the right, and then a policeman jumped out in front of me.

181

This was no ordinary Egyptian copper in tatty khaki fuzz, but a man wearing a magnificent uniform, with twill riding breeches, a smart olive-green tunic, gold epaulettes, polished Sam Browne belt and holster. This last was empty, for the .45 that usually lived in the leather was now in his hand, pointing straight at my heart. My heart didn't like being pointed at; it began to beat very rapidly indeed.

'All right,' said the policeman quietly and in English – after all, if he'd spoken in Egyptian I wouldn't have understood a word. I looked up from the mouth of his revolver. Hassan's face leered at me. Or was this his cousin, the chief of police?

'Who are you?' I asked, because I wanted to know.

'Hassan,' he replied. 'Drive right on and stop behind the car in front. It's about fifty yards away.'

'That rock?' I began.

'I put it there to stop you,' he said. 'Get moving.'

'But . . .'

'Don't talk. Drive. And don't try anything clever.'

There was nothing clever I could think of to try; if I were clever, I wouldn't be where I was. My mouth felt dry as the desert all around, and my body was shaking with reaction. Hassan jumped up behind me and dug the muzzle of his gun into my back.

I drove on. We came through the bend and the sea was pounding only feet away on a beach scummed with driftwood and dark green strips of seaweed. A few seabirds, the first living things I'd seen since I left the hotel, apart from Hassan, floated on the water, watching us, or maybe watching fish. I didn't know. All I knew was, I envied them; they were free and I was captive.

Ahead of me, pulled half off the road, stood the big Bugatti, yellow as the yolk of an egg in the early sunshine. The bonnet was open. Sabry perched on its huge tail, smoking a cigarette. He jumped down and came towards us, hands in his pockets.

182

'So you came, yes?' he said, which is about as good, or as bad, an opening as any.

I half expected him to offer me a cut rate for attar of roses or musk, or some other rubbish, because even in the desert he looked what he was, a dabber of scent on the lobes of other people's ears, a ponce perfumier, or a perfumed ponce, if you like that better. I didn't like him at all; and as for Hassan, if he were burning to death I wouldn't bother to pee on him.

I had a sudden wild idea of running Sabry down, but Hassan would have fired. I know that in a film I would have ducked just before he fired, and then swung around and pitched him into the sand. I've seen this sort of thing happen on the box so many times – and so have you – but in real life you don't write the whole script, only your own lines, so you can't guarantee the end of the action.

'Switch off your engine,' ordered Hassan, jumping down to the side of the road. 'Then get out and stand by the car with your hands behind your neck.'

'Why don't you say please?' I asked him.

'Because you're a cocky English bastard,' he said. 'And I hate the English. Why should you come and make money out of my country's old cars?'

I couldn't follow the fellow's reasoning, but this didn't seem the time to tell him so. Cocky, possibly; English, agreed; bastard, not actually – but a deal, surely that's another thing altogether?

He spat at me. I could feel his spittle cold and vile on the side of my face. I've never been spat at before, at least by anyone on target. I didn't like the feeling.

I reached out, turned the ignition key. The red warning light flickered and died. As I eased myself slowly out of the car, I put my right hand down, felt for the petrol tap by the side of my seat and pushed it to 'Off'. Waste not, want not, is as good a motto as any, and better than most. There must have been a petrol leak somewhere at sometime, or else this tap would never have been fitted. Hassan didn't see the motion, and he would have learned nothing from it if he had.

The sand felt very soft and powdery to my feet, and I immediately sank in it over the tops of my shoes, and stamped my feet and shook them, but my shoes were already full. At the other side of the car, Maria was climbing out, a forlorn figure. Sabry crossed over to her.

'I'm sorry about this,' he said. He might even have meant it, but more likely he meant he was sorry for himself, stuck by the side of the sea, on the edge of the sand in a monster car forty years old.

'We've had a breakdown. You will not be harmed in any way.'

'What the hell *is* all this?' I asked Hassan. 'Why are you dressed up in that rubbish?'

Hassan said nothing. He turned to Maria.

'Throw your handbag back into the car,' he told her.

He obviously thought she had a gun or some weapon. The only weapon I was carrying, I had been provided with at birth, and I could see no use for it whatever in my present situation.

Hassan jabbed his gun into my stomach. His face was very close to mine, with his too-white teeth, his thick lips and the tiny moustache. The sweat was pouring off him now; no scent in all the world could sweeten his smell. I wondered what it would be like to be a woman, and wake up every morning of your life with that face on the same pillow. I decided no woman would endure it. No wonder he was king, as George would say. King Lear – queer.

'You're the old-car expert, or so you claim,' Hassan said, 'so get this car running.'

He jerked his head towards the Royale.

'I've no tools,' I said, and I hadn't, either, apart from the one mentioned a few lines up.

'There are some in the car,' said Hassan, convincing himself

184

as much as me. But in his pale blue eyes I could see a tiny flicker of fear and doubt, the same sort of flicker I've often seen in the eyes of someone after they've signed a cheque for one of my old cars and then belatedly wonder whether they've committed themselves to something far too expensive.

If the Royale had a broken half-shaft or a cracked distributor, or something else as serious, whatever tools were on the car would be useless; Hassan could be stuck there for hours. Virtually the only traffic would be military convoys, with drivers who wouldn't stop, or maybe a truck carrying provisions for the hotel. Add a taxi or two with foreign tourists having a quick *shufti* at the sea and the sand, and that would be about the lot.

We stood looking at each other. Then Hassan moved the gun from my stomach, for which my stomach was very thankful, and so was I.

'Have a look at the engine,' he said, and as I started to walk towards the Royale, Sabry called: 'Wait, we'll frisk him first.'

He ran his hands down my jacket and my trouser pockets, but I was carrying nothing more lethal than a handkerchief and a few hundred-piastre notes in a money clip.

'I can't work with that gun around,' I told Hassan.

'You'll bloody work,' said Hassan and kept the gun in his hand.

So, I worked.

At least, I looked under the bonnet at Ettore Bugatti's masterpiece of engine design, at the two sets of plugs to each cylinder, at all the engine-turned metal that glittered like jewels. The whole engine appeared to be a solid metal ingot; there had never been one so beautiful before, and there never would be another made like it now.

'How did it stop?' I asked Sabry. The less I had to do with Hassan, the better. I couldn't look at him without my feelings showing in my eyes.

185

'Hassan was driving,' said Sabry, as though this made a difference. 'The engine gave a cough, and then it began to whir inside and all the power went out of it. We just stopped.'

This sounded to me as a patient's symptoms must sound to a bored family doctor: 'I've got this strange pain, see, that starts in my left elbow and sort of goes all round my body and then gets worse here, in my right ankle.'

'Come on,' said Hassan. 'We haven't got all day. The heat will be up in an hour.'

He had command of the situation, but I also had one card to play; my mechanical knowledge, such as it was. I didn't fancy working on the engine, maybe persuading it to start, and then being shot in the back of the head for my trouble. Hassan hadn't told me he'd do this, of course, but then nations declare war on each other without informing their opponents, and I didn't trust Hassan any more than I'd trust a rattlesnake that hadn't had a good rattle in far too long.

'I know nothing about this car,' I said, which was more or less true.

'It must be the same as any other,' said Hassan, but with a welcome twinge of doubt in his voice. After all, if the Royale was twice as large as any other car, mightn't it also be twice as complicated?

'You know nothing about it,' I told him, pressing my tiny advantage, as one dwarf told the other.

'This is one of the most complicated designs in the world.'

Certainly, the engine looked so huge that it must have been unlike any engine he had seen before.

'I'll do my best,' I went on. 'But not if you're flashing that gun about. You might fall or trip, and then I'm dead.'

'I have never fallen with a gun,' said Hassan seriously. 'I was the best shot in Farouk's court.'

For shot, read shit, I thought, but didn't say the words. We stood looking at each other, and either he must have

186

realized I was harmless, or he thought I meant what I said, because he slipped the gun into his back pocket.

'Now,' he said. 'Get going on that engine.'

From the symptoms Sabry had given me, I didn't need to be a senior wrangler or even an A.M.I.C.E. to guess that the cause of their stop was either no petrol or no spark. I turned the ignition key on and off quickly, before Hassan could see what dial I was watching, which was the petrol gauge. The needle flicked up from empty to show three-quarters full. So they had plenty of juice.

Perhaps there was a blockage in the pipe; maybe some fluff or sediment was blocking a bend after years of being unused? Then I had another think and flicked the switch again. The needle did exactly the same, as I expected it would. Hassan said irritably: 'Don't waste time. Do something mechanical.'

'I must check everything,' I told him. 'Either I do it my way or no way.'

I was stalling for time, because the longer I could spin things out, the greater my chance – not much of one, admittedly, but the only one I had – that someone might come along the road and stop to see if they could help us. And, if that happened, I could conceivably get an outsider involved, and the odds might shift a little more in my favour. As I viewed things, I was right down on the deck, so the only way I could go was up.

'Where do you keep the tools for this thing?' I went on.

I knew exactly where they were; in one of the torpedo-shaped wings, with their recessed nickel hinges and carriage locks. Hassan and Sabry looked at each other doubtfully. I pretended to make a discovery of my own.

'Are they in one of the wings?' I suggested to them both. 'Perhaps you'd like to see?'

If either bent down, I'd boot him hard right up the jack with one foot, and kick him in the side of the head with the other, executing a neat *pas de deux* meanwhile, and then try

187

my luck with whoever was left. But Hassan didn't give me the chance.

'Open it up yourself,' he said, and put his hand into his back pocket to grip the butt of the gun.

I squatted down in front of the old-fashioned lock, pressed the button so that the lid flipped open, and took out a black leather tool roll which contained all the tools, each one nickel-plated, and stamped with the name, Bugatti. I didn't think they'd ever been used.

'Never had a spanner on her,' I thought, that old claim of so many used-car dealers, who buy a new roll of tools to drop into the tool-box of each old car they sell, so that they can open the roll and show the innocent prospective buyer how the car has never been in any mechanical trouble.

Of course, if the buyer has any sense at all, he retorts that, after thirty or forty years, a car must indeed be in a bad state if it has never had a spanner on it. But, somehow, in all my experience they never do. There's something about the statement that mesmerises them, so remember that, next time you hear it.

I selected a plug spanner, pulled off a plug lead, slipped the spanner over the plug, gave the Tommy bar a jerk, and the plug began to turn easily. I took it out. The points were pale grey, another indication that the mixture had suddenly gone weak and died. But how, if the tank was three-quarters full?

I loosened the union nut outside the carburettor, turned on the ignition again, pressed the rubber solenoid button on the starter motor switch to spin the engine, and watched the blue spark jump across the points of the plug. This was just play-acting. The loose join didn't even grow wet, so no petrol was passing from the pump. If the original petrol tank had been removed, so that the huge container necessary to conceal a human being could be fixed in its place, it was likely that a small petrol tank, holding only a couple of gallons, had been

188

substituted. This would be connected to the five-inch filler, for, after all, two gallons would have been more than enough to propel even this gigantic car from a house in Cairo to the Palace, carrying a girl in the back.

The petrol gauge had probably not been altered, because this would be an unnecessarily complicated operation. If this were the case, the original unit, designed for a large tank would have a float moving up and down perhaps three feet. But the float would bottom in a tiny tank, four or five inches high, and when that happened, it would still register three-quarters full. The three-quarters it referred to would be notional, as the Income Tax people like to say about some-one's profits, when they haven't had any.

I had had this experience of a false reading years ago with an old three-litre Bentley, which had been fitted with a replica body, and what was apparently a forty-gallon tank at the back, shielded by wire mesh grilles against an almost non-existent risk of puncture by flying stones.

The tank was just a hollow shell, and hadn't even a bottom, and inside we had fitted a much smaller tank, from a Vaux-hall, with the original rheostat mechanism, so that when this replacement tank was empty the original petrol gauge still registered nearly half full.

Now that I'd satisfied myself as to the reason for their breakdown, I felt quite irrationally relieved. Maybe this was a professional thing, or maybe it was because I knew something the others didn't. The man who said knowledge was power knew a thing or two.

'Hurry up,' said Hassan. 'I can see you've a spark there. It must be a fuel blockage, for there's plenty of fuel.'

'So you know about cars?' I said. 'If you're so good, why don't you get it going?'

'I'm guessing,' he admitted.

I screwed back the plug, tightened up the union, then undid the bolts in the float chamber, slipped it down

half-an-inch, peered inside. It was as dry as my own mouth.
I bolted it up again.

'You're out of juice,' I said.

'We can't be. The gauge says we're three-quarters full.'

'Then why doesn't it work?'

He said nothing.

'We'll take some of your petrol,' said Sabry.

'Be my guest,' I said. 'But how are you going to manage
that? I've no can.'

I guessed there was no can, no hose or other container in
the big Bugatti, either. Hassan bit his lip, in lieu of anything
else to try his teeth on.

'Use my hat,' he said, and pulled the peaked cap from his
head.

'It'll run through that. You'll just be wasting your time.
You'll need nearly ten gallons at least to get to Alex, and my
car hasn't got a lot more in its tank.'

For the first time since I'd seen him, Hassan looked really
worried. A shadow darkened his already dark face, and his
eyes were hard as prune stones.

'Take one of the headlamps off,' he told me. 'Use the shell
as a scoop.'

'Useless,' I said quickly. 'The drain plug in my tank has
been soldered.'

It hadn't, so far as I knew, but I spoke with such certainty
that he believed me.

'Why not take the whole tank off, then?' suggested Sabry.
'Put it on the big car and connect it up?'

'Be your age,' I told him. 'It'll take half a day to get those
nuts undone after forty years. And we'd have to empty the
tank in any case before we could move it. Back in square
one.'

I stood there watching them, relishing their discomfort,
feeling the sun grow warm on my back and my face when I
turned into it. In an hour, the desert would be like an oven.

190

'Have you got any water?' I asked Sabry. 'I've an idea.'

'Let's have the idea,' said Sabry.

He leaned inside the Royale, pulled out a plastic container, and filled two plastic mugs with water. He handed one to Maria and the other to me. I drank mine gratefully, swilling it round in my mouth, feeling it soak into my parched throat.

'Well,' said Hassan. 'You've had your water. What's your idea?'

'Before I tell you,' I said, trying to keep my voice calm, as though I was making a business proposition, 'What's going to happen to us?'

'That depends on whether you help us,' said Hassan, but I knew from the way he smiled, with his mouth just a muscular contraction of the lips, that it didn't depend on anything but his own whim.

'If I do get you to Alex, what then?'

Maria was looking at me with surprise in her face, and disappointment, too; almost contempt. Surely I couldn't be such an idiot as to attempt to make some deal with them, when I had no bargaining power at all? I knew what she was thinking, and I let her think it. I'd have thought the same in her position.

'Then you can go back to England,' said Hassan smoothly.

Possibly, but dead or alive? I wondered.

'Why did you kill Kent?' I asked him. This had to come out in the open sooner or later, as the games master told the choir boy, and it was better to come out now. I didn't think that Hassan would bother to lie to me, because you only lie to someone if you want to go on dealing with them, and maybe deceiving them. You don't trouble to lie if they're no more use to you; they're simply not worth the effort of inventing an excuse or a reason. But in every life there is always at least one moment for truth. For Hassan, this was that moment.

'We didn't mean to kill him,' he said.

'We?' repeated Maria.

'Yes,' said Sabry. 'We were working on this car, cleaning it. I was polishing the lamps and I suddenly realized that the red lenses in the sidelights and the headlamps weren't red glass at all. They were rubies. So we looked at the green lights on the dash, and the red lights on the side of the tail lamps. They were emeralds and rubies. Even the radiator name plate was made of precious stones. There's a fortune in this damn' car.'

'But you left the cigar lighter?'

'Yes. The lens in that was glass.'

'And so?'

'So Kent came in when I was prising the jewels out. He must have guessed what they were. We had an argument. We struggled. He fell and hit his head.'

'Convenient,' I said. 'Maybe you pushed him?'

I turned to Hassan questioningly.

'Maybe I did, and what the hell does it matter?' he asked aggressively. 'I've a witness who'll say differently. And Kent's dead, so he can't contradict me. And you're in no position to talk, either, Englishman. Your fingerprints are all over that garage. I pressed your tiny hands in Kent's blood myself and dabbed them on all kinds of things – walls, doors, those petrol cans. So come on, fellow. How are you going to get us out of this?'

'You still haven't told me what's in this for me if I do?'

As I stood there, I suddenly – belatedly, maybe – realized why they didn't just abandon the Royale and take off in my car.

They had kidnapped François – probably imagining they were the only people to think of doing so. He'd have been waiting for Maria's signal, and when they came instead, he would have thought it was only a change of plan.

They couldn't just abandon the Royale. François was hidden inside it; and if they left him, they also forfeited their chance of a fortune. The jewels from the lights would only represent small change compared with the amount he could be forced to pay them for his freedom.

I also guessed they wouldn't give me any deal, because they didn't need to. I was expendable. I remembered the advice an American buyer of a Lorraine-Dietrich once gave me: 'Never get into an ass-kicking contest with a three-legged man.' Which means, don't play out of your league, don't fight if you've no chance of winning. But the longer I could drag this out, the more chance I had of winning; in fact, this would give me my only chance of winning.

'What do you want?' asked Hassan.

'Safe passage for Maria and for me. My passport and the papers, so I can export this Type 57. After all, I've paid you for it.'

'You get us to Alex,' said Hassan, 'And you both go free.'

'I'll have your hand on that,' I said. As I stretched out my hand, I thought that if I was a fictional superman, I'd have him over my shoulder as our hands touched. But fact is like a new river; it never runs the way you would expect it to, and I wasn't a superman. Indeed, I felt so depressed I was barely a man at all.

He shook hands, puzzled by my gesture, obviously expecting a trick, because I could see his muscles harden under the silk of his shirt.

'You don't imagine he'll keep his word, do you?' asked Maria contemptuously.

I didn't, of course, but this was no time for telling anyone. I couldn't bear to look at her. From the way she looked at me, she'd spit on the other side of my face, and I couldn't really blame her. I felt so low I could have walked under a slug's belly on stilts, and the slug wouldn't even have noticed.

'What's your plan, then?' asked Sabry.

He was the sharper of the two, but if I could fix Hassan I'd have no trouble from him. Sabry had spent too long among

193

his scents and perfumes and pomades, too long hunched-up, peering at jewels through a magnifying glass, offering ridiculously low prices for things worth ten times as much. He was a one-punch fighter, and, if I had the chance, that one punch would be mine. For if, read when.

'I'll tow you,' I said. 'It's the only way. Outside Alex, we can stop at a petrol station, and you can fill up and buy a spare can to keep you going.'

Sabry looked at Hassan.

'It makes sense,' he said.

And, of course, it did – for them. I wouldn't know whether it did for me for some time yet.

Hassan glanced at his watch. Two minutes after six o'clock. Six hours before the boat sailed, but only four hours of useful time, for we should be there at least a couple of hours before they cast off. He nodded.

'Have you a rope?' he asked me.

'Yes.'

I still had the tow ropes I had told Kent to buy before we set off from Cairo. I lifted up the trunk lid at the back of the Type 57, pulled one out, and looped one end round the nearside spring shackle.

'Drive the car in front of the Royale,' Hassan ordered Maria.

He took out his gun and held it about a foot away from my stomach, so close that a blind man couldn't miss, and with his skill he'd give me a second navel in no time. As if I needed such a thing.

'Don't try anything,' Sabry warned Maria, as though she might. 'Hassan just wants an excuse to fire.'

She shook her head. She looked so miserable, so disappointed in me and my pathetic showing, that she had no words left to express her feelings. She started the engine, drove in front of the Royale and then slowly backed up to it.

'Switch off,' I called to her. I'd turned off the petrol, and it

194

could only run for a few minutes on what was already in the carburettor. I didn't want them to find out about that tap. I bent down, tied the rope to the front dumb iron of the Bugatti. Maria moved over to the passenger seat, still not looking at anybody, simply staring straight ahead.

'I'll drive,' I told Hassan as he came towards me to order me out. 'I know this car. I drove it up from Cairo, and you've got to nurse it.'

'Then I'll ride in the back,' said Hassan. 'And don't get any ideas about putting us off the road, because I'll shoot. It's a long time since I shot a man.'

'I thought your thing was birds,' I said. 'Feathered birds.'

He hit me across the mouth with the back of his hand, luckily not with the one that held the gun, but I felt my lips split against my teeth, and my blood tasted salt on my tongue.

Another debt to pay, I thought. He was the only creditor with whom I'd looked forward to settling accounts in a long, long time.

'Get moving,' said Hassan. 'And only stop if Sabry blows his horn twice.'

Sabry could do what he liked with his horn, for my money.

I gripped the serrated rim of the steering wheel, sitting low in the now familiar leather seat, looking out through the faintly tinted windscreen, down the long narrow bonnet to the radiator cap. My heart was thumping like an S.U. pump with an air lock. I felt tired, and desperate for a way out. Hassan climbed in behind me and sat with his gun pressed into the nape of my neck.

'There's no need for all that crap,' I said, moving my head.

'You just drive,' said Hassan coldly, but he took the pistol out of my flesh, although I guessed it was still aimed at me. I hoped he hadn't a twitch in his trigger finger, but then if he had, I'd know nothing about it.

I switched on the engine, put my right hand down carefully under the seat and pushed over the petrol tap to 'On'. Then I pressed the starter button. The engine fired. I let in the clutch gently and the rope took up the strain. The car jerked as the other Bugatti began to move, and then we were off.

Every few hundred yards I pushed over the petrol tap with my hand, and the engine coughed and spluttered and we stopped, and Hassan cursed us. I shrugged my shoulders, waited for a few moments, and then turned on the tap again and we started off. If I had to explain in a court of law why I did this, I couldn't give a rational answer. But then isn't that true of an awful lot of things in life?

I had a customer once, a psychiatrist, who bought, of all things, a Bean, a car about as dull as its name, and he told me that every time he rode alone in a lift, just as he was leaving, he'd press all the buttons for the other floors, plus the 'up' and 'down' buttons. He'd no clear idea why, he just liked to do it. So if he can't say, when it's his living, why we do the odd things we do, how can I? I suppose I wanted to bitch things for Hassan, and this was the only way in which I could annoy him. There was also another reason: the longer we took on the journey, the longer we stayed alive – and the greater chance that someone would stop and offer to help.

'We haven't all day,' complained Hassan, at the fifth stop.

'I know that,' I said. 'But I can't help this damn' car. It wasn't built to tow something twice its weight. If you can do better, you drive it.'

'I've a bloody good mind to,' said Hassan.

'All right,' I said, opening the door and climbing out.

He covered me with the gun. For a moment I thought he really would take my place, and then he'd soon discover my trick with the petrol tap, so I said hastily, and quite slanderously, 'If you let the clutch in too quickly you'll snap the half-shafts like sticks. They're a weak point on this model.'

196

'Get in again,' said Hassan, believing me. 'And take it gently.'

By a quarter past seven, we had covered fifteen miles. One or two Skoda trucks were coming towards us now, being driven down from the docks of Alexandria, part of an Iron Curtain consignment of military equipment. They blew their horns impatiently and roared past, enveloping us in dust so that I had to stop until it had settled, and I could see the way ahead again.

We drew near to a railway that ran alongside the road for a few miles. A train overtook us, crowded with soldiers, some of them hanging outside, some even sitting, legs wide apart to keep their balance, on the roofs of the carriages. They waved to us as though we were in some kind of a race, and I suppose in a sense we were. I wondered uneasily whether their movement north was anything to do with our attempts at a diversion a few hours earlier.

We passed road blocks, giant squares of concrete with rusty metal loops, that had been dragged up, ready to be rolled across the road in the event of an Israeli invasion, and a few hutches at the edge of the beach, dried black skins stretched over driftwood boards. I don't know who lived there, but even if the shacks didn't look like split-level, gracious living as advertised in the home section of Sunday newspapers, at least their tenants were free, which was more than I could claim to be.

We were nearer the sea now, and the spray was rising, and the waves pounded other blocks of concrete, like the foundations of submerged citadels. One of the wasp-coloured taxis, black and yellow, came surging down the road from Alexandria, and I had a brief glimpse of two middle-aged tourists, unmistakably American, in horn-rimmed glasses, flowered shirts and nylon sunhats.

One of them waved to us and Maria waved back, but they didn't stop. I wondered what they made of our two old cars roped together, grinding along on the side of the road in their dust. I wondered what they would have said if they had known the truth. Obviously, they wouldn't have believed it, because truth of this kind would be far beyond the frontiers of their comfortable, air-conditioned, package-deal world, and I wished to hell it was outside mine.

I glanced down at the mileometer. We were only eleven or twelve miles out of town. In the long, dim distance, now, I could see a few faint jagged shapes on the rim of the shimmering desert – Alexandria. Even at our pace, we would be there within an hour. Then either Hassan would keep his word, or he wouldn't. There were no other options, but I didn't feel optimistic about the matter, for every turn of our wheels diminished our use to him.

He must have been thinking along those lines himself, because he suddenly jabbed the muzzle of the automatic into my neck.

'Pull off the road,' he ordered.

'Why?' I asked. 'We're miles away yet.'

'You talk too much. Do as you're told.'

I did.

'Get out,' he ordered, as the wheels stopped turning. I did that, too.

It was hotter now in the sun than under the old tattered hood, which was bad enough. My shirt was stained dark with perspiration. I saw my face in the outside driving mirror; lips swollen, dried blood down my chin, dark shadows under my eyes, and in them a look of resignation and defeat. I must say, if I'd been in a competition for salesmen and how they could influence new clients, I wouldn't have made first base.

'Undo the tow rope,' Hassan ordered.

I went round to the back of the car, crouched down in the sand, and wrestled with the knot. It came undone finally, with reluctance and at the cost of several torn finger nails. I saw a beetle crawl across the sand, and bombed it with drops

198

of my own sweat. I spun out the job as long as I could, but nothing lasts forever, and this didn't last more than seven or eight minutes.

I stood up, and the desert looked so hot that it shimmered in the distance, sand melting into sky. The sea was blue as melting glass and looked as warm. I had a vague idea I might use the rope as a lasso or a stock whip, but Sabry stopped that. He took it from me, threw it into the back of the Royale, then poured himself a mug of water from a canister, handed one to Hassan and another to Maria. When she finished drinking, he poured some more in it for me. I drank it gratefully and perspiration poured out of my forehead and forearms. But I felt better, not quite so parched. I hadn't won yet, but also I hadn't entirely lost.

'Throw the rest away,' Hassan told Sabry.

Obediently, he turned the canister upside down. The water glug-glugged into the sand. It made a tiny pool, then there was nothing but a darker stain where it had been, and then even that disappeared. Within minutes there might have been no water at all. The desert was also thirsty.

Sabry handed me the empty container. I shook a few drops out into my mouth. Some ran down my chin, and I licked at them greedily.

'We'll use that can for petrol,' said Hassan. 'Drain some off from your car's tank.'

'I told you, the plug's jammed,' I said.

'Punch a hole with a screwdriver. And hurry. That can will hold enough for us to reach Alex now.'

I didn't really know that the plug was jammed, but when I looked, I found that it had been soldered over. They often do that in old cars, because the plugs weep petrol. I suppose the threads become distorted; after all, most cars are built to last for two or three years, not forty or more, in the nineteen-twenties as today.

I went back to the Royale, opened the tool box, took out a

screwdriver and a hammer, and started to walk towards the smaller car. I walked slowly, for my legs under Hassan's gaze felt like logs, and my feet sank into the sand. I once read of a wartime spy who had been captured by the Nazis and made to dig his own grave; I was beginning to understand how he must have felt.

I was certain now that neither Maria nor I would go free. We knew too much, and our knowledge was the only thing that kept Hassan and Sabry from a fortune. This was our bad luck, but it didn't make the thought of approaching death any easier. My mind spun uselessly round the problem as a slipping clutch on a one in four hill. And then I had an idea; the clutch gripped; I went back to the Royale with a little more alacrity.

'What's wrong?' asked Hassan suspiciously.

'Thought I saw a funnel in there,' I said. 'It would save us wasting half the juice.'

I'd seen nothing in there, but I wanted to look behind the front seats to see whether there was a control lever to release the lid of the dummy tank. There must be something somewhere. There was. I saw a small nickel-plated lever, like an old-fashioned motor-cycle throttle control, before they thought of twist-grips. It was connected by a Bowden cable to the dark recesses of the car. I moved down the lever as far as it would go and scrabbled noisily about, as though looking for a funnel.

'No good,' I told Hassan, my head still down, for I've an old-world idea that it's easier to make someone believe a lie if you don't have to look at them while you tell it.

I walked back to the Type 57, crouched down under the tank at the back, and scooped out a hole in the sand for the base of the container, to hold it steady. Then I put the end of the screwdriver blade against the tank and tapped it gently with the hammer. The metal was thin and old, and at the third blow the point went through it and petrol gushed out.

200

I filled the container, then screwed one corner of my handkerchief into a spill and stuffed this up into the hole. It would still leak, but it wouldn't leak so quickly, and if Hassan was, by any unthinkable chance, going to keep his part of the bargain, I would need some petrol to reach Alexandria.

The smell of leaking petrol was very strong, and I wondered about the danger of fire, but that was the least of my problems. I picked up the container, took it back to the Bugatti, opened the filler cap and poured it in. Not entirely to my surprise, the couple of gallons or so in the can filled the tank completely. So I had been right; they *had* run out of fuel because of the smallness of the tank. Not that this confirmation did me any good at that particular moment in my life, but if you're a pro it's always cheering to know your diagnosis is correct.

'Now get back in your own car,' said Hassan. He had his pistol out in his hand which, in some quarters, would be considered better than having something else out in his hand, but I wasn't in those quarters or even halves; I was in the hell of a mess, and the sight of that blue barrel did nothing to slow my heartbeats to a healthier speed.

'Turn your car round,' he said.

'Why?' I asked, watching his eyes for that tiny flicker towards the pistol that would mean he was going to fire. 'Alex is this way.'

'You're not going to Alex,' he said. 'You're going somewhere else.'

'Where?'

I leaned against the door and felt the warmth of the metal through my thin damp shirt, and I knew where I was going: to the graveyard. I was suddenly cold all over; cohorts of men could be walking over my grave, and if I didn't do something to help myself at once, or sooner, that's just what they would be doing. The long day seemed nearly done, and so was I.

'All right,' I said hoarsely, 'I'll turn it.' I moved towards Maria.

'You wait there,' I called to her. 'Guide me if the wheels are too near the sand.'

I started the engine, moved the car forward a few yards, turned and then backed so that I was facing Hassan. He stood about eight feet away from the radiator, gun pointing at me. On the floor, halfway under the seat, was the crank handle. I carefully put my left foot on the clutch, pushed the gear into second and brought up the crank handle until one end was resting on the accelerator pedal. This had a rubber cover, so it didn't slip. I pushed the crank slightly; the engine began to rev.

'Come on,' called Hassan. 'Park over to my left. Then get out.'

He wants all the work done for him, I thought. Then, when I'm out of the car, he'll kill me. That way, there would be no bullet-holes through the doors, no messy bloodstains on the seats. Just a body on the sand; a mad Englishman who'd killed one of his countrymen, stolen a car and then shot himself.

As Hassan spoke, I jammed the crank handle hard against the accelerator, and at the same time threw myself down under the dashboard.

The car bounded forward. Above the scream of the hundred odd horses under the bonnet, I heard a crack like a stock whip, and then a splutter as the engine died, and then another crack, and then silence, broken only by the distant thunder of the sea on the shore. The car rolled slowly to a stop. I had failed again.

Hassan had fired at the radiator, and by some incredibly lucky chance for him – or maybe because he really was as good a shot as he claimed – the bullet must have shattered the distributor, or the coil or the main lead or one of the other vulnerable and vital parts that a single well-aimed bullet could destroy.

Well, I'd tried. I still held the crank in my right hand. I had lost everything now except the last battle, and no bookie would have given me any odds on that.

I lay where I was for a moment, for I'd nowhere else to lie, and then slowly I levered myself up. I'd be in a better position to ward off a counter-attack sitting up than lying down.

As I moved, I half expected a bullet to splinter the windscreen.

I could feel it in advance, boring through my shoulder, puncturing the bone, shattering the muscle, tearing apart the tendons. Imagining it was nearly as bad as having it happen; what did Shakespeare say about cowards dying many times before their death? I was practically part of my own instant funeral kit – the corpse part.

Finally, I was sitting upright behind the wheel, still alive, and gripping the crank, and looking at Hassan. He was standing only feet away, bewilderment on his face, holding his right wrist in his left hand. His pistol lay on the sand near his feet.

I climbed out of the car, watching him. We were like characters in one of those pictures with which they used to illustrate the adventure stories of my schooldays; everyone would stand staring at everyone else, arms half bent, but nothing actually happening, because the artist hadn't got the gift of action. If he had, of course, he wouldn't have been drawing such deplorable pictures.

I saw Sabry standing up in the passenger seat of the other car, both hands carefully above his head as though he'd been frantically waving to someone and they had suddenly frozen like that. Just behind him, I saw that the lid of the tank had opened, like the turret top of a tank. An old man stood there, a plastic mug in one hand, sipping from it. In his other hand he held a toy pistol with an ivory butt.

Good for dad, I thought, if this was Maria's dad. He

certainly wasn't mine. Good for someone. He called to me in English.

'I'll deal with this – person.'

He spat out the word, so I gathered that he wasn't exactly a fully paid-up member of the Sabry supporters' club.

As the old man spoke, Sabry took a swing to the right with both his hands gripped together like a flail. He hit the old man in the stomach. The mug of water flew over the side of the car, and his pistol arm went up into the air, but he didn't drop the pistol.

Sabry started to run, taking great steps, but not covering much ground because of the sand, like a man running in a nightmare. It was all happening in slow motion, which made it worse for him, although not for me. I liked to see him run, and so far as I was concerned, the slower and longer he ran the better, for there was nowhere in all the world he could run to now. He was running to eternity.

He held out his hands in front of him, as though he could drag himself along by will power only, desperate to be out of range of that tiny gun.

The old man steadied himself with his left hand against the open lid of the tank, and then, taking his time and his aim, he fired twice. Then he put away his pistol. I suppose it only held three shots. The pistol was a toy unless you knew how to use it, but like the man with the twelve-inch hampton, François knew how to use it.

Sabry ran on for a few more paces, but his legs had turned to rubber, and his knees folded, and his whole body rolled forward, and he fell on the hard road and slipped sideways. He lay where he fell, and I didn't need a coroner's qualifications to know he would never get up again, because whoever moved Sabry would have to carry him off in a box with handles on its sides.

'I've left Hassan to you,' said the old man casually. 'I expect you'd like to deal with him yourself.'

He climbed out over the back of the car and jumped down on to the sand. He might be a bit long in the tooth, but he was no arthritic bathchair boyo.

Hassan made a sudden dive for his F.N., near his feet, and I threw the crank at him. It hit him across the top of the head as he bent down, and he staggered back and fell. I picked up his pistol and put it in my own jacket pocket. If anyone was going to use it, I was going to.

'You bastard,' I said, and as his face came up, I hit him hard, right on those china teeth. Maybe what George would call his Hampstead Heath – his teeth – were the best china, for he kept grinning at me. But this was only a muscular reaction, for his lips were drawn back like an animal's over those firm gums that must have gammed many a game young Egyptian boy.

He stood now, bent forward, his arms out, fingers hooked. As we faced each other, he kicked out with his right foot and tapped at my left kneecap. I don't know what this was supposed to do, except to throw me off balance, which it might well have done had my kneecap been where he aimed at. But years in the old-car trade have taught me some crude cunning, if nothing else, for you never know how customers can react when they feel a deal's going against them. I stepped smartly to one side as I saw his foot approaching.

I seized his shoe as his foot came up and twisted it as though I wanted to break it off at the ankle, and so, like that character in the Old Testament who digged a pit and then fell into the midst of it himself, Hassan, the thrower, became Hassan the thrown.

This time, as he jumped up, I clobbered him on the side of the head, and as he reeled, I hit him twice hard, left and right, in the guts.

They wouldn't have stood for those blows at the National Sporting Club, and neither did Hassan. He dropped on his hands and knees, and I trod on his fingers and ground them into the sharp hot sand before he could grip my ankles and try to bring me down.

The Marquess of Queensberry wouldn't have liked that, but then I wasn't asking him to. I must be honest and add that Hassan didn't like it, either, but he was tough and he knew, as I did very clearly, that, on his feet, he could cripple me in seconds. I was therefore determined to keep him off his feet, and at mine, as much as possible, for I was tiring. I'd have to finish him soon, or he would finish me.

Hassan lay for a second as though out, and then, unexpectedly, for he'd taken more punishment than I'd have liked to receive, he jumped up and came at my throat. My hands went up between his and then out, breaking his strangle hold, and then, body to body, I brought up my right knee hard in his groin.

He gave a whimper of pain and in his giant agony, his mouth opened like a gargoyle, and he sank rather than fell, and scrabbled in the sand, half turning like the bent spoke of a living wheel.

'Get up,' I told him.

He scooped up handfuls of sand as he struggled to his knees. I kicked him in the crotch to make him move more quickly, thinking as I did so, of George's old adage, 'Never kick a man when he's down – he may get up.'

Maybe Hassan had heard it, too, for he crawled to a squatting position and crouched there. I'd never trusted him, but now I didn't have to. I took out his automatic, blew the dust off it, fired once into the sand to see that it hadn't been damaged. It hadn't, so I pointed it at Hassan's stomach.

'Get up,' I repeated.

This time, he unwound himself and stood up shakily, his face matted with sand and blood, streaks of sweat running down from his hair. It could run where it liked so far as I was concerned. My own running days were over.

I kept him covered, and called over my shoulder to Maria, because I wasn't sure whether her dear old dad, François, was still around.

'Has your father reloaded?' I asked her.

François replied: 'No. I only carry three bullets.'

'They're enough,' I told him. 'Put all Hassan's and Sabry's stuff in the little Bugatti. And quickly, before someone comes.'

I felt like that fellow in the story who's screwing a young girl and she suddenly gets agitated and asks: 'Ooh, what if my mother comes?' And her lover sternly replies: 'Apart from you, the only one who's coming round here is me.'

I was in charge now, and I was staying that way because that's the best way to be; more, it's the only way.

François pulled two suitcases, a brief-case, and an airline bag with the neck of a bottle sticking out, from the Royale. I fired into the bag and the bottle splintered and lime juice poured across the sand.

'Ever heard of the first Rockefeller?' I asked Hassan, only rhetorically, you understand. I didn't care whether he had heard of him, but he was going to hear about him now. He was what one might call a captive audience.

Hassan said nothing.

'Well, I'll tell you about him,' I went on generously. 'He was very rich, very hard, very tough. One day, he realized his associates were trying to screw him, so he called them all together, and he said: "Gentlemen, you have conspired to swindle me. I won't sue you, the law takes too long. Instead, I'll ruin you!" And he did.'

I don't know whether Hassan absorbed the message, which was that what was good enough for Rockefeller, was good enough for me. Hassan and Sabry had tried, and very nearly succeeded not only in swindling me, but in landing me on a possible murder charge. Sabry was now where I didn't want to go for a while yet, but Hassan I could handle.

'I'm going to leave you here in your uniform with Sabry's body,' I told him. 'You can talk your way out of that one – as you wanted to make me talk my way out of being found with Kent's body.

'Just to even the score, I'll also leave you a gun.'

François had moved up to my side. Out of the edge of my eyes, I could sense rather than see he was grinning; the poetic justice of the thing must have appealed to him, as keeping him a poor man had no doubt appealed to the Egyptians. Odd what a kick we can all get from making life hard for other people, isn't it?

I put out my right hand, still keeping Hassan covered, and took François's empty pistol from him, and threw it in the sand at Hassan's feet.

'When people want to know how Sabry died – if anyone cares – you can tell them that two shells from this gun are in his body. Or perhaps they'll find out for themselves if they do a post mortem. The empties are still in the breech.

'But then again, maybe no one will want to know. There's not much traffic that comes along here, so you have a fighting chance. Now, take off your shoes.'

He bent down, and began to unlace them.

'Throw them into the back of my car,' I told him.

He did so. They landed in the front seat.

'Now, all your money and identity papers.'

He unbuttoned an inner pocket and pulled out a yellow wash-leather wallet.

'Throw them one by one into the car, too.'

'But I must keep my identity card,' he protested. 'Otherwise, no one will know who I am.'

'I know,' I told him. 'And I wouldn't want to change you, darling. Chuck them in the car or I'll do it for you.'

I jerked the gun slightly. Hassan opened the wallet as quickly as a spinster opening her arms to a night intruder.

208

He threw the car's papers, my passport, then a cheque book, then some currency notes clipped together, finally, the empty wallet.

'Now,' I said. 'I'll tell you how you sprang François here. You borrowed or stole that uniform from your cousin, the chief of police, and you simply told the guards you were taking him out. It was very simple, no strain at all. They thought you were the chief of police, and, of course, they released him at once. Right?'

'Right,' said François.

Hassan said nothing. I threw him a few more lines of dialogue. I liked the sound of my own voice. It made a change from being ordered about.

'First, you killed Kent, though.'

'It was an accident,' Hassan insisted.

'So you told me. But now your only witness, Sabry, is dead, too. So we've only your word for that accident. The court will only have your word, too.'

'What do you mean?'

Hassan seemed genuinely puzzled, or maybe the genuine look of concern he gave me was as phoney as anything else he'd given me.

'Just what I say. We're leaving you here to explain to your good Egyptian friends how you came to be wearing the uniform of the chief of police – without any shoes or any identity papers, and with a man dead here, shot by two bullets from this gun.'

He stood staring at me, his eyes as big as onions in his head. I stared right back at him. He hadn't told me why he had beaten me up in Rosemary Court, so long ago it seemed now it was practically out of this century, and yet it was less than a week ago. If I didn't find out now I never would, because I hoped I would never see Hassan again this side of Jordan, and I didn't mean the river or the country, but this side of the tomb. The fact is, I wasn't so keen on seeing him the other side, either, so before we said goodbye, I had to know the reason for his roughness.

'You never told me why you clobbered me in that flat in London,' I said. 'The one Maria was using. I'll give you three to talk.'

'And if I won't,' said Hassan.

'I'll shoot you first through the left knee-cap, then the right, then where the bullet falls.' It sounded kinder to use George's rhyming slang.

'What do you say?'

'I'll talk,' said Hassan.

I was relieved, for this saved me three bullets, and there was no guarantee that I would have hit him, even at that distance.

'I had to get to London,' he said. 'I deal in guns, and there are no guns here any more, except the ones we buy and sell among ourselves, but they're not enough. I needed new stock, but I had no currency.'

He paused. I threw a couple of lines into the pause.

'So you went to your cousin, the chief of police, and gave him a long spiel about doing a job for him, and so he let you have some official currency. Right?'

'Yes. I saw that Maria had a job with Kent. I knew who her father was. I told my cousin she was planning to smuggle him out. I needed to watch her. He'd get all the praise if we caught them both just going over the border. But first of all I had to go to London.

'He gave me the authority to take out some money. When I got to London I thought I'd go over Maria's flat first to see if I could pick up anything like a letter, even any cash. She came back unexpectedly, and when I heard the key in the door, I jumped into the cupboard. She ran out again before I could escape, and then you came.'

This made sense to me. The letter in the Delahaye had obviously been from Maria's father. If Hassan had found that in her flat, then he would have realized that what he had imagined and invented was actually happening.

If he'd discovered this, then he could have helped smuggle François out himself with Maria; but then if we all had different turns of mind we wouldn't be where we are.

I felt sorry for him in a way, but not that sorry. I was glad I wasn't in his stockinged feet.

'Get in the Royale,' I told Maria. François was already behind the wheel.

'You can't leave me here,' protested Hassan.

'Why not?' I asked him. 'You've a sporting chance. More chance than all those birds you used to shoot.'

I handed Hassan's gun to François; he was a better shot than me, and there was a special reason why I wanted him to fire, which I'll come to later.

'Shoot,' I told him, and nodded in the direction I wanted him to fire.

'No!' shouted Hassan. 'No, I beg of you!'

He closed his eyes as he prepared for death.

François fired once, twice, not at Hassan, but into the petrol tank of the small Bugatti. For a second, nothing happened, and I thought nothing would. Hassan opened his eyes, and with a roar like instant thunder, the rear of the car erupted into a ball of flame.

The petrol, leaking out of the tank, past my handkerchief, had vaporized in the heat. As any schoolboy will tell you, if you can grab an articulate one for long enough, a mixture of petrol and air is heavier than air alone, and so the petrol vapour hung beneath the car like a dangerous and invisible fog.

Hassan would have a long walk on his bare feet – and some interesting explanations to make at the end of the trail.

I heard a crackle of exhaust as François started up the Royale's engine, and I vaulted over the back of the car.

'Drive,' I told him, as he must so often have commanded his own chauffeur in years long past.

He drove, with me sitting astride the tail, like a split-arse mechanic. Behind us, a column of thick oily smoke grew taller in the sky, the funeral pyre of Hassan's dream. He ran after us in his stockinged feet, screaming with rage, and then, as we drew away, he bent down and hurled handfuls of sand after us. I gave him the old V-sign. It cost me nothing, and aren't we told somewhere that it is more blessed to give than to receive?

I felt blessed all right as François coaxed fifty out of the old Royale, and we trundled along for a couple of miles. Then he pulled to the side of the road and switched off the engine.

'What's wrong?' I asked him. I couldn't believe that he was simply stopping to admire the scenery, which wasn't worth a postcard home.

'Nothing,' he said, 'But don't forget I'm still the most wanted man in Egypt. And there's a police post only a mile ahead.'

'Once more into the tank, dear friend,' I said, and leaned down behind the seat and pulled the release lever. We lifted up the lid. The dummy tank was lined with felt, and had a strip of thick sorbo rubber on the floor. A plastic water bottle and a mug were clipped to one side of the wall. He might be hot in there, but he'd survive until we were aboard ship and well beyond the twelve-mile limit.

Maria and I locked the tank lid shut, and I drove. The car felt heavy at slow speeds, but as the speedometer needle climbed round the dial, the steering grew lighter – not that I worried much so long as the thing would carry us to the docks. I never wanted to drive it again.

We stopped at the police post with its radio aerial, the trestle table covered by the inevitable army blanket. Two shabby soldiers stood up as we approached. One had a rifle over his shoulder. The other waved us down with a cigarette in his hand.

'I'll do the talking,' said Maria, as I cut the engine to save petrol, and we coasted the last hundred yards.

212

'Do that,' I agreed, because I can't speak a word of Arabic. 'But make it clear that if these two guys want promotion, then they can arrest an imposter – doubtless an alien spy – disguised as the chief of police.

'Tell them he's only a few miles behind us in the desert with a burned-out car and a dead man. Don't spare the details. Give it to them rich and thick, just like the soup mother used to make.'

'Whose mother?'

'Everyone's.'

Both men looked around the car as though they'd never seen one like it before, and no doubt they hadn't. After all, why should they have done? I hadn't seen one myself, and I'm in the business.

Maria climbed out and began a long spiel to the character with the rifle. He didn't appear greatly interested. Maybe he wasn't promotion-orientated. She held out her hand, and I saw the pink edge of a thousand-piastre note between her fingers. The soldier saw it, too, and shook hands with a bit more enthusiasm, palming the note with a practised ease that any head waiter would have envied.

Here, I was sure, stood no upright fighter for the worthy cause of Egyptian solidarity. Here was a man like me, who wanted to do a deal, and who now saw his chance. Even so, he went through the motions of examining the car. He peered under the bonnet, patted the huge tail appreciatively, and then waved us on.

'Did you tell him?' I asked Maria.

'Everything. Just as you said.'

I pressed the starter button, and the motor gave a sad whine and died.

I pressed the button again, and nothing happened except that the petrol gauge needle swung down its dial, and I didn't have to be a paid-up member of the Motor Trader's Association to realize we had a dud battery.

Heaven knows how long the battery had been in the car when it was on show, and this business of starting the gigantic engine a number of times in the baking heat of the desert, had made it realize its age. It also made me realize mine, and what an awkward spot we were in, for I didn't under-estimate Hassan's powers of survival, or his tennis-ball ability to bounce back.

'What's wrong?' asked Maria.

'Battery's down. They'll have to push us.'

It was impossible to think of swinging that engine on a crank, even if I had one, which I hadn't. Maria spoke to the guard, who listened gravely and then shrugged his shoulders. However, he called to his companions, and together they leaned against the body of the car. It didn't budge an inch. They were old soldiers, of course, and only leaning, not actually pushing.

Maria spoke sharply to them, and they called out two other men from inside the post. They also leaned on the car, without much enthusiasm, but at least it did begin to roll forward very slowly. I put my foot on the clutch, engaged third, and then let out the clutch sharply. The engine fired, and I kept it running while we shouted mutual congratulations at each other.

The soldiers crowded round Maria. She handed out a hundred-piastre note to the nearest, who saluted her, as well he might. He looked more intelligent than his companions. Maria thought so, too, for she began to talk to him urgently, pointing back at the desert behind us. I had no idea what the hell she was saying, and so I asked her when we were on our way.

'I gave him a revised version of what I'd told his companion with so little effect. There's been an Israeli raid back up the road. Our people had been engaging them with heavy anti-aircraft fire. A plane had been shot down and burned itself out. And only a few miles away was a traitor, wearing

214

Egyptian police uniform, with a burned-out car and an Egyptian patriot he'd shot.'

'Hassan,' I said approvingly, hoping we'd be well away and out of sight of land before any of these characters learned the truth. 'Hassan.'

'Who else?' she asked.

Who else, indeed, I thought. It might have been me. I beat on the petrol tank.

'You all right down there, dad?' I asked. 'François, art thou sleeping there below?'

He certainly wasn't sleeping, but whatever he said I couldn't understand it. He sounded as though he were speaking from the middle of a gasometer, and, frankly, I didn't care how he sounded so long as he was near me, for the thought that I would soon have twenty thousand pounds was growing ever more rosy in my mind.

Alexandria in the morning was like Alexandria in the evening, but a bit busier, with more cars, and masses of bicycles, and a whole string of camels walking in line. Each held in its mouth the tail of the camel in front, which was one way of keeping together.

I would have liked a coffee or some breakfast, but there was no time. We had to reach the docks first; business, as I've said earlier, before pleasure. Maria knew the back streets away from the sea front where we'd pass fewer people. I rather missed the hotel names, The Gordon, The Cecil, The Ivy, but I felt that maybe my conduct had not been quite up to their high aristocratic standards.

We came into the docks behind a crowd of workers arriving on bicycles, all showing their passes, which was better than showing anything else, but no doubt they did that, too, when the mood overtook them. They looked a villainous lot.

The same man with the hat was in the little house with the window by the gate. He might never have gone home; perhaps that was his home. He came out when he saw me, and we shook hands. I handed over the papers, and Maria did her spiel in Egyptian.

Up went the Royale's bonnet. He checked each digit of the chassis and engine numbers on the plates and on the papers. Luckily, he didn't glance too closely at the engine, and the dust of the desert, caked on the oil leaks, had effectively concealed Hassan's handiwork with paint and putty on the previous evening. He stamped the papers, examined Kent's passport which I offered as my own, and called up the same man who had driven the other cars into the docks.

We'd made it. All that remained now was for the ship's captain to cast off or pull his anchor out or whatever else he'd got in, and we'd be away. François would be free and I'd be richer by twenty thousand little green men. It was a happy thought and I enjoyed thinking it.

'What now?' I asked Maria.

'All the cars are being loaded immediately,' she said. 'We can go aboard any time.'

'The sooner the better,' I said.

With a bit of luck, Kent's body would still be undiscovered, and even if we hadn't that bit of luck, I'd cut the telephone line, so how could they contact the police here? And even if they did contact the police by semaphore, runner, pigeon, flag or heliograph, or even by any other unexpected means, how could they trace us to the docks so quickly? The answer seemed reassuring enough. They damn' well couldn't.

I walked with Maria to our ship, between wooden crates just unloaded from Russia. The blue peter was already fluttering at the masthead, and a wisp of steam grew like a beard from the exhaust behind the funnel. Only minutes now, and we would be away – and suddenly I remembered something.

My mind must have been slipping, or maybe it was the change of life, or a change of sex or heart, for I'd forgotten one most important thing I had to do before I boarded the

216

ship – the real reason why I'd asked François to set the Type 57 alight rather than do it myself.

'One minute,' I said to Maria.

'There's a lavatory aboard,' she said.

'No, I don't want that,' I told her. I knew exactly what I wanted, for I'd seen a sign in English above a small hut: *Telegraph Office*. I ran towards it, hoping it was open. Inside the wooden room, a clerk sat at a table surrounded by sheets of telegrams held down by crystal balls. I counted three of them. He could have been going into the pawnbroking business.

'Please?' he asked, looking at me with the pained irritation of all Post Office servants when a member of the public approaches.

'I want to send a telegram,' I told him.

He pushed a form towards me.

'You have a pen?'

Yes, I had a pen. I wrote out the telegram, handed it back. He read it aloud suspiciously in case it contained a code.

It was to: MIDLAND WIDOWS INSURANCE CO. FENCHURCH STREET LONDON STOP ATTENTION CAR INSURANCE DEPARTMENT STOP MUST INFORM YOU THAT BUGATTI CAR INSURED WITH YOU AGREED VALUE 5,000 POUNDS THROUGH ARISTO AUTOS BELGRAVIA TOTAL LOSS IN EGYPTIAN DESERT STOP AM INFORMING LOCAL POLICE STOP.

'That will be three hundred piastres,' he said.

'Cheap at the price,' I told him, and sent another telegram to the Chief of Police to tell him where the car was now.

'A total loss?' asked the clerk sympathetically.

'Absolutely total,' I agreed.

'But it was insured?' he went on hopefully.

'To the full amount,' I assured him thankfully, which was why I couldn't very well have set fire to the thing myself, I mean, could I? That would have been arson. We must have some standards, that's what I always say. That's what's so wrong with everything today: no moral code, no sense of honour.

I walked back towards the gangway. Maria was waiting for me, standing in the sun. I could see she hadn't a slip beneath her dress, and I wondered what else she'd be wearing, or not wearing. Well, I'd have time enough and money enough to find out.

I thought about that, too, and about the voyage through the warm wine-dark Mediterranean to Marseilles – a touch of the old Homer there. And once we were at sea there'd be a touch of the old this-and-that, too.

I was also thinking of my old family motto, or what I'd have chosen if I'd had either an old family or a motto.

For too long it had been, business before pleasure. Well, I'd had the business. I'd collect £5,000 on the insurance, and at least as much again on these three cars, and half as much on the jewels, and then there was also the prospect of Maria's £20,000.

Moneywise, as the financial writers in newspapers like to say, it hadn't been an entirely unproductive trip. But otherwise, how would I rate it? That remained to be seen; the journey was not over yet. So much for business, I thought. Now for pleasure. Maria's pleasure. And mine.

We went up the gangway together.

London – Cairo – Alexandria.